VOYAGE of the

FROSTHEART

VOYAGE of the

FROSTHEART

•••°

JAMIE LITTLER

VIKING

VIKING

An imprint of Penguin Random House LLC, New York

First published in the United States of America by Viking,
an imprint of Penguin Random House LLC, 2019
Published simultaneously in the UK by Penguin Books Ltd.

Visit us online at penguinrandomhouse.com

LIBRARY OF CONGRESS CATALOGING-IN-PUBLICATION DATA IS AVAILABLE.
ISBN 9780451481344

Printed in Canada

1 3 5 7 9 10 8 6 4 2

Text set in Bohemia LT

VOYAGE of the

FROSTHEART

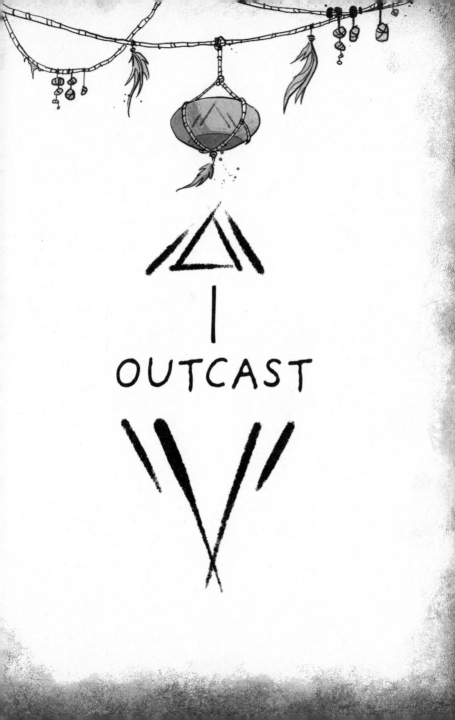

OUTCAST

Song

They shouldn't have been out on the snow.

"The snow hides death," the Fira people would claim, one of the many cheerful sayings taught to their children as soon as they were old enough to learn. And with good reason. The snow was a deadly place to be.

But the ball wasn't *that* far away.

A quick jog and grab, and it would be theirs. And yet it might as well have been a million miles away. There it sat, a dark speck against the endless white plain. The four children looked at it in silence. They didn't move. They didn't dare. Each of them was tensed, ready to run at the slightest noise.

Ash, the smallest of them, gave a shiver, and tucked his hands under his armpits, trying to soak up all the warmth he could from his furs. His breath puffed out in a white cloud. Behind him his friend Flare sniffed, and wiped the snot dribbling from his nose with his sleeve. Flare always had a snotty nose. It was almost as if he wasn't used to the cold, which was strange, really, as there hadn't been a warm day in living memory.

"We could get that," he said, sniffing his large nose again. "It's not that far."

And it wasn't. But still, no one moved.

"You get it," Shyne told Flare, her freckles doing nothing to soften the hard scowl that seemed forever etched onto her face.

"*What?!* I'm not going out there! Ryse kicked it over the battlements—it should be him who gets it!"

"Ash passed it too hard! He always does—he lost loads of balls when he lived with me," Ryse said, his chubby cheeks raw from the chill.

"Yeah, he lost all mine when he lived with my family too," Shyne agreed.

"OK, OK! I pass too hard. I get it!" Ash said.

"Anyway, it's *your* stupid ball," Ryse pointed out to Flare.

"Exactly! It's *my* ball, and *I* want it back!" Flare retorted.

"There's another ball back at your house, Flare," Ash said, trying to stop the argument. "Why don't we just play with that? We're already too close to the snow. We're not meant to be here . . ." He was shivering terribly now, and not just because of the cold. He gazed at their Stronghold high above them, nestled safely on its cliff-top perch. From this distance it looked even smaller than usual, trapped and isolated amid its endless white surroundings. Ash wanted nothing more than to run back up the winding, raised wooden stairway and in through the front gates. Back to safety.

"Ash is right. Leviathans have been seen about, *Lurkers* no less, and I don't want to become any stupid Lurker's *breakfast*," huffed Shyne.

"We'll just be a second!" Flare snapped.

Still no one moved. A cloud passed over the morning sun, strengthening the shadows across the snow plain. It got colder. Quieter. There wasn't a sound. Nothing, except for the whispering of the wind, and the occasional sniff from Flare. The cold breeze bit into Ash's face.

"Guys—" he began.

"Fine! I'll get it! Wow, you guys are such cowards!"

Ryse said. "Keep watch. If the grown-ups see, they'll kill me."

"It's not the grown-ups I'm worried about," Ash muttered. Looking out at the snow, he saw only unbroken, glistening white. It didn't seem possible that anything could be hiding beneath. *But that's what Lurkers do best . . . they hide.*

Ryse stretched his arms out and rubbed his hands together, preparing to make the trek to the ball. It was probably a whole two hundred steps away. That was far. Far enough to have the children shaking in their boots.

After a moment's hesitation Ryse finally made the first careful step off the wooden platform and onto the snow.

He froze.

The other children held their breath.

Nothing happened.

The children breathed out in relief. As quietly and quickly as he could, Ryse trotted over to the ball. His ulk-fur boots made a gentle *pff pff pff pff* noise as he padded through the snow. He was about a hundred steps away from the ball now.

Fifty.

Twenty.

Ash could barely watch, yet

he couldn't bring himself to look away. Sweat trickled down his neck, despite the cold.

Ten steps.

Five steps.

One.

"I've got it!" Ryse cried, hoisting up the ball. He quickly covered his mouth with a hand, shocked at the volume of his voice.

"*Bring it back!*" Flare whispered as loud as he dared. With a nod Ryse began to jog back.

"He's gonna make it!" said Shyne.

Ash laughed in relief.

Then: *FWOOM!*

Snow erupted into the air like water from a geyser. The children staggered back as freezing slush rained down upon them. Out of the snow-chasm rose three large shapes. "*Lurkers,*" Ash gasped, his voice strained with fear.

The creatures were wet, sleek, and serpentine, longer than two men, with six frost-white eyes that blinked slightly out of order, and gaping jaws filled with ice-sharp fangs and drool-slick tongues.

Despite their graceless scram-bling gait, they moved with terrible speed—so quickly, in

fact, it was hard to make sense of their spiny crests, scrabbling claws and whip-long tails—they just looked like a writing mass of horror to Ash.

"They've cut him off!" Shyne screamed. And she was right. The Lurkers had blocked Ryse's path back to the village and were already racing hungrily toward him. He was frozen to the spot in fear.

"We need to tell the grown-ups!" Ash yelled, but he needn't have bothered. A lookout on the watchtower above had already seen the commotion.

"*Lurkers!*" he bellowed. "Hunters, to the battlements!"

Meanwhile the Lurkers were nearly upon Ryse, who simply stood there, whimpering in terror.

"Ryse, RUN!" Ash yelled at the top of his voice. This seemed to snap Ryse out of his trance. He dropped the ball and began to sprint, trying his hardest to skirt round the approaching Lurkers.

Suddenly a hungry, violent noise grew, echoing across the plain, terrifying in its fury. It was the Song of the Lurkers. Harsh ragged howls and screeches pierced Ash's ears, and his belly gave a sickening lurch as he *felt* the hateful emotions of the Leviathans. This was a war Song.

"HUMAN. CATCH. KILL."

Ash and the rest of the children clutched at their heads as the Song tore through them. The air around the

Lurkers shimmered with blood-red energy, an aura of snakelike tendrils writhing and reaching for Ryse with as much ferocity as the monsters themselves.

On the battlements Fira hunters used slings to launch rocks at the beasts, but they did little damage as they bounced off their slimy hides. Cumbersome harpoon-launchers fired too, but the beasts were too close to the wall and the giant harpoons flew wide of their mark. One Lurker was almost upon Ryse, its jaws open wide . . . but before it could chomp down on him, another Lurker leaped in its way, determined to be the first to get the meal. They fell in a tangled mess and collapsed to the ground in a wave of snow.

Ryse used the opportunity to sprint around the writhing mass. He headed straight for the wooden platform where the other children were waiting in terror.

"Come on, Ryse!" Ash shouted.

Ryse ran as fast as his little legs could carry him. The monsters finally untangled themselves, snapping and hissing at each other in frustration, before continuing the pursuit. Ryse was nearly at the platform, but the Lurkers were inches behind him.

"They're . . . they're coming this way!" Flare said. "I don't want my ball *that* much!" And with that he turned tail and legged it up the staircase, Shyne close behind.

Ash, however, remained, waiting for Ryse with his arm outstretched. Ryse *finally* made it to the platform and grabbed Ash's hand. Ash pulled him up, screaming, "GO, GO, GO!" Together they ran up the rickety stairway that led back to the safety of the village gate. But they'd taken only a few steps when a Lurker tore through the wooden posts that held the stairs aloft, shattering the wood in a shower of splinters. The staircase gave out a low groan before it started toppling toward the snow.

"Keep going!" Ash shrieked. The two boys tried to outrun the collapsing stairway, but they were too slow. The stairs trembled and swayed beneath them, and then Ryse lost his footing, sliding down toward the waiting jaws of the Lurkers below.

"*HUNT. KILL. EAT.*"

"HELP ME!" screamed Ryse.

Ash didn't know what to do. Ryse had managed to catch hold of the edge of a step, but the stairs were falling down around them. The gate was still so far away. The hunters were streaming through it, but they wouldn't make it in time to help. Ash's head spun, and the sight of the writhing Lurkers below made his belly churn.

Ash was desperate. Desperate to survive, but that wasn't all. He could feel an overwhelming urge bubbling up inside him, something that had been tugging at his spirit for as long as he could remember.

It was the desire to sing.

It would have seemed crazy, absurd, *funny*, even, had he not been feet away from a pack of ravenous beasts. But it also felt like the most natural thing to do. He couldn't have said why, but deep down inside he felt certain he could stop this if only he sang at the Lurkers—something to fight back against their terrible Song. He could see no other way out.

I shouldn't.

His people would exile him for sure. All the terrible rumors . . . they would be proved true. He would show himself to be the monster the Fira had feared him to be for so long.

No. I can't . . . I won't. I'm normal!

The stairs creaked and groaned as they drew the boys closer to the gaping, snapping maws below. Ash gritted his teeth and made a decision. He opened his mouth . . .

And then there was a terrible *thwack*, and below them a Lurker reared up, shrieking in pain, an arrow protruding from one of its many eyes. The creatures spun to face their attacker, and Ash followed their gaze.

A hunting party had returned from the wilds, and they were racing across the snow toward the children. At their front stood Ash's guardian, the mighty yeti warrior Tobu, bow in hand, already reaching for another arrow from his quiver. As he approached he shot Ash a terrifying glare—almost as if he'd somehow sensed Ash was about to sing.

Even among all the chaos, Ash's heart sank. *Another thing I'll be in trouble for.*

"*This way!*" the hunters called, waving their hands, whooping, and making as much noise as they could to attract the Lurkers. "*Come on, you horrible things!*" The Lurkers howled and scrabbled toward them, and the hunters scattered in different directions so the frantic Lurkers didn't know whom to follow. Almost immediately a large spear tore from the battlements into the side of one of them, pinning it to the ground with a deep *thunk*. It screeched a final bloodcurdling scream before going limp and still. Blue lifeblood began to envelop its entire body, like frost freezing over a puddle, and in mere moments the creature had turned into glistening ice. It was dead.

Realizing the danger they were in, the remaining Lurkers dived under the snow, burrowing away and out of sight, their prey forgotten.

Ash felt the world go quiet, silent but for the sound of the hunting party rushing toward him and Ryse.

They were the last thing he saw before his head hit the wood, and everything went black.

2

A Rude Awakening

Song Weaver.

The name had flashed through Ash's mind like an accusation the moment before he'd blacked out, and now he turned it over and over in his head, dimly aware that someone—no doubt Tobu—seemed to be gently carrying him home. The term was like a shadow, following him wherever he went. And Ash didn't even know what it meant. He just knew it was bad news.

Truth be told, Tobu was just the latest in a long line of reluctant guardians who had been tasked with looking after Ash since his parents had disappeared. His parents had been Pathfinders, a fact that filled Ash with both pride and sadness. Pathfinders were fearless traders, and also the last hope of human-kin, a final effort to connect the scattered Strongholds into some sort of unified civilization. Only a few years after he had been born, Ash's parents had set off aboard their sleigh, the *Trailblazer*, leaving him in Alderman Kindil's care as they had so many times before. It was the last the Fira ever saw of them, and so began Ash's time being fostered by the Stronghold. Before Tobu, he had been living with Charr and her family, and it had all been going fairly well. Right up until he'd sung.

Song Weaver . . .

Ash *knew* he shouldn't have. The Fira were so scared of singing—of *Song Weavers*, whatever they were— that music was forbidden in the Stronghold. And there had already been rumors going around about who Ash was—*what* he was. But he had done it anyway.

In his defense he had only sung a lullaby—the lullaby his parents had used to sing to him before they left. Ash couldn't help singing it to himself, as much as he tried. The urge came so often, he rarely realized he was even doing it.

Ash would sing it for comfort, to feel like his parents were still around. It was almost all he had left of them after all. He would hum it quietly to himself when he pulled on his animal-hide tunic and fur cloak in the chill mornings. He'd sing it under his breath while at lessons, learning to hunt, practicing archery and hunter sign language—though he would clap his hands over his mouth when he became aware of the fierce looks the other villagers were giving him. He would roll the few words he remembered through his head at night, a warming blanket of memory to send him to sleep. It was innocent. It was harmless.

But that wasn't a good enough excuse.

Not for his guardian Charr, at least, who had whipped Ash right out of his bed and taken him to Alderman Kindil's stone lodge in the dead of night. "He was *singing*!" she'd whispered, her voice strained with fear.

"I—I wasn't!" Ash had squeaked in a very small voice. It was a lie, but it was all he could think of to say.

"I can't do it, alderman!" Charr had said. "I have children of my own to think of. I can't risk it. My home is no place for a"—Charr's eyes darted from side to side, as though she was afraid to say it—"a *Song Weaver*."

The hairs on the back of Ash's neck had prickled. That name again.

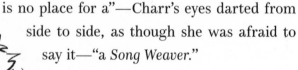

Ash had stood beside his guardian before the large wooden doors of the alderman's lodge. Warm, inviting light spilled out through the opening the alderman stood in, but he made no motions to invite them in.

"I am no *coward*," Charr continued, though she had certainly looked scared. "But I am no fool either. The Leviathan attacks are getting worse. Every winter that passes, they get more hostile, and we lose more of our people. You can barely hear yourself think for their singing these days—and the boy sings more 'n' more too—just like them! The Leviathans *hate* us, and they'll use the boy for evil, you mark my words. I'm sorry, but he can't stay with me."

Alderman Kindil, the large, imposing hunter leader of the Fira people, had let out a long sigh. He looked tired. While he might have had shoulders as wide as a sleigh, his beard was touched by gray and wrinkles etched his face, creasing his many scars. The air of wisdom and strength he carried was only slightly ruined by the big fluffy slippers he was wearing.

Ash had felt like his heart was in a terrible, painful grip. The tears were becoming harder and harder to hold back. *Moved on again . . .*

Seeing his expression, Charr had reached out as if to hold him, to comfort him, as she had used to. But she had hesitated, before pulling her hand away. "I am sorry, Ash. Truly."

Kindil had scratched his head, thinking. "Although he *has* broken Fira law, I can't imagine his singing was anything more than some childish rhyme he's made up." Ash had gazed up at the alderman with hope, but was met with a look that suggested he was still far from off the hook. "As much as it pains me, I clearly cannot persuade you to look after the boy. But it is the duty of the Fira people to care for Ash. If you will not look after the child, we must find someone who will."

Ash's face had flushed red with shame. He knew the alderman was running out of options. He gazed at the still, empty village around him. Passing Pathfinders considered it to be a small Stronghold compared to those farther south, and Ash guessed that must be true, but it was the only Stronghold he had ever known. It consisted of fifty or so stone dwellings that surrounded the alderman's central lodge like a protective ulk herd, all nestled behind the high stone walls, upon a snow-covered cliff that raised the Stronghold from the dangerous snows below. Tall watchtowers stood at each corner, connected to the walls by bridges made of stone or ice—stoic sentinels that guarded against the hidden enemy that threatened them all. The Stronghold also had a tannery and a sleigh dock (which was empty more often than not), but that was pretty much it. Everyone knew everyone and they did what they could to help one another. You had to when you practically lived on top of each other and were cut off from everyone else in the known world.

Ash had spotted a giant walking close by carrying a large ulk carcass over its shoulders as though it were nothing but a sack of redroot. The figure had snow-white fur and a long tail and was clad in ornate armor, a spear slung over its muscular back. It was Tobu, the mysterious yeti outsider. All Ash knew about him was that he'd been outcast from the yeti lands in the World's Spine Mountains years ago and been accepted into the Fira Stronghold before Ash had been born. Yeti were rarely seen outside their own lands, and were rightfully respected as powerful warriors. Even Alderman Kindil had to look up at him, and Kindil was the biggest man in the Stronghold by far.

Ash was scared of Tobu. Most of the Fira were.

Kindil must have spotted Tobu too, as the next

thing Ash knew, he was hailing the beast.

"Tobu!" Kindil called. "A word, please?" Tobu looked surprised but strode over and grunted a greeting, his white fur matted with the blood of the ulk he was carrying. "Tobu," the alderman began, "you are a valuable member of our Stronghold, a staunch defender of our walls, and an unsurpassed hunter. We are happy to have you." Tobu seemed a little taken aback at the compliments but nodded his thanks. He was a yeti of very few words. "You will remember that you swore an oath to do whatever the Stronghold required of you in return for sanctuary within our walls?"

"I remember," Tobu had said. For a creature so large, he had a very quiet voice. This made him all the scarier to Ash, who took a step away.

"Well, the Fira have great need of you now. This boy, Ash, needs a guardian, to raise him, to protect him, to turn him into a strong Fira hunter. I'm delighted to announce that this guardian, Tobu, is now *you*."

Ash's heart felt like it had stopped. Tobu dropped the ulk carcass, which fell to the snow with a sickening *thwump*. The yeti flexed his considerable muscles, balled his huge fists, and gritted his fangs, taking in a deep breath. Even Charr looked like she might intervene.

No, no, no, no, no! Ash thought in desperation. *This*

can't be! Anyone but him! PLEASE. *He'll have me for his dinner! I don't want to become boiled-boy broth!*

"I—I must object," Tobu's deep voice rumbled, as he held up his blood-soaked hands in protest. "I'm no child-carer. It is. . . ." The yeti had looked at Ash with distaste, Ash careful not to make eye contact. "It is a task that I am not equipped for."

But Alderman Kindil was having none of it. "Now, now," he said, raising his hand. "We have taken you in, Tobu. We have given you a home, safe from the terrors of the wilds. And in return this is what you must do for us. I thought a yeti's oath was as immovable as the mountains from which they hail?"

A low growl came from deep within Tobu's chest. He breathed hard, his nostrils flaring. But finally he relented, giving a small nod. "It is so."

"Excellent!" the alderman cheered.

But Ash had thought it anything but.

❧ ❧ ❧

And over the next month Ash had become quite familiar with that feeling. Tobu's drafty watchtower home lay on the outskirts of the village, just beyond the Stronghold's eastern wall, the small space they shared filled with the strong bestial, tangy scent of the yeti. It was cold and lonely out there, away from the village fires, with only a long, narrow bridge of ice connecting the tower to the rest of the Stronghold. All Fira children were trained in the arts of survival, but Tobu trained Ash harder than anyone else in the Stronghold, and he made it quite clear how he felt Ash's progress was going. "I have seen rocks with more agility than you," he said.

Indeed, the morning of the fateful Lurker attack had started like any other—with Tobu shaking Ash awake at the crack of dawn, violently swinging his hammock to and fro.

"*It's so early* . . ." Ash had groaned, squinting at the cooing pigeons who lived in the rafters of the tower.

Tobu grunted. "Let us hope it is not too late to make you into a hunter."

Tobu had been as keen as ever to fit in a training session before breakfast. "Breakfast" was perhaps a bit of a strong word—it was more a collection of roots Tobu had gathered, still dirty and unwashed from the wilds. Including redroot, Ash had noticed, pulling a face. Ash *hated* redroot. It was the favorite food of the Fira people, who respected strength and perseverance above all else. Like them, the redroot was tough, and it required great amounts of strength and perseverance to chew the stupid thing. And just like the flames that the Fira worshipped, the redroot was as hot and spicy as placing a burning torch in your mouth. Passing Pathfinders would trade furs and fabrics for it, but always with slight reluctance.

"I don't really like redroot," Ash said. He wouldn't normally complain, but Ash felt he needed to make a stand against at least *one* of the bad things that was happening in his life, even if it was just his breakfast.

"Thought all Fira liked redroot," Tobu replied.

"I don't think I am Fira. Not anymore," Ash mumbled. Ever since he'd been chucked out of Charr's dwelling, the villagers had given him a wide berth, whispering about what he'd done as he passed. They avoided making eye contact with him, and if they did, their smiles would quickly disappear. Ash had become used to this, but it didn't stop him from feeling like he had a stone in his stomach. *I don't even know what I've done wrong,* he would think to himself. *It can't just be my singing, can it? I know I've broken the taboo, but it was just a lullaby. I've never hurt anybody!*

"Don't eat it then," Tobu had said, picking up a wooden stool that seemed no bigger than his giant hand. He laid it down carefully and managed to almost delicately balance his considerable bulk on the seat, the stool's wooden legs creaking and straining. He tucked into his own redroot. With grim satisfaction Ash noticed a spice-induced tear well up in one of Tobu's eyes.

Ash had tried to take a bite from his root, but the ruddy thing was so tough he had to gnash and gnaw at it, until he finally succeeded in ripping a bit off, his hand slamming painfully onto the table with the sudden release. He had held his throbbing hand, looking down at his plate and breathing hard.

"I have told you before," Tobu noted, "you must practice patience and perseverance, boy—you must—"

"Why did you leave your clan?" Ash interrupted, deflecting another lecture. Tobu was very fond of them. But Tobu said nothing. He crunched through his root.

Ash tried again. "What are the yeti clans like?"

"Eat," Tobu answered, furrowing his brows.

Ash gulped down a piece of the root he'd been chewing for at least ten minutes. He took another bite and winced. So Tobu wasn't in the mood for chatting then. No surprise there. . . .

After they had choked down "breakfast," and Ash had floundered his way through another lackluster morning training session, it had been time to join the other children of the Stronghold for yet more delightful training. Tobu and Ash had walked into the village together, as Tobu was going to join the daily hunt for food and supplies vital to keeping the Stronghold alive. As they parted Tobu had given Ash what was clearly meant to be an encouraging push to send him on his way, but instead sent him flying.

Ash could've sworn he saw the closest thing to a glimmer of humor he'd ever seen in Tobu's eyes. "I'm sorry, Ash. It is easy to forget just how light and frail you are. I will do better to remember."

"Hurry up there, young Ash!" called out the cracked, elderly voice of his teacher, Light Bringer Hayze, who stood close by with the other giggling Fira children. "'Tis no time to be lounging in the snow; you have a lesson to attend. Yes, yes indeed!"

Light bringers, the clerics who spoke with the fire spirits, were responsible for keeping alight the flames of the Stronghold, which was sometimes the only light the village had in the dark, cold north of the Snow Sea. They were also charged with bringing the light of *knowledge* to the Stronghold's children.

"Now gather round, children. If you blizzard babies don't want to end up as monster food, I suggest you clean out your ears and listen good to what I tell you, yes, indeed!" declared Hayze. Ash joined the rest of the class atop the southern wall. The old man leaned on his staff, sunstone shards hanging from his furs like glowing amber rain. He nodded at his own wisdom, flecks of spittle glinting in his beard. "To be a hunter—to leave the safety of our walls—is to face near-certain death!" The children gulped as one. "As you all know, there is no greater enemy to the human-kin of the scattered Strongholds than the Leviathans. Lurkers, Hurtlers—no matter their type, they're all deadlier than starvation, worse than any Wraith raid. Yes, more deadly even than the freezing fury of the Ice Crone herself!" Hayze gestured dramatically at the barren snow plains around them. "The ravenous beasts hide under the snows, always watching, indeed, always waiting, ready for anyone brave or foolish enough to set foot upon the snows. To survive such a threat you must learn the tried and proven secrets of the Fira hunters, passed down for generations, indeed!"

As he spoke the light bringer paced in front of the class, his chin frantic in motion as his mouth pulled up a line of drool that had tried to get away. Ash stood beside Ryse, Shyne, and Flare, the only children in the Stronghold who didn't seem to believe that he might be a Song Weaver. They were the closest thing he had to friends, and they were all doing an outstanding job of avoiding eye contact with Hayze in case he asked them a question.

Suddenly one of the children called out in alarm, pointing over the side of the battlements. "Light bringer! Wh-what's that?"

The snow below had been disturbed. Something was moving underneath it.

"Aha! What did I tell you?" crowed Hayze. "They're here! Gather round, children, and you will see something so awful it may turn your hair as gray as mine."

Ash was shoved hard as the class surged forward to get a closer look. "Outta the way, Song-freak!" sneered Thaw, a lanky, smug-looking older boy. Thaw was by far Ash's least favorite person in the Stronghold, followed closely by his guffawing, bootlicking lackeys Raze and Frai, who stepped in line behind their leader. Ash said nothing but got as far away from the bullies as he could before peering over the battlements.

The children held their breath.

All was still.

All was quiet.

Then: "*There!*" cried Hayze in his most spit-spattering whisper. The snow had surged forward, leaving a trail behind it. There was something below, something that had sensed the sounds of the Stronghold, perhaps the vibrations of the western gate creaking open as the hunting party had set out. The trail moved fast, snaking toward the Fira cliff. The children gasped.

Ash's throat had gone dry, and his fingers gripped the stone wall. The trail was almost there—it was so close, and then suddenly . . . a tiny snow hare popped his head out from under the snow.

The children let out a collective groan of disappointment. The hare hopped over to the base of the cliff, twitching its nose. It left a few little droppings to show that the cliff did not interest it, and with a last adorable twitch of its nose it burrowed back under the snow out of sight. Hayze cleared his throat. "Yes, well. *Ahem*. Of course, the Leviathans are unpredictable beasts, and you can't always be certain when they'll attack. But rest assured they *will*, yes, yes indeed!"

"Erm . . . sir?" one of the children said, pointing at a friend who'd had a bit of an accident in the heat of the moment.

"Spirits above, what a mess!" Hayze cursed, pulling at his beard. "This is not how you become a brave hunter, no indeed!"

"Come on," Ryse hissed at the gang. "This'll take a while. Fancy a quick game of sparkball while the old man's back is turned?" The friends smiled at each other. Of course they did. And what could go wrong?

As it had turned out, rather a lot.

3

The Sound of Wind

Ash came to with a start, gasping and thrashing before realizing he was back in the safety of his hammock, no longer dangling for his life above the hungry jaws of Lurkers. He must have passed out properly after Tobu had brought him back to the watchtower. His head hurt, and he felt as though every muscle in his body had been thumped by a walloping walrus.

After getting dressed, Ash pulled back the hanging furs that offered him the smallest amount of privacy and found Tobu waiting for him on the other side, frowning with a confusing mixture of disappointment and concern. Ash waited, but the yeti said nothing.

"Tobu, I-I'm sorry," Ash said at last. "I know we shouldn't have been messing around out there. I tried to tell them, but—"

Tobu interrupted. "You must learn to control the urge."

Ash was confused. "What? To play *sparkball*?"

"The urge you have to sing," Tobu growled.

Ah.

"I didn't—"

"You *nearly* did. I saw it in your eyes."

There it is, Ash thought. *Proof Tobu has super yeti senses. You can't hide anything from him!*

"You were moments away from ruining everything for yourself. For us both," Tobu said. "You know the Fira laws. You are forbidden to sing. And it was no mere child's song that nearly escaped your lips."

How did Tobu know all this? "No—but . . . it felt like I had no other choice! I wanted to save Ryse . . . to save myself . . . and I-I don't know why, but I felt like singing would've helped, as if . . . I dunno . . . as if . . . singing would've . . . calmed the Lurkers down . . ." Ash trailed off, realizing how ridiculous this must sound.

"It does not matter what you *felt*. You know the rules, and you must obey them."

"When the Leviathans sing . . . I can hear them. I can hear them saying things," Ash confessed.

For the briefest moment Tobu looked shocked.

Ash went on. "I tried telling one of my other guardians about it once, and they just looked at me like I was insane. But I'm not—I know I'm not. The Leviathans talk to me . . . and I think I could sing back if only—"

"*No.*" Tobu's voice was low, but firm. "You must never do that, Ash."

"What do you know about it anyway?" Ash mumbled, deliberately too quiet for Tobu to hear.

He heard it all the same. "Enough to know you should *never sing.* Whatever you might *feel,* you will need to find other ways to defend yourself against the Leviathans, the same as the rest of us." Tobu turned and headed toward the weapons rack that leaned against the wall. His every move was filled with strength and purpose, reminding Ash just how scared he was of his new guardian. Tobu chose a sling from the rack. "Come," he said.

Ash was aghast. More training? "I was nearly *eaten* today! Can I not have a bit of a break?"

"Do you want to be a hunter?" Tobu growled. "Do you want to survive the next time a Lurker attacks you?"

"Y-yes," Ash replied in a small voice.

"Then come."

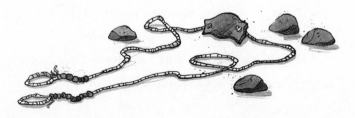

Ash squinted at the pebbles Tobu had piled up as a target a fair distance away. He took a steadying breath, then began to swing his sling, the stone pulling at the cord, forming wide swooping circles.

"You're too tense. *Breathe*," Tobu advised, standing ominously behind him.

I am breathing, Ash thought, his temper rising. *I'd have trouble being alive if I wasn't.*

He let the stone fly, and watched it gracefully arc into the air, then clack off a nearby boulder. Ash cursed.

"You're too impatient. You're not concentrating, as usual." Tobu really was excellent at telling Ash what he was *not* good at.

"I'm much better with a bow!" Ash complained (though this was not *entirely* true).

"You are not using a bow. *Focus.*"

Ash huffed, then placed another stone in the pouch of the sling.

"You must listen to what the world is telling you," Tobu said. "Feel the shift of the snow beneath your feet, the sturdiness of the earth far below that. Feel the caress of the air around you, the way it cradles you, moves you. Listen to the sound of the wind, and what it's saying."

Tobu was meant to be teaching Ash how to survive, and he was talking about *wind*? If Tobu wanted to hear wind, he should hang out with Flare.

Still, Ash tried having a little listen. He heard the wind all right, but it didn't seem to want to tell him anything. He felt the snow underneath his boots, sure— he felt how cold it was, and how much he wanted to go back inside. He felt the air, sharp and harsh with every breath he took.

He released the stone, and missed the target again.

And again.

And *again*.

Spirits, he *hated* slings. He ground his teeth in frustration.

"You're not *listening!*" Tobu growled.

"Well, it doesn't help when you're yelling at me!"

Tobu looked as though he was about to yell something, then stopped, and sighed. "It was wrong of me to shout. But did the Lurkers stop roaring as they hunted you?" Ash remained silent. "They did not," Tobu answered for him. "It is when things are most chaotic that your focus must be at its strongest."

With that Tobu took the sling from Ash, gave it one smooth swing, and sent the stone flying toward the target, neatly knocking off the top pebble. Ash became aware that his mouth was hanging wide open.

Handing the sling back to Ash, Tobu climbed up the ladder back to the watchtower.

"You can do it if you concentrate. Continue until you hit the target—you might surprise yourself."

Unlikely, thought Ash.

And he turned out to be right.

4

Keepsakes

Later that night—much, much later—Ash slumped into his hammock, exhausted. He'd finally managed to hit the stupid target, and pain cramped his calloused fingers. High up in the rafters, Tobu lay silent and still in his hammock. But despite how tired he was, Ash could not sleep. Every time he closed his eyes he saw slithering serpentine bodies, glistening fangs, and frantic rending claws.

Tears burned their way down his cold cheeks. The Lurker attack had been terrifying, and he wished more than anything that someone would just hold him and tell him it would be all right. He thought of Tobu and laughed bitterly under his breath. *Not likely* . . . It was at times like this that Ash missed his parents the most. He might never have known them, but he felt sure that they must have loved him and would know how to comfort him now.

Where are you? he called out in his head. *Mom, Dad . . . I* need *you.*

Rubbing at his eyes, Ash got up, dressed, and slipped out onto the watchtower roof, the chill air biting into his furs. The village lay ahead, so close and yet a world away. Ash had always felt disconnected from the other Fira, but he now felt further away than ever. He could see lantern light shimmering behind the high walls, shining like stars amid the night sky, the only light within uncountable leagues. It looked comforting, Ash thought, *beautiful*, even, if a little lonely. Or was that just how he felt?

The clustered dwellings were too numerous to count. And yet, no matter how big the village seemed, when you were forced to remain behind its walls, it began to feel very small indeed. It began to feel a lot like a prison.

It was cold, but Ash rather liked it up here on the roof.

It was peaceful . . . and it was the only place he could go to secretly listen to the mysterious songs that were carried to him upon the icy breeze.

And he was in luck, for tonight the Leviathans were singing in chorus.

Unlike the rest of the Fira, Ash found the sound soothing. He couldn't hear what they were saying—maybe they weren't saying anything—but the song itself was calm and mournful, the deep howls and eerie keening a world away from the rabid war cry they'd screamed that morning. As snow whipped through his messy black hair, Ash dug inside his furs and pulled out an ocarina. It was the one gift his parents had given him before they disappeared, and he treasured it.

He raised the ocarina to his lips. No one would hear him play up here. Not if he played quietly.

Besides, Tobu said no singing; *he said nothing about playing instruments.* Ash began to join the Leviathans' melancholy melody. He allowed the Leviathan song to envelop him, and, for a moment which seemed to last an age, it took him to another place. Somewhere away from Tobu, away from his loneliness, away from his problems. A place where he felt safe. A place that felt like home.

And despite what Ash had been through earlier that day, he felt the familiar craving to answer it with a song of his own.

Ash pulled the ocarina away and shook his head to clear it, to try to break himself from the song's spell. *I have to stop doing this. I have to. It's dangerous. Tobu made that clear enough.*

He settled for murmuring his parents' lullaby under his breath.

"This is not farewell, this is not goodbye.
Our love for you will never die.
Over the horizon, to Mother Sun's light,
We'll be waiting to hold you tight.
Walls can be broken, and left behind.
Follow the paths and you will find . . ."

He could remember only a handful of the words, but he was positive the melody would be something he remembered forever. Ash's heart swelled every time he heard it, the loving message wrapping him in a blanket of calm, protecting him from all the terrible things that had shaken his world. It felt like there was a kind of magic to the words, a magic that filled him with hope. And sometimes when he sang he thought he could see vague, blurred visions of faces. And if he tried hard enough, he could sharpen the edges. Like the memories could be touched, and lived in.

Warm, cozy firelight. Two smiling, happy faces, looking down at him with nothing but joy. It was his parents, he was sure. But just as it seemed like they were crystallizing into focus, they would blur again, lost to the blizzard of time, and Ash would be alone again.

Sometimes he even dared to believe the lullaby was a message left by his parents, some kind of hidden secret telling him where they had gone and why. He had obsessed over the lyrics he remembered, going round and round in circles, trying to find their meaning.

> *Walls can be broken, and left behind.*
> *Follow the paths and you will find . . .*

It wasn't hard to think it was telling him to leave the walls of the Fira Stronghold, and perhaps head east, to *Mother Sun's light* . . . She did awaken in the east after all. But of course that was impossible. East, west, south, or north, no one got far beyond the walls, not even the hunters. There had to be more to it, something he was missing.

But deep down he knew it was all nonsense. It was a fantasy born of his loneliness.

After all, it was only a lullaby.

Suddenly a shadow fell upon him.

Ash whipped round and with a gasp saw Tobu standing behind him. The images of his parents' faces still burned in his mind's eye, but they were disappearing like ghosts in the sun.

"I told you not to sing," Tobu said.

"I-I'm sorry. It's just a lullaby my parents used to sing to me . . . It's all I have left . . ." Ash's voice broke as he slipped the ocarina back into his furs. Was it his imagination, or did Tobu's expression soften just a little?

"It is for your own safety that I tell you not to sing."

"I know," Ash replied.

Tobu grunted. "Especially this . . . *lullaby*. And you would be wise to think carefully whom you share it with . . . the World Weave tells me that much. Now come in to bed."

Ash scrunched his eyes shut, trying one last time to conjure the faces of his parents, but it was no use. They were gone. The Leviathans' song seemed to echo his sadness as he followed Tobu back into the watchtower, where he finally fell into a deep, dreamless sleep.

➤ ❢ ⸖

The next morning, Ash decided to see if he could wheedle any more information out of his yeti guardian. It was clear he knew *something* about singing—and perhaps he could tell Ash more about this mysterious World Weave. Tobu seemed to be in a relatively good mood. During the few free moments Tobu had to himself, when he wasn't busy with chores, hunting, or meditating, he had taken to sculpting. Quite *what* he was sculpting, Ash had still not figured out. They looked like little wooden . . . *blobs* maybe?

It must be a yeti thing, Ash thought to himself. Whatever it was, Tobu's heavy brows were slightly less knitted, and Ash took this to mean he was happy. Happy*ish*? It was hard to tell.

So, feeling bold, Ash looked up from the spear Tobu had made him sharpen, took a breath, and asked: "What is a Song Weaver?"

Tobu looked up from the small chunk of wood sculpture he had been whittling. He'd already set aside three previous blobs, apparently unsatisfied with their blobby-ness.

"It is a human-kin matter," he said after some time.

"*Please*, Tobu," said Ash, sitting up. "I know you know something, and I have to know. I have to know what people think I am . . . and *why*."

Tobu let out a heavy sigh. Just as Ash began to think he'd get nothing out of his guardian, Tobu began to speak. He spoke slowly, as if he was choosing his words very carefully.

"Song Weavers are those who can Sing the Song of the Leviathans. It is no mere verse or chant they Sing, but the very Song of nature, the World Weave. Song Weavers are said to have the ability to 'speak' with Leviathans, if their skills are honed enough."

Ash felt a chill run down his spine, all the way to the tips of his fingers and toes.

He felt a connection to the Leviathans when they Sang.

He had a near uncontrollable urge to Sing along with them.

But *he* wasn't a Song Weaver. Was he?

"Why's that so bad?" Ash asked, trying to still the trembling of his hands. "Why are the Fira so afraid of me, if that's what they think I am? Surely . . . surely being able to speak to the Leviathans would be a good thing? We could ask them to leave us alone!"

"A shadow lies upon the history of the Song Weavers. What goes

one way goes the other. The World Weave is nothing if not balance. Song Weavers speak to Leviathans, so Leviathans can speak back to them. And given . . . past events . . . most human-kin fear that Leviathans can bend a human mind to their will and use them as tools against the Strongholds. This fear results in Song Weavers being shunned in the Strongholds, and shapes Fira law so that it bans all music, just to be safe."

Ash shook his head in disbelief. His hands were properly shaking now.

I'm not a Song Weaver. I can't be.

"What could I—What could a Song Weaver do to stop it? The mind-control, I mean," Ash asked, trying his best to contain the cracking in his voice.

"I do not know," Tobu said. He seemed about to leave it there, but he saw the fear in Ash's eyes. "The best thing a Song Weaver could do is to keep quiet, and to not Sing. As I have told you."

Ash felt like he'd been thrown from a great height, his belly left at the top. That was it then. He would have to stop Singing. Even the lullaby, which made his heart hurt. But maybe . . . maybe then nothing would happen to him? Maybe any tiny bit of Song Weaver that might have been in him would dwindle and disappear, and he would be normal again?

"Do you think I'm evil?" Ash blurted out. "If I am a Song Weaver? Do you think that makes me evil?"

"I don't know much about that," Tobu said, which wasn't exactly reassuring.

Ash was quiet for a moment. "I don't feel evil. I try to be nice," he said eventually.

"The world exploits weakness," grunted Tobu in reply, his face an expressionless mask as he cut his dagger into another wooden blob.

"I don't think being nice is weakness," Ash retorted. "Maybe Song Weaving could be used for good, if people were just more open-minded. It could save people. It—it could clear the way for Pathfinder sleighs, it could help deliver food and medicine to all the Strongholds of the world! It could—"

"Enough!" Tobu cut right through the wood, his carving ruined. (Or had it been made better? It was hard to tell . . .) A fire burned in his eyes. Ash braced himself for an explosion of yeti fury, but instead Tobu took a deep breath . . . and reached for a new chunk of wood. Ash let out a quiet sigh of relief. "Do not get your hopes up, boy. People can't see past what scares them."

"You don't seem to be scared of me," Ash ventured.

"There are many things I do not understand in this world. It does not mean I should fear them." Ash thought on this. "I have also seen your hunting skills. I do not see any reason to fear you based on that."

Ash rolled his eyes. *What an awful, awful last few days. At least it's the festival tomorrow. At least there's that to take my mind off all this.* Ash looked forward to the Festival of a Thousand Fires every winter. It was a great celebration in honor of Mother Sun, and the whole Stronghold dressed in elaborate costumes that represented the fire spirits to help scare away the Ice Crone.

Then, almost as if he was reading Ash's mind again, Tobu said, "I think it would be best for you not to set foot in the village for a time."

"*What? But why?!*"

"We must be confident you can control your urges. The villagers are scared. I am worried what they might do to us if you lose control again. If you try to Sing." Tobu looked up from his sculpture, noticing the disappointment in Ash's face. "Do not worry," he said, his expression the closest to sympathetic Ash had ever seen. "I shall continue your training here. You will not miss out on any fun."

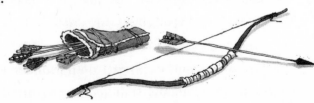

5

Festival of
a Thousand Fires

Fire spirits danced in the night sky, shimmering like luminous turquoise flames against the star-studded blackness. Despite Ash's pleading protests, Tobu had insisted that Ash not go to the festival, saying that he should stay home and practice his bow work. Ash was not surprised, but it didn't stop him from feeling furious about it.

It was *one* night. One night, and Tobu couldn't even let him have that.

The rumble of excited, happy voices drifted over from the village, as did the mouthwatering smell of a banquet being cooked. Ash knew torches of all sizes were being lit throughout the Stronghold. The festival marked the end of the coldest winter moons, and the coming of Mother Sun's warming embrace (which, in truth, only meant that the days would be teeth-

chatteringly cold instead of mind-numbingly freezing).
The whole village would feast and celebrate till dawn's
welcome light. Tobu hated festivals. *Something to do
with all the dancing and people having fun no doubt*, Ash
thought. But Tobu was invited every year, and like the
rise and fall of Mother Sun herself, he would attend, as
though his honor depended on it.

The moment Tobu had left, grumbling under his
breath about what a waste of precious resources the festival was, Ash lowered his bow and climbed to the roof to
think about the options that lay before him.

"Maybe I should sneak back?" he said to himself,
looking west to the village. He could see the warm, in-

viting glow of bonfires rising above the walls. Sitting on
the roof next to him was Tobu's latest sculpture. Tobu
was getting better. This one looked like a blob with eyes.
"What do you think, Eye-blob?" Ash asked the sculpture. "I know Tobu's worried about me being around
the others, but maybe he's just being his usual glum self?
Maybe the Stronghold will have realized it was pretty
mean to kick me out here with a grumpy yeti, and they'll
invite me back to be a normal Fira after all?" Ash placed
his hands on his hips and did his best Alderman Kindil
impression. "'I was so wrong, Ash! So, so wrong. Can
you ever forgive me?' Then he'll get down on his big ol'
knees and say, 'Please come back, we beg you! You are a

hero of the Fira—stories of your strength and valor will be told for centuries!' 'OK, OK,' I'll say. 'I'll come back to the village, if you insist, but on one condition: Get off the floor. You're embarrassing me!'"

Ash went silent as he thought about this. His smile faltered. "Yeah, right, Eye-blob. I don't think so." His fingers cramped with pain, a reminder of his intense archery lessons. "Maybe if I tell them how horribly Tobu is treating me, they'd save me from his evil clutches?" The sculpture stared back at him with sad, mismatched eyes. "I know, I know. He made you, I get it. And I guess he's not *that* bad. But you have to admit he's nothing but a big hunk of grump. And what's the worst thing the Stronghold could do to me if I go back? Cast me out into the wilds?" Ash paused as he saw a flock of white birds take flight on the Snow Sea. Seconds later a gigantic dorsal fin broke the surface of the snow, leaving a hazy white mist in its wake, before diving back into the depths. Ash stared at the patch where it had emerged, but it was now nowhere to be seen. He shuddered.

"OK, so maybe being cast out into the wilds *would* be pretty bad." Ash drummed his fingers upon the roof. Eventually he threw his hands up in the air. "Nope, I've decided—I'm going in! Don't try to stop me, Eye-blob, I'm doing this! I have to. Look at me, I'm sitting here, talking to a piece of wood!" And with that Ash rushed inside to his hammock, and, from under its furs, grabbed the ramshackle mask he'd managed to make in secret. It was of Rayj, his favorite fire spirit. It wasn't much to look at, but it would hide his face, and that was all that mattered, right?

I'm not missing this, Tobu, no matter how big and scary you are.

Then he slid down the watchtower ladder, had a quick glance around to make sure that Tobu was nowhere to be seen, and scampered across the bridge toward the village.

➤ ❗ ◄

The Stronghold hummed with excitement and activity. Ash couldn't drink it in fast enough, although he certainly tried. A large man with a grinning spirit mask stumbled through the crowd with a platter of candied roots. He barged into Ash, nearly dropping the sweets all over Ash's head. "Sorry about tha', little one!" he boomed.

"I-it's OK," Ash replied, checking his mask.

"Here, can I offer you one o' these in payment? Snagged 'em straight from the kitchen, I did!" Just as he finished, an angry voice bellowed over the laughing crowd.

"Where's that lug gone with my roots? I'll stick him in the hot-sugar barrel if I ever catch him, I swear it!" the cook said.

The man lifted his mask up and revealed a weathered, bearded face that winked at Ash. "Go on, lad, before she finds me!" Ash took a candied root as the man jogged off with the platter to cheers from the crowd. Turning to face one of the dwellings so there was no danger of being spotted, Ash lifted his mask up just enough to pop the sweet into his mouth. It tasted beyond amazing. It was sweet, of course, but smoky too, with a crunchy texture that seemed to melt in his mouth the more he chewed. *Beats redroot, that's for sure.*

As he wove through the celebrating crowd he spotted Flare, Ryse, and Shyne putting on their masks. Plucking up his courage, he made his way over.

"H-hi, guys!" Ash greeted them.

They squinted as though that would help them see through his mask. He lifted it up, careful not to let too many people see the face behind it.

"Ash?" Ryse asked.

"Yeah. You don't mind if I hang out with you, do you?" Ash said. Tobu's warning that the Stronghold was becoming ever more fearful of what Ash might be echoed through his mind. Had Ryse noticed Ash had been about to Sing during the Lurker attack, like Tobu had?

The friends looked at each other. Flare cleared his throat. Ash held his breath.

"Well, we survived a Lurker attack together . . . That makes us practically family, right?" Ryse said, a large smile spreading across his face.

A hot glow of happiness bloomed within Ash. He felt so relieved he burst out laughing. "Yep, I'm pretty sure that's the rule," he replied. "Cool masks, everyone!"

Flare had made a grotesque Ice Crone mask, Shyne had created a beautiful fire-spirit face, complete with dyed hawk feathers, and Ryse had made . . . well, Ryse appeared to have stuck a load of snow hare fur round his face. "Thanks! And you're just in time," he said. "Tell me what you think my mask looks like. It's obvious, right?"

Ash took a closer look. "Mm, er . . . are you trying to make it look like you have a beard?"

"*What?* No! It's clearly a frost bear!"

"Oh, right," Ash said. "Yeah, that was going to be my second guess."

"Exactly! Shyne said I looked silly." Ryse shook his head in disbelief.

"I didn't say you looked silly," Shyne corrected. "I said you looked *stupid*. There's a difference."

"Oh, ha ha," Ryse replied. "I told you my mask was

gonna be even better than last winter's!"

"Your mask last winter was you wearing your cloak back to front with your hood pulled over your face," Shyne pointed out, and Flare burst out laughing.

"Your mask looks great!" Ash lied, not wanting to hurt Ryse's feelings, aware of Shyne's eyes rolling again from behind her wonderfully crafted mask and Flare giggling behind his monstrous one.

"Well, enough about Ryse and his inability to make anything at all. Shall we get this party started, or what?" Shyne said, leading the way into the crowd.

6

Fire

Everywhere they looked, the Fira ate, drank, and laughed, their extravagant masks as varied and colorful as the spirits they represented. There was food the likes of which Ash had only dreamed of back in his tower, and the smells of roasting meat, cooking spices, and flame-baked cakes made his mouth water. And all around the village, in every nook and cranny, were lights. Torches and candles, hanging lanterns and bonfires . . . the village was almost as bright as Mother Sun herself!

People waved and greeted Ash and his friends as they passed. It felt strange to Ash at first. He clung to his mask for dear life, worried that they might see through his disguise, but it soon became apparent that no one was any the wiser. He even spotted Tobu standing alone in the shadow of the alderman's lodge, his face as bright and chipper as dirty brown snow slush. A kind passerby offered him a mask to wear, and Tobu pushed it aside with disdain.

Yikes, just try to relax for once! thought Ash, before hurrying past.

Farther on, a storyteller held a group of children and adults enraptured by the tale of a Pathfinder's journey to the greatest Stronghold of them all: Aurora. "And thus our hero traveled farther than you can imagine, gliding across the oceans of ice upon his mighty sleigh!" The storyteller stooped low only to leap up high, making hand gestures to represent a sleigh traveling the great distances across the Snow Sea. "Until his journey at last came to an end, the jewel of the Snow Sea shining bright before him. His heart lifted high at the sight of fair Aurora's might!"

Ash's imagination ran wild at these stories. He would often dream of leaving the Fira walls and following in his parents' footsteps on the path of adventure, setting off into the wilds on a sleigh. What wonders must lie out there. What sights! And in the center of it all: Aurora. The biggest settlement in the world. The central Stronghold, the meeting place of the Pathfinders. Ash had heard wondrous tales of the place, of its soaring spires and monuments that could have been built only by giants—but of course had never seen it with his own eyes. Spirits, he would love to go there one day!

Next, the friends gathered round a thrilling display of fire dancing. Each dancer held a long stick, both ends ablaze, twirling them round in complicated motions and wide circles. Just as it looked as though one dancer would strike another with their flame, they would deftly weave between each other to the gasps of the audience. The whole dance was done in an almost eerie silence, the dancers moving only to the sound of the crackling bonfires and the whooshing of the fire sticks. Ash couldn't help but think how impressive and stirring the show would've been with music. Drums, ocarinas . . . *Singing*.

"Fancy giving it a go?" asked a laughing girl dancer, pointing a spare fire stick in Ash's direction. She was about his height and wore the mask of a snarling wolver spirit.

"M-me? I don't really—" Ash began, but it was no use. The girl pulled him into the circle of dancers, placing the fire stick into his hands and raising her own. Ash tried again. "I don't know how!"

"I'll show you!" the girl answered. She spun her stick slowly round and round, and Ash did his best to copy. He felt like his arms were getting tangled, that the flames were too close to his mask, which suddenly felt far too big and flammable. But it didn't seem to bother the girl one bit. She ducked and wove about him, laughing and cheering the whole while. Her happiness was infectious. Ash started laughing too, even though he probably looked more like a demented ulk than a dancer. "Now you're getting it!" the girl encouraged. People clapped and urged the dancing partners on.

Ash didn't want the dance to end. He felt like he could've danced all night, danced forever. But eventually

he and the girl had to stand to the side to catch their breath. He leaned his fire stick on his shoulder, sweating despite the cold air.

"Wow, you're on fire!" the girl said.

Ash grinned. He suspected she was being generous, but he appreciated it nonetheless.

"I think I started to get the hang of it there at the end, right?" he said.

"No, I mean, you're actually on fire," said the girl.

Ash's eyes widened as he realized the ember-hot end of the fire stick had set the furs at his shoulder alight.

"Argh!" He dove down into the wet snow and rolled around, desperate to put the fire out, the girl helping to pat out the flames. When it was clear that Ash was no longer alight, nor likely to set anything else aflame, they both started laughing.

"Hey, so who are you?" the girl asked in between giggles. "I mean, under your mask?" She raised her own and revealed her face. It was Borea, a girl who would never normally give Ash a second glance in lessons.

Ash's stomach tied into a knot. "Erm," he began. "Sorry, I—I just remembered—I—"

"Hey!" came Ryse's voice just in the nick of time. He slipped between Ash and Borea. "May I have this dance?" he said, wiggling his eyebrows up and down at Borea and taking Ash's fire stick. Borea didn't look convinced, but her features became friendlier as she took a closer look at Ryse.

"Are you dressed as a frost bear?" she asked, taking up her own fire stick. "I love frost bears!"

"As a matter of fact, I am!" Ryse said, leading her back into the dance.

Ash could almost *feel* Shyne rolling her eyes at the whole scene.

"*Thank you,*" Ash whispered to Ryse.

Ryse grinned and nodded, before spinning his fire stick in such a wide circle he managed to knock Borea's mask off.

But before the children had time to laugh, a sudden hush fell over the crowd. As if by an unspoken word the villagers began to stamp their feet as one. It felt like the Fira Stronghold had a heartbeat of its own.

BOOM.

BOOM.

BOOM.

"It's time!" called one villager.

"Fira, prepare your offerings!" called out a light bringer silhouetted against the Great Pyre, the most sacred spot in the Stronghold. It was a giant flame that was said to have been burning for two hundred years. As the village gathered round, an old lady passed something to Ash. It was an object made of woven twigs in the shape of a five-pointed star. *A star offering . . .* The Fira would sculpt these offerings and set them alight just before dawn, scaring away the Ice Crone's night and welcoming in Mother Sun.

The light bringers began their prayers as the crowd marched forward and dipped torches into the Great Pyre. One by one, the Fira lit their star offerings. "Make a wish!" the old woman said to Ash as he pulled his own torch from the bonfire. He hesitated before stealing himself away to a shadowed, unwatched corner. Ash lifted the mask from his face, just in case the spirits would get confused as to who was making the wish. Swallowing back a lump in his throat, he nodded.

I wish that I could find my parents. I wish for a proper home . . . for a family.

With that he touched his torch to the star offering, and soon it was ablaze. All around him the Fira watched their offerings dance and flicker in flames. It was so beautiful—Ash felt like the stars had come down to visit the Stronghold. As if hearing her children's call, Mother Sun began to awaken on the horizon, and light pierced the night sky.

But as he watched the sun rise, Ash couldn't help but feel sadness pulling at him. The festival was nearly over. He would soon have to go back to his tower, back to Tobu, before the villagers began to take their masks off. Before the people saw who he really was.

AHWOOOOOOO.

So lost in his thoughts was Ash, it took him a while to notice the horn sounding from the battlements. Distant calls and shouts could be heard. The crowd shifted nervously. "What's happening?" someone asked.

AHWOOOOOOO.

AHWOOOOOOO.

Ash's heart caught in his throat as he realized what he was hearing.

The warning horn. The Leviathans—they're attacking!

7

No Other Choice

Ash joined the crowd in their stampede to the top of the battlements, everyone desperate to see what was happening. His heart raced as he climbed the wooden gangplank, pushed and shoved by the crush of people, nearly throwing himself over the battlements in his hurry to see out. *There!* Racing toward the Stronghold from the south, snow trailing behind it like a long white tail, was a Pathfinder sleigh.

Ash's heart jolted. *Pathfinders.*

All Fira were thrilled when Pathfinders arrived, especially since it was incredibly rare to find them so far north these days. But it was always particularly exciting for Ash. Deep, deep down in his heart he couldn't help hoping that his parents might be returning for him, to scoop him up and make everything right.

He reached into his furs and grasped his ocarina. *Could it be them?* He didn't have long to wonder. The sleigh was under attack from four Hurtlers, particularly hideous Leviathans that looked like jaws on legs. Hurtlers didn't hide under the snows to catch their prey like Lurkers and other such Leviathans. They were so fast, they didn't need to—they simply ran them down. But this time they seemed to be well matched. The enormous sleigh they were chasing was like a mini Stronghold in itself, its huge bulk as high and mighty as Stronghold walls, its massive runners as long as the alderman's lodge. Tall red sails rippled in the wind, the symbol of a snowflake woven into their designs. Large propellers and a sunstone-powered enjin thrust the vessel forward at an incredible speed. The build-knowledge of such a thing was beyond what normal Strongholders could create, of course, and came from archeomek—mysterious technology and artifacts that were unearthed from the ruins of the World Before. But despite this technical marvel, the Hurtlers had no trouble keeping up with it, charging through the snow with their powerful legs, biting at the runners like wolvers snapping at the feet of ulk. Ash could see their Song-aura, a mess of frantic lashing shapes that trailed behind them like crimson smoke.

"*Hunters! To your positions!*" ordered the hunts-master.

"Man the battlements! Load the harpoon launchers!"

Ash watched the hunters take defensive positions along the wall, Tobu alongside them, reminding Ash to yank down the mask he'd fogotten he should be wearing amidst all the excitement. The Fira hunters scrambled, bows at the ready. Others pulled the cranks and aimed the large harpoon launchers that squatted on the walls.

Tobu drew an arrow from his quiver and nocked it to his bow.

The sleigh itself was badly damaged, but the Pathfinder crew— little dots from this distance— were doing their best to fend off the monsters. Ash saw one jab a spear right at a

Hurtler's great maw. The creature wrapped its long serpentine tongue round the shaft, twisted its head, and wrenched it from their hands, nearly pulling the defender over the side to their certain doom.

Another Hurtler screeched and rammed the sleigh, arrows clacking off its thick hide as the crew desperately tried to drive it back. Yet another tore deep rents into the sleigh's side, sending it swerving in the snow. The captain was clearly skilled, however, and pulled it back on course with a skid. They sped toward the ramp that the Fira were now lowering from the wall, the large ropes that held it up creaking from the strain of the heavy wood.

The Pathfinders *had* to make it or they'd soon be torn to pieces.

"*Fire!*" the hunts-master roared.

Arrows and stones tore through the air. Some struck true and impaled the hard flesh of the Leviathans, their blue lifeblood leaking from the wounds, but most of the missiles sank harmlessly into the snow, the Hurtlers dodging the attacks, weaving and leaping out of the way without losing momentum. A harpoon launcher propelled its huge bolt with a loud *ka-chunk*, but this too hit nothing but the ground in a huge explosion of snow.

"They're too fast!" Ash said aloud.

"They'll rip the sleigh to shreds before we manage to hit them!" agreed a man beside him, raising his mask to get a better view. The Hurtlers were ramming the sleigh in unison now, biting gashes into the splintering rudder, vicious, serrated tongues tearing chunks out of the runners with frightening force. The sleigh swerved and shook, the captain desperately trying to keep it on course.

Dread swept through Ash. It was bad enough to see anyone under attack like this, but what if his parents *were* on the sleigh? So close to returning after all these years, only to get eaten by Hurtlers on the last leg?

"They're not gonna make it," he gasped. *I have to help them. But . . . how?!*

Sing, said a voice in his head.

He went cold. *No. The Stronghold would absolutely lose it! So would Tobu!*

There was a loud shredding sound as the Hurtlers tore the rudder from the back of the sleigh. The captain had no control over it now. They were in serious trouble.

Ash couldn't bear it. *I—I might be thrown out into the wilds! I wouldn't stand a chance. Not against Leviathans! And what if the Leviathans can control me?* Ash began to panic. *But . . . what if Song Weaving can save their lives?*

Now the Hurtlers keened and shrilled with pleasure, sensing they had nearly brought down their prey. The crew were close enough to hear from the battlements now. They were screaming, shouting, doing everything they could to survive.

No. *I can't let this happen.* Ash balled his hands into fists. *It's now or never. Now or never! Oh, spirits . . .*

Ash tore his mask off, took a big gulp of air, and began to Sing.

It was strange how easy it was, considering it was something he'd tried to restrain and hide all his life. Low at first, but growing in volume, in strength, Ash Sang his Song. There were no words; at least, they weren't words he knew. It was a raw sound, primal and simple, but haunting and utterly enchanting. Ash could feel it in every muscle and tendon in his body, and deep within his bones. He was dimly aware of the crowd parting along the battlements, gasping and yelling in horror. But Ash didn't care. For him the world appeared to change, the falling snow gleaming like stars in the night sky. Lights danced in and out and around his body, passing through him like ghosts, but warm to the touch. They gave him strength, connecting him to his surroundings in a way he had never felt before. He had his own aura now, this one the color of stars. After all these years of having to bottle up his Song, denying it even existed—at last he was able to release it, and it burst out like a torrent. He felt like he was flying, like the fears that had clouded him for so long were burned away in the light of his Song.

It felt *amazing*.

"*Peace!*" Ash Sang, channeling his emotions into the thread of the Song. "*LEAVE!*"

His Song-aura swirled forth like a blizzard of starlight. It crashed against the mass of the Hurtlers' Song-auras, which immediately pushed back, resisting him, trying to block him from their minds.

"*RESIST, FIGHT, DENY!*" they roared.

Ash felt his brow crease, his fists shake. *Come on, guys—work with me here!*

He Sang harder. "*PEACE, CALM, FRIENDS!*"

"He's calling them upon us!" he heard someone scream.

"STOP HIM!" came a voice a million miles away. To Ash there were only the Hurtlers and him. The monsters shrieked and roared.

His Song-aura swirled around the thrashing red war cry, trying to get the Hurtlers to calm down. He could see, if it could be called seeing, that there were gaps and cracks in their squirming auras. His warming Song-aura surged through the cracks like a tumultuous river, and to Ash's delight, instead of resisting, it felt like the Hurtlers were *calming*. They began to join their Song with Ash's, diving and swooping and entwining round it, two very different auras suddenly Singing the same tune. The blood-red of their auras turned into a tranquil ice-blue, the thrashing shapes withering away into glowing sparks, dancing with Ash's Song like snowflakes in a flurry. The Hurtlers dipped their heads, their serpentine tails drooping.

"Go," Ash Sang with all the focus he could muster. The thought was channeled from deep within his being, and the Song carried his message. "*Go. Please leave us. We're not your enemies.*" The Hurtlers mewed and grunted.

It was working! Ash couldn't believe it, but it was *working*! It was like he was pouring water onto the

burning flames of the Hurtlers' hunger and fury. They began to slow, and the sleigh managed to pull away.

Exhaustion suddenly washed over Ash. He could feel his Song getting weaker, his aura flickering in and out of existence. But he'd done what was needed.

The sleigh tore up the ramp into the safety of the Stronghold.

Ash began to laugh weakly. *I've done it! I've let the Pathfinders get to safety! This—this is incredible!*

Which was the last thing he thought before two hunters rudely tackled him to the ground.

8

Friend and Foe

"*Song Weaver!*" someone roared in anger as Ash was brought down from the wall and back into the village. The villagers encircled him, buzzing with tension and anxious murmurs, all in the shadow of the sleigh that was busy docking at the gate close by. Ash tried to squirm free but was thrown to the cold ground for his efforts.

"Be still, *Song Weaver!*" grunted the hunter who had held him.

Ash's head spun. This wasn't what he'd imagined at all! He'd thought his success would've changed their minds. He'd helped the Pathfinder sleigh get to safety—surely they could see his Song had been used for good?

"I don't believe it. The Song Weavers are a dying

people; there are barely any of them left. How can there be one *here*?" Alderman Kindil rumbled quietly as he approached Ash.

At last, Alderman Kindil! Ash thought. *He's always fair. He'll sort this out!*

"We all saw it, true as flame," said the hunter, lifting Ash up and pinning his arms behind his back with rough hands. The hunter's rugged face was scarred from past scrapes with Leviathans. "We've all suspected for years that the boy was one of them—and now we have proof! He Sang their Song, spoke with the Hurtlers. 'Twas clear as day." The crowd was in an uproar, and the alderman furrowed his brow.

"Fire spirits protect us. So the rumors are true."

"I—I was trying to help!" Ash called out, desperate for support. He looked from his old guardian Charr to Shyne's parents, but none would meet his eye. Even his friends couldn't bring themselves to look at him, though they stood a short distance away. "Ryse, *please*! You have to tell them! Tell them I'm not like that!" He struggled to break free from the hunter's grip, managing to reach out for his friend, but Ryse tore away from his grasp, his eyes wide with fear and disgust.

"It makes sense—we long suspected his father was one of *them* too," a light bringer said as the hunter pulled

Ash back into a hold. "The filth runs in the blood! The tales do not lie."

Ash's ears pricked at the mention of his father, despite the awful insults.

My father . . . So they suspected him *of being a Song Weaver. Is—is my mother one too?* Somehow the idea that they might have been made Ash feel better. A little less alone in the world. But only a little.

He could feel the ocarina hidden within his furs, and he clung to the small amount of comfort it offered. How he wished his parents were there right then.

We'll be waiting to hold you tight . . .

Mum . . . Dad . . . where are you?

"We need to act, and fast, yes indeed!" declared Light Bringer Hayze. "The young 'uns won't remember the last time a Song Weaver schemed with the Leviathans. She helped them break into the Bora Stronghold, our neighbors. The entire Stronghold was torn to pieces! The Leviathans will use their Song to control *any* human-kin susceptible to their voice, yes indeed! We must cast him out! Cast him out, I say!"

A chill stabbed through Ash's body. To hear Hayze, his teacher, say these horrible words . . . He felt that the whole scene was happening to someone else, and that something had grabbed his heart in a painful tight grip and wouldn't let go.

"I-I'm not like that! I would *never* do something like that, I promise!" he squeaked. "I didn't mean to—"

"*Quiet*, boy!" commanded one of the hunters. "We've heard enough from you already." Ash's face flushed—he was trembling. They spoke as if he were one of the Leviathans.

"Why don't you leave us and live with your monster friends, monster-boy?" Thaw sneered from the crowd to a rousing cheer.

"Yeah, go live in the wilds like the rest of your kind!" said another. "You have no place here!"

"*Freak!*" someone shouted.

"*Monster!*" spat a man.

The angry, frightened crowd grabbed, pushed, and jostled toward Ash like a snowstorm. He cringed in terror—and then a flash of white sped through the teeming villagers, separating Ash from their reaching hands. The crowd parted as fast as it had formed.

"T-Tobu?" Ash stammered. The yeti was low and taut, his spear held ready behind his back. His muscles were straining, prepared to strike. As the crowd made room for him he rose, slowly, to his full imposing height, and then hauled Ash toward him.

"You shame yourselves," he growled. "He is just a child!"

The crowd shifted uncomfortably. Ash may have been a Song Weaver, but, as their anger cooled, they realized that Tobu was right.

"I only tried to help!" Ash said. He couldn't help it— he began to cry. "I don't want to be used by the Leviathans, I don't want to be like this, I—I promise! You have to believe me!"

"*Enough!*" demanded Alderman Kindil. "I'm sorry, but the boy cannot stay here, Tobu. I will not put my people in danger. But he is not without hope. I have heard rumors of a place where his kind gather—the boy's father himself mentioned it once. A Stronghold of Song

Weavers, so the legends say." The crowd rippled with fear at the idea of such a place, many touching the sunstone pendants that hung from their necks for protection. "He would be welcome there, unlike the other Strongholds. It is where I would go, were I in his boots." The alderman gave Ash a firm look—though one that wasn't entirely unsympathetic.

Ash's ragged breaths caught in his throat at the mention of this place. Could a place like that exist?

Tobu broadened his huge shoulders and growled dangerously. "If you will act so low as to abandon him, then so be it. But I will *not* let you send him to his death alone."

Protests and grumbles came from the crowd, but Alderman Kindil silenced them with a raised hand. "As you wish, Tobu. You shall follow him into exile."

"It would seem this place is not as honorable as I had thought," Tobu said, and Ash saw the hunters in the group bristle in response.

"Once an outcast, always an outcast," one spat.

If at all possible, things were becoming even more tense, when—

"Floundering *fish farts!*" came a loud voice. The Fira crowd turned as one to see a gangplank pop out from over the top of the Pathfinder sleigh and bang down to the ground.

9

Pathfinders

A large mursu stepped from the deck and began clunking down the gangplank. Ash had seen a mursu Pathfinder many moons ago, but it didn't lessen the wonder at seeing one of these strange walrus-like creatures again. She had a peg leg, which was so big it looked to be more of a log leg, and a very casual swagger for someone who'd so nearly been chomped by Leviathans. Her scrappy armor revealed bare, leathery arms. A mursu's blubber kept them from feeling the cold like human-kin did, or so Ash had been told, but it was still a surprising sight. "By Aurora, did you see how close that was?" she asked the crowd. "Course you did, course you did, you were right there after all! Thought I was going to lose more than my rudder there, isn't that right, Master Podd?" she asked a small upstanding-looking vulpis, who followed close behind, his fox-like ears and bushy tail poking out of his patchwork clothing.

"Indeed, captain," he said in a surprisingly deep voice.

"That's why you're my first mate, Master Podd—you know what you're talking about, make no mistake."

"We are delighted to welcome you to the Fira Stronghold, Pathfinders!" Alderman Kindil boomed, opening his arms wide in greeting, hiding the tension of moments ago well. "Captain Nuk, of the sleigh known as the *Frostheart*, if I remember correctly?"

"You do indeed, alderman!" said the mursu Pathfinder, shaking his hand so vigorously it looked like he might be pulled off his feet. "Pleasure, as always!" The rest of Captain Nuk's crew joined her before the expectant villagers. Ash's already very sad heart sank even lower when no Fira Pathfinders stepped off the sleigh to scoop him up into their arms. He knew it had been a long shot, hoping for his parents to be aboard, but he still felt a stab of disppointment.

Instead, there were a few shaken-looking men and women who looked like they hailed from Strongholds all around the Snow Sea, dressed in the ragtag clothing Ash only ever saw with the rare arrival of such crews. To Ash's surprise there was also a girl only a little older than

him. Her head was half shaved, half sprouting dread-locks. Oddest of all was a man in dark tattered robes laced with ancient archeomek, who followed the rest. He looked like he'd walked straight out of the wilds. His turquoise eyes were so bright they seemed to glow, made all the brighter by the dark sockets they were set within; they darted about the Stronghold, taking it all in like a hawk searching for its prey. He seemed amused at something, a wolvish grin never once leaving his narrow, sharp face. While all of the crew looked like hardened travelers, Ash thought this guy looked like he'd seen more than most. Tobu had spoken of giant mountain cats back in the yeti lands, and this was how Ash imagined they would look if they had long matted hair. And a beard.

Alderman Kindil stepped forward importantly. "It has been, what, six, seven years since your last run here? But your timing could not be more fortuitous. We are in desperate need of supplies from the outside world!"

"Try telling that to my sleigh. Poor pup," Nuk said. As if in response, a plank fell from the sleigh's ruined frame.

"Indeed," Kindil said. "That was dangerously close, although all too common in these parts sadly. There was a time when we were visited by many a sleigh, but we're lucky to see any but you these days. The Leviathans around here have become ever more hostile over the last few decades, though what's stirring them up is anyone's guess." The Fira crowd watched the exchange in awed silence. Ash seemed to have been forgotten for the time being.

"Same all over the world, I take no pleasure in telling you," Captain Nuk said. "Ever more livid they get, and they were already ruddy fuming to begin with! Still, I must say, I'm not at all surprised we're the only Pathfinders who've made the run out here in a while. You really are out in the middle of nowhere, I'm sure I don't have to tell you. Took us moons to get out this far, but we assumed you could probably do with the help up north. Oh!" A shadow fell over the captain's face. "Have your lookouts keep their eyes peeled—you have Wraiths prowling nearby. The scoundrels nearly spotted us, but we were lucky enough to give 'em the slip. I certainly hope we've not used up all the luck we have."

Wraiths. A threat nearly as terrible as the Leviathans, or so it was said. Ash had never witnessed a raid from the monstrous pirates himself, which was a good thing, really, considering the tales Pathfinders told. They were not stories you wanted to hear while you were eating your dinner.

"And as for those blasted Hurtlers running us ragged," Captain Nuk continued, "one thing after the other, I tell you! They followed us for miles, which is highly unusual, I might add. They're racers, not stamina beasts, although you wouldn't know it from watching that lot." She shook her head as though she could still scarcely believe it.

"Well, we thank you for your great bravery and honor," Kindil said.

"I'm glad, alderman, I truly am," Captain Nuk said. "But I'd sooner ask who it was that saved *us.* We would've been *Hurtler chow* were it not for them!"

The crowd shifted uncomfortably.

"Well, it was our courageous hunters, of course! No finer marksmen will you find in these parts," Kindil replied, a bit too loudly. Ash noticed him making a get-him-out-of-here! gesture to Tobu, who was more than happy to oblige and began pulling meaningfully on Ash's furs. Clearly the Stronghold didn't want to let the Pathfinders know that the Fira were harboring a Song Weaver.

Probably because he thinks I'll scare them off. Ash was trying to resist Tobu's less-than-subtle tugs on his hood, but it wasn't doing him much good.

"I was most impressed with their shooting, most impressed indeed!" said the mursu captain heartily. "But it is not what I mean, appreciated though it is. I mean the one who was Singing their lungs out from atop the wall."

The crowd held its breath. Alderman Kindil was at a loss for words. A shot of excitement whipped through Ash. The captain didn't seem scared of him—quite the opposite! Tobu began to pull harder on his furs, pushing through the crowd. Ash wriggled in protest, trying to hear what was being said.

Kindil gave a nervous laugh. "Singing . . . ? Oh, I don't think so. There's no *Song Weaver* here, if that's what you mean."

"Oh. I suppose it must've been the Valkyries of my clan Singing me to the afterlife as my days came to a close then. I'm getting old, you see; I hear them Singing quite often these days. Unless, of course, I'm not dying yet and the boy that yeti over there is so eager to get away from us happens to be the one that saved me and my crew . . . ?"

Tobu froze. Ash didn't know what to do. Should he agree, or keep quiet? He looked to the alderman, who opened and closed his mouth like a fish, obviously feeling at as much of a loss as Ash.

"OK, fine. The boy *is* a Song Weaver," Kindil finally admitted.

The villagers stirred around them, many gripping their sunstone talismans for protection. Ash saw someone spit on the ground not too far from where he was standing. *Eurgh!*

"Bouncin' blubber balls! Is that so?" Captain Nuk looked impressed. "Well, now. You don't see too many of them running around the place and that's a fact Master Podd wouldn't mind telling you."

The small vulpis gave a little nod at her side. "I wouldn't, indeed, captain."

"Yes . . . but the boy is . . . is of the Fira," Kindil said. "And we'll deal with him the Fira way, you can rely on that."

And what way is that? Ash wondered with a shudder.

"There is no reason for this to affect future visits

from your sleigh," Kindil continued, speaking a bit too fast and betraying his nerves. "Aurora does not have to concern itself with us in that regard!"

"Aye, well, calm yourself, alderman, I shan't be blabbering to the Council or anything; of that you have my word." Captain Nuk looked toward Ash. "Many thanks to you, dear boy! You did a brave thing, and we, the crew of the *Frostheart*, won't soon forget it."

"*Aye!*" the crew yelled, raising their fists in thanks.

"Hear, hear!" called out the wild-looking man, despite the clear discomfort in the Fira audience. Ash suspected the man might've even been *enjoying* it. Ash too couldn't help himself. He grinned from ear to ear and nodded back at Captain Nuk and her crew. The wild, bright-eyed man's grin seemed to grow even larger. He stared with great intensity at Ash, who was then yanked away by a grim-faced Tobu.

If the Pathfinders are grateful for my Song Weaving, surely the Fira will have to see the good I did too? Ash thought hopefully. *They'll have to understand . . . . right?*

10

Lunah

Wrong.

Ash and Tobu had tramped back to the watchtower in silence, Ash not daring to say a word to his guardian. They arrived to find that the watchtower hatch refused to open—frozen shut, as it often was. Tobu was not in the mood for stubborn hatches. With a grunt he burst it from its hinges with his shoulder, climbing within as though the hatch had never been there. Ash gulped and followed Tobu inside.

The watchtower was cold, as always. The family of pigeons who lived in the rafters (and who did their very best to poo on Ash's head whenever he least expected it) bobbed their heads and cooed in surprise at the sudden commotion. Tobu didn't say a word, he just huffed and growled, stomping from one end of the tower to the other in quick, angry strides, banging some bowls together, apparently preparing food for the two of them to eat.

Ash was at a loss for words. He didn't know what to feel. On the one hand, he'd Song Woven for the first time, which had been incredible. And he'd saved all those lives! But, on the other, he'd doomed Tobu and himself to an eternity of exile. His mind was barely keeping up with the terrible situation.

"We are no longer welcome with the Fira," Tobu said, stating the obvious. "Your rash thoughtlessness has seen to that." Ash felt he should defend himself, but he was far too tired to try. "We must prepare for the journey ahead," Tobu continued. "To survive the wilds, to travel to another Stronghold, you will have to draw on every lesson I have taught you. You will need to have all your wits about you."

Ash knew Tobu was an expert. He was the only person the villagers had ever known to have survived a journey through the wilds on foot. It had been why the Stronghold had accepted him—anyone with that much strength and grit had a place among the Fira.

"We will go south. There are more Strongholds down there. And *if* we arrive safely, we shall keep your Song Weaving a secret."

If.

And even if we do somehow survive, it still doesn't end well. I'd still have to hide my power. Still pretend to be something I'm not.

Ash and his guardian sat and ate their redroot in silence. The sad otherworldly Song of the Leviathans could be heard outside, calling out into the new day. Tears ran down Ash's cheeks. He told himself it was because of the spice of the redroot.

Ash sat very still. A snowflake landed on the tip of his nose, but he didn't flinch, not a bit. He was far too absorbed with watching the Pathfinders as they made the much-needed repairs to their sleigh and unloaded crates and barrels for trade with the Stronghold.

The Fira had given Ash and Tobu two weeks to make their plans and collect supplies before they had to leave, and so Tobu was out on a hunt, gathering valuable rations for the dangerous journey ahead of them. Ash had been ordered to stay out of the village, so of course he had snuck in. He was fascinated by the Pathfinder crew. Ash had seen only a few Pathfinder arrivals in his whole life, so far from Aurora's Embrace were the Fira, and he'd been so young at the time. But the thrill and wonder never grew old. The crew were so strange, so *different*, covered in weird and wonderful tattoos, their clothes decked with mysterious talismans. Ash's belly rolled with excitement. He'd spent his entire life in the Fira Stronghold, and to see all these outsiders, these people who came from lands so distant they were almost unimaginable . . . It was no wonder that the arrival of a Pathfinder crew was often the most exciting thing that happened at the Stronghold.

One of the crewwomen spat on the ground.

Whoooooa.

Ash watched in wonder. They looked so wild. They looked like adventurers. They looked like they were *free.* Surely this was the only way to travel the Snow Sea—aboard a sunstone-powered sleigh. One of the Pathfinders Sang happily as she gazed out to the east with a seeing-glass.

"The horizon looms before me now, waaay-ho, waaay-ho!
We slice through ice with our forward bow—"

"SHH!" hissed a nearby Fira tanner, waving the knife they had been using to scrape an ulk skin. "It is forbidden to Sing here!"

"Right you are!" the Pathfinder said, imitating a sealing motion across her lips. The sound of another Singing had been, quite literally, music to Ash's ears. He hadn't expected quite how pleasant it would sound. The Pathfinder's Song about distant horizons made Ash think of his own lullaby, the last few lines of which he'd dwelled on since he could remember:

Over the horizon, to Mother Sun's light,
We'll be waiting to hold you tight.
Walls can be broken, and left behind.
Follow the paths and you will find . . .

Leave the walls behind, follow the paths, Ash thought, beaming. *The Pathfinders.* The hidden message—could *this* be the answer he'd searched for? Most people can't leave Stronghold walls behind, but Pathfinders could! *They could be my ride out of here!* Ash didn't know what he would find once he left, but he felt sure his parents were guiding him toward them—and he would be far better off looking for them on a sleigh than in some random Stronghold. Besides, *anything* had to be better than this walking nonsense Tobu was going on about. Ash gazed in renewed wonder at the *Frostheart*. It looked longer than fifteen Fira dwellings lined up side by side. A confused tangle of ropes hung high above from the curved masts, the hull poised like an arrow, promising to carry the crew wherever they wanted to go. *If only I could find a way on board. If only I could convince the Pathfinders to take me with them, to allow me to follow in my parents' footsteps . . .*

"You spyin' on us or somethin', fire-boy?" came a voice from behind.

Ash spun round, letting out a little yelp. It was the Pathfinder girl with the half-shaved hair. She had her arms folded across her chest, one eyebrow raised.

"Oh no, no!" Ash said, putting on the most high-pitched, ladylike voice he could muster to help further his ruse, "I'm just working here on this . . . this *urine* . . ." He realized with horror that he had been hiding behind a big barrel full of the golden liquid the tanners used to treat animal hides.

What am I doing? Ash screamed in his head. *Why am I putting on a* woman's *voice?* He dared to look up to see if the girl was buying it, angling his face so that it was mostly hidden by his furs. Her eyebrow rose even higher. She might have been around Ash's age, but she had the confidence of someone much older. Ash noticed that the long cloak she wore over one shoulder had been woven with patterns resembling constellations, and small star-shaped trinkets glinted amid her dark hair. "I—I was just interested, that's all," Ash confessed. "It's been moons since I've seen Pathfinders. I mean, I have seen Pathfinders before, my parents were—*are*—Pathfinders, but I don't know my parents, I—I mean, I do *know* my parents, but I haven't seen them for a

long time and I just thought that maybe—"

"Stars above, calm down! I was just messin' with you," the girl interrupted. "Thanks for savin' us back there, by the way."

Panic rose in Ash. "I don't know what you mean. That wasn't me!" he said, backing away.

"Really? Because yer height, yer hair, yer voice, it all sounds mighty familiar, and I'd recognize those scrawny legs from a mile away."

"S-scrawny . . . ?"

The girl screwed her face up and paced around Ash, inspecting him with squinted eyes. She began to poke him.

"Hey, what are you doing?!" Ash asked, swatting her probing finger away.

"You don't look that scary," she replied, clearly disappointed.

"I'm . . . not trying to look scary?" Ash said, puzzled.

"*Huh*," she said, folding her arms. Ash couldn't tell if that was a good "huh" or a bad "huh." From her expression he suspected it was the latter. Suddenly she lifted his lips up with her fingers to examine his teeth, Ash spluttering with shock.

"No fangs," she said, before pulling at his furs. "No scary armor"—she raised up his hands—"no claws! Some Song Weaver you are."

"Song Weavers don't look like that!" Ash said, stepping away. With a jolt he realized he didn't know if this was actually true or not. He'd heard the frightening legends grown-ups told of a mysterious thing called *puberty*, and how awful it was, and how much your body changed . . . what if it was even worse for Song Weavers? Was he going to grow claws and fangs as he got older? Ash gulped. He really didn't know much about being a Song Weaver at all.

"Don't matter if yer not scary, though; you obviously have guts on the inside," the girl said. "That was somethin' brave you did in front of all them people, 'specially for someone of your . . . well, yer, y'know, yer *kind*." She punched him in the shoulder, a strange way to say thank you, Ash thought, but the fact that she had said "yer kind" had hurt Ash more than the punch.

Apparently she saw this reaction in his face. "I don't think there's anythin' wrong with Song Weavers, you understand? Well, I mean, yer the only one I've ever met, but, just—y'know what I mean—no one *likes* Song Weavers." Ash's shoulders slumped even lower.

Is she trying to make me feel better?

The girl suddenly looked behind her. "Look, I gotta shoot, before Cap' has a go at me. Enjoy your wee-barrel, fire-boy!" She waved as she turned back to the dock.

"Goodb—"

THWACK.

A snowball smashed into the side of Ash's face.

"Ow!" he cried out, and the Pathfinder girl whipped round to see what had happened. Ash put his hand to his stinging cheek. It hadn't been a soft, powdery snowball that signaled the beginning of a friendly snowball fight—it was one that was more ice than snow, the type used as a declaration of war. The type that had been launched from a sling.

Ash turned his stinging head to face his attacker.

It was Thaw and his friends, Raze and Frai, who were far bulkier than anyone on Fira rations had a right to be.

Of *course* it was them. "*SONG WEAVER!*" Thaw called with an infuriating smile. "Still Singing love Songs to monsters?"

"We know how much you love 'em, monster-lover. You smell like one. You even *live* with one," Raze chipped in.

"Too much of a freak to live with us humans," Thaw agreed. "Better off running to whatever hole other Song-freak monster-lovers like you call home. Though I'd be surprised if they wanted you either."

Ash tried his best to ignore them, suddenly very focused on his feet. He had been thrilled that a Pathfinder was talking to him, let alone being *nice* to him, even though she knew he was a Song Weaver. It had made him feel like less of a, well, *weirdo*. But now he was being ridiculed in front of her. He couldn't help but notice her take a step away from him, frowning as she did so.

"*Ooooh, monsters, I'm Ash and I love you all so much!*" Frai trilled in a high-pitched voice, fluttering his eyelids. The other two laughed and began dancing around daintily, Thaw puckering his lips and making kissing sounds. Ash was trembling, but didn't react. He didn't want to provoke them further. But this annoyed them even more. Thaw came over and nudged him hard. "You not hear us or something, monster-lover?"

"Y-yeah," Ash murmured.

"Really?" Thaw pretended to ponder. "Sounds to me like you're having trouble hearing us. Maybe because you're too busy playing . . . *this*?" Ash tried to pull away from Thaw's reaching hand, but Thaw was too fast, and he snatched his ocarina from his belt. "This is a monster-caller if ever I saw one," Thaw said with a vicious grin.

"Give it back! Thaw, please, my parents gave me that!" Ash said, reaching for the instrument, but he was held back by Raze and Frai. He felt tears stabbing at the back of his eyes.

Thaw chuckled, twisting the ocarina round his fingers, before shrugging.

"Y'know what, Ash, if this means so much to you, you can have it back." He placed his hands on either side of the ocarina, and snapped off the windway, before throwing it down. Ash cried out as though he'd been struck. His body froze in horror. Thaw and his lackeys laughed and pushed him down.

Ash picked up the pieces of his ocarina, his whole body shaking, but said nothing.

Thaw smirked a crooked smile, before turning to the Pathfinder girl, who had been watching the whole scene unfold in silence.

She's probably trying not to laugh along with the rest of them, Ash thought miserably.

"I'd get outta here fast, Pathfinder, or he'll probably try to bore you to death with a Song he wrote," Thaw

scoffed. "He's no Fira. Visiting travelers should talk to real Fira, not freakish wannabes."

The Pathfinder seemed confused, looking from Thaw to Ash. "An' where would I find a *real* Fira?"

"Don't have to look far." Thaw lifted both thumbs toward himself and his friends.

The Pathfinder's eyes brightened. "*Really?* I can hang out with *you* guys? That would be amazin'!" she said, clutching both sides of her face in excitement, framing her huge smile. Ash could do nothing but look at the ground, his heart sinking.

"Course you can," Thaw said, smug in his triumph. "We can show you the Great Pyre, show you how good a *real* Fira hunter shoots a bow—"

"'N' maybe then we could pick on some other poor small kid who's done nothin' wrong 'n' has no knuckle-draggin' mates to back him up? That would be great fun, wouldn't it?" the girl asked, her eyes glinting.

Thaw's smile faltered. He was beginning to suspect a trap. "Um—*yeah?* I guess . . . ?"

"I mean, it *does* go against everythin' us Pathfinders stand for. Helpin' people out, unifyin' all the different Strongholds an' all that borin' wholesome stuff. Yeah, it's waaaaay more fun to be an absolute cowardly drool-dribbler!" said the Pathfinder, stalking right up to Thaw and staring him in the face, fists clenched and a storm raging in her eyes.

"You'd better be careful—" Thaw began.

"Oh, I know! I should be *very* careful of warriors as brave 'n' powerful as you guys! I've already seen how you valiantly defeated this mighty intimidatin' foe! A Pathfinder crew would be lucky t'ave lads like you aboard!"

The bullies stood flabbergasted. This girl had fast become Ash's favorite person in the whole wide world.

"You don't scare me," Thaw spat, backing away. "You're as bad as each other."

"So, you're not gonna show me around the Stronghold? Aw, what a shame!" the girl shouted after the bullies as they fled.

"Th-thank you," Ash said, finding his voice at last. "Those guys are idiots."

"Pssh, that was nothin'. You should try fightin' Yorri, our enjineer, for the last scrap o' dinner. Anyways, I'm glad you're all right, but I'd better go . . ."

"Wait! Please. I-is it true what they said?" Ash asked the girl.

"What, that you smell like a monster? Maybe. Don't really have a nose for it, to be honest, spending weeks on end with a crew of sweaty, grimy, unwashed—"

"No, no, I mean, about the Song Weavers gathering out in the wilds. Our alderman mentioned it too, a—a Song Weaver Stronghold? Have you . . . ever come across anything like that out there?" Ash's heart fluttered with hope.

The girl thought on this for a moment. "*Huh*. Well, there *are* rumors. It's a legend, really. No one's actually ever *found* the Song Weaver Stronghold, so it's probably just a story."

"But there's a chance it exists?" Ash asked, his eyes shining. *Could that be where my parents have gone? They said my father might've been a Song Weaver, that he mentioned this place . . .*

"Er . . . yeah? I guess there's always a *chance* somethin' exists. I mean, you Fira are so far out, people don't think *you* exist, but look at you all here, existin' away regardless. It'll be out in the middle of nowhere, if it's anywhere, but, hey, that's exactly where we tend to go. I'll let you know if we ever find it, if we ever come this way again. But now I really gotta go. Sleigh won't fix itself!"

"R-right," Ash said, not really sure what else to say.

The girl headed back to the docked sleigh but stopped before she got too far. "Hey, fire-boy!" she called, filling Ash with hope. "Always stand tall, yeah? Don't let 'em get you down. My name's Lunah by the way!"

"Lunah," Ash repeated.

She stuck her hand out in front of his face. He hesitated, then shook it. "My name's Ash."

"Ash the Terrible, Ash the Destroyer, Ash the Eternally Grim and Slightly Peckish, am I right?" she said. Ash's smile left his face, but she nudged him with her shoulder. "Only messin'. It was good to meet you, Ash the Kinda-Small-Sized."

And with that Lunah ran back to the sleigh to help her crew prepare to leave.

Star Sign

The *Frostheart* loomed high over the village, silhouetted against the twinkling lanterns of the Stronghold. The repairs were complete, or at least the damage was patched up enough to set sail again. In exchange for the materials needed, the Pathfinders had given over all the food and supplies they could spare. Ash watched the far-off hustle and bustle from his spot atop the watchtower roof.

Same as the Pathfinders, this was the last night before he and Tobu had to set out. They'd already come to the end of their two weeks in the Fira Stronghold.

They'd packed what little they had: Ash his bow, dagger, spare cloak, and the pieces of his ocarina; Tobu his weapons and sculpted blobs, plus enough rations to last a few weeks, if used sparingly. Fear clawed its chill fingers down Ash's spine. The lessons Tobu had been trying to fit in before the day of their exile hadn't exactly filled him with confidence about his chances out in the wilds. There had been the archery lessons, where Ash usually struggled to hit a single target. The climbing lessons that more often than not ended with Ash falling headfirst into a snowdrift, legs flailing. And then there were the stealth lessons. The distance between the Strongholds was huge, and Ash couldn't even sneak from boulder to boulder without being seen by Tobu.

"Tobu, what—what are we going to *do* . . . ?" Ash had asked in desperation during one lesson.

Tobu had knitted his brow and looked out at the Snow Sea. With a heavy breath he had given his answer. "Survive."

Now Ash's brain was racing, weighing the consequences of the decision before him. The lullaby seemed to be guiding Ash, but doubt kept gnawing at him. What if he was wrong? Pathfinder runs were incredibly dangerous. Many sleighs didn't make it back. Perhaps trying his luck with Tobu would offer him the best chance of starting a new life? If anyone could get them

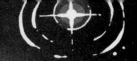

to safety, it was Tobu. And a lullaby, guiding him? It sounded crazy. He Sang the words to himself once again, as much for reassurance as for trying to make sense of it all.

"This is not farewell, this is not goodbye.
Our love for you will never die."

But this time, as the words left his mouth, something strange began to happen.

He could hear a type of buzz, a low hum that he realized was not coming from the outside world but from within his own head. His vision began to blur, with his other senses seeming to sharpen, as though his very being was focusing in on something. The sensation became stronger and stronger as he Sang. He stopped Singing with a yelp.

His eyes cleared and the buzz in his head faded, until all he could hear was the whisper of the wind. Cold beads of sweat were dripping from his forehead, his breathing heavy as he trembled.

He had Sung the lullaby many times before, but *this was new.*

Despite the shock of it all, Ash was unable to ignore his curiosity. Building up his courage, he began to Sing the lullaby again.

Once more, his vision began to blur, and, yes, there was the buzz, getting louder and louder in his head.

All at once, the stars dimmed in the clear sky, a sky usually so full of light and color it could make one dizzy if one looked long enough. They all dimmed, that is, except for one to the east. This one grew brighter, so bright it seemed to hum an underlining melody to Ash's lullaby. He found himself unable to look away. The hum pulled at him, at his very core, beckoning him to listen.

What was happening?

Ash snapped out of the Song-trance, his heart pounding, his body damp in a cold sweat.

This is insane! What've I done to make this happen? Ash's mind raced, retracing his recent past. Obviously the biggest change had been his exile. His exile for having Sung to the Leviathans for the very first time after years and years of bottling up what he really was. Could that be it? How could it *not* be? That was a pretty major change in anyone's book. Could the lullaby be reacting to him because it was indeed not just a lullaby at all, but a Song Weaver Song?

He had no answer, but he knew one thing, and that was that the lullaby's words—no, his *parents*—were trying to tell him something. His hopes weren't just fantasy! Seeing this amazing sight, he'd never been surer of it.

His parents had left him a message hidden away in the lullaby, a clue as to where they'd gone.

I'm a Song Weaver, as much as I wish I wasn't, and it sounds like my parents were too. And I'm sure my Song Weaving is the key to finding my parents—how else is the lullaby changing the way I see that star in the sky? What if they were in danger and had to hide the message so that it didn't fall into the wrong hands? If I follow where the lullaby guides me, I might be able to find them at last!

Mother Sun had just begun to wake, peering over the horizon, doing her very best to fight back the chill of the Ice Crone and warm up her children.

It was now or never. Ash had made his decision.

Gliding back through the window, as silent as a ghost, Ash darted through the shadows of the watch-tower. Tobu was in his hammock, unmoving. *Asleep, probably, resting for today's journey.* Ash snuck over to his own hammock and picked up his pack and weapons. A floorboard creaked, making him grimace. He looked up to the rafters, but Tobu remained still. Breathing a sigh of relief, Ash slipped out of the hatch. He had to be quick. He slid down the ladder without a sound and made for the bridge, but stopped in his tracks just as he reached it.

With a pang of guilt he looked back at the lonely

watchtower that had been his home. His breath misted in front of his face.

Tobu. They might not have got on—*spirits*, they might not have even *liked* each other very much—but Tobu had cared for Ash in his own sort of way. He had been the only one of Ash's guardians who had not given up on him. Tobu had even accepted exile so that he could keep watch over him. Ash felt terrible for not even saying goodbye, but he knew that if he did Tobu would stop him from doing what he was about to do.

Ash swallowed. No. This was the right decision. It would be better for them both. Tobu was getting exiled only because of Ash. With him out of the picture Tobu would be allowed to stay with the Fira. He could even redecorate, maybe put a new weapons rack or something where Ash's hammock had been. It would be great.

My parents are out there somewhere, Ash reassured himself. *I have to find them! And I have to find out about who I am—who the Song Weavers are. I can't do that from behind Stronghold walls. If there really is a Song Weaver Stronghold, I have to find it. That's where I belong.*

"Goodbye, Tobu," he whispered. Then he crossed the bridge and did not look back.

12

All Aboard

Many Fira had gathered at the dock in the early morning light to say farewell to the Pathfinders. There was always an air of sadness when a sleigh left. Once more the Fira would be cut off from the rest of the world, forced to fend for themselves until the next sleigh came by with news and resources. And who knew when that would be?

"May the fire spirits lend you haste," Alderman Kindil said to Captain Nuk, bowing low. "We thank you for all you have done, Pathfinders."

"And we thank you for your fine hospitality. We wish we could stay longer but we've got to keep moving. We've been delayed long enough and must head back to Aurora's Embrace to resupply. Our cargo hold is looking terribly sorry for itself."

"Surely you should ride for Skybridge, then?" Alderman Kindil asked. "That's the closest Stronghold to us, I believe, as far as that may be."

"Perhaps, if we were searching for scraps, dross, 'n' dregs. Not much in the way of good food in that vulpis mine, though. Hooo, no. Better we head straight back whence we came." Captain Nuk began to walk up the gangplank after her crew. "Keep fighting the good fight, Fira. Know that Aurora hasn't forgotten you!"

"*Wait!*" came a desperate yell. The crowd recoiled and gasped as Ash pushed his way through them. Nuk paused, her eyebrows raised.

The nearest hunters closed in on Ash, ready to tackle him.

"Ash?" the alderman said in surprise. "You are forbidden from entering our village. Not that rules are a thing you make a habit of obeying, it must be said . . ."

"I know—I'm not. I just want to talk to the captain!" Ash said.

The hunters looked to their leader, who gave them a small nod. With some reluctance the hunters allowed the boy to step forward and speak. Ash spotted Ryse, Shyne, and Flare. There was no friendliness in their eyes now, no sympathy in their expressions, just fear and contempt. He drew in a deep breath.

"What is it, my new, melodious friend?" Captain Nuk asked with a smile.

This is it. No turning back. "Take me with you." It sounded stupid now that he heard it out loud. *Why in the Snow Sea would they want me aboard their sleigh? A child putting the whole crew in danger with his uncontrollable urge to Sing the Leviathans' Song . . .*

To his surprise Captain Nuk actually seemed to think about it. Ash had expected her to laugh at him, to scoff at the idea, but she did neither.

"It could be that I'd have a use for a beastie-tamer such as yourself on my sleigh," she answered. Ash reeled. But a number of the Pathfinders shared uneasy glances, and Ash could've sworn he heard one particularly dangerous-looking crewwoman grumble disapprovingly under her breath. The dark, wild-haired man Ash had seen the morning the *Frostheart* had arrived pushed his way to the front of the Pathfinder crew.

"If I may say, I think you are making an incredibly wise decision, captain," he said, smiling down at Ash. "In these dangerous times in which we find ourselves, I believe we should be looking to Song Weavers for what they can offer us, rather than fearing what we do not understand."

"Aye, well, there's no word of a lie that it's dangerous out there," Nuk said to the man, before turning to Ash. "But what about your people, my boy? Your family? You're willing to leave them to take to the paths?"

"I have no family here. Not anymore," Ash said. The gathered Fira shifted uncomfortably, but no one tried to deny it.

"We have *tried* to look after you, Ash," Alderman Kindil muttered.

Ash ignored this. "My parents, my *real* family, are out there. They're still alive, I'm sure of it—I have to find them!" His voice became more desperate. "Setting off with you Pathfinders is the best, no, the—the *only* chance I have!"

Captain Nuk eyed the crowd curiously. No one said anything. No one stepped forward to argue.

"Any objections then, if I take the young lad with me? Anyone going to be crying tears of woe and loss later?" she asked. The crowd kept their eyes to the ground. Someone at the back coughed. Ash half expected to hear Tobu's low voice call out, but he was nowhere to be seen. Ash couldn't help but feel a little sad, even if Tobu's appearance would've ruined all his plans.

Alderman Kindil bowed his head. "You must walk your own path, Ash." Then, to the boy's surprise, he strolled up to him and whispered hurriedly in his ear. "I am sorry it has come to this, my boy. I know you won't believe me, but we have tried to keep you out of harm's way. Listen. Before he left, your father gave me a message for you, saying that I would know when the time was right to deliver it. I had no idea what he was talking about. He was not himself then, and a lot of things he did and said seemed strange to us at the end."

Ash stood in shock. People never talked about his parents, despite his best efforts at asking. His father had left him a message? Why couldn't the alderman have given it to him before? But before he could think about this too much, Kindil continued.

"I now believe *this* is the time your father meant. This is goodbye for us after all. The message was thus:

"*'A drifting star to light the dark,*
To an ancient beacon, cold and stark.
Guard it true, protect it well,
Lest shadow break through prison's shell.'

"I hope it means something to you, Ash, for the meaning certainly escapes me."

Ash's confusion turned to elation. He was pretty sure he did know what this was. It was the next verse of the lullaby, the next clue on the path he had to take! That's why his father had delayed the message—so it didn't get confused with the first verse, not before Ash had solved it. He knew that once Ash had, he would leave the Fira, and the alderman would give him the next clue! If ever he had proof that his parents were guiding him, this was it. Ash grinned, suddenly feeling as though everything was falling into place.

"Thank you, alderman, I think it does," Ash said.

Kindil smiled, though it was full of sadness. "Spirits guide you, Ash."

"So it is settled then!" announced Captain Nuk. "Now if you'd all be so kind as to make way for the young lad, I'd be much obliged," she said, motioning with her large hands. "That's my new Song Weaver you're all crowding! Welcome aboard the *Frostheart*, young Ash!"

❧ ❦ ❧

Only minutes later, Ash stood on the *Frostheart*'s deck, unable to close his mouth in awe at the sheer size of the thing. The wooden masts of the sleigh, rising above like the tallest of pines, groaned in the chill wind, their sails furled. A large bolt-thrower was fixed to each side of the sleigh, a small comfort against what awaited them. The vessel's giant archeomek propellers, each blade longer than two men standing on top of each other, were whining in eager anticipation, their archeomek build-knowledge seeming more like magic to Ash than human-kin inven-

tion. What those ancients had created was truly a marvel. The sunstone enjin hummed, warming up and supplying the lifeblood the sleigh required to move, like the glowing heart of some mighty Leviathan. Sunstones were said to be fragments of Mother Sun herself, and were used across the Snow Sea for a variety of reasons, though mostly for power. The Fira considered them to be sacred objects, and the tiny shards they managed to find were usually too small to use for anything other than decoration anyway. But it was said the vulpis mined sunstones the size of boulders, and the one powering the *Frostheart* was impressive indeed—it was as big as Ash's dinner bowl!

Up close the sleigh looked a tad worse for wear, chipped paint, scraps of random metals, and materials creating a patchwork of surfaces and textures across the sleigh's hull, dampening the image of the glorious sleighs told of in tales. But to Ash it could not have looked any more glorious if it had tried. The sight of a single thumb-sized painted star nestled amid the snowflakes on the sleigh's mast sparked the memory of the fantastical sight he'd seen in the sky the previous night.

A glowing star. This is my path.

A crow cawed at him from atop a mast. Ash looked at it with curiosity, its black shiny eyes staring back. It was unusual around here to find crows, who were seen as bad luck. He touched the broken pieces of his ocarina within his furs, warding off any bad omens the crow might have brought.

"Are you ready, young Song Weaver?" Captain Nuk asked, stepping to his side and looking upon her vessel with pride. Lunah was waving to them both from up in the rigging. "It's not an easy life out there. You may find yourself longing for the comforts of a Stronghold after all."

Ash looked at the village. It had been his home. But he was no longer welcome there, whether he wanted to be or not. He wasn't sure if he ever had been.

He took a deep breath. "There's nothing for me behind Stronghold walls. But there could be everything for me out there."

Captain Nuk put her massive hand over Ash's small shoulders. "I could tell you didn't belong with the Fira, but be under no illusions that the wilds are merciful. But those brave enough to become Pathfinders are few and far between, and goodness knows I could do with an extra hand. You've made a courageous choice here, Ash; you've grabbed your destiny by the horns and are showing it who's boss. That's certainly the attitude we take to kindly here, dear boy. We'll make a Pathfinder of you yet!"

Despite his nerves, the thought of the incredible things he might discover made his belly do a somersault, his butterflies stirring up a storm. Ash couldn't help but smile.

The Fira watchmen upon the watchtowers on either side of the docks signaled that there were no signs of Leviathans close by. The *Frostheart*'s enjin stirred the propellers into roaring life, the large sunstone in the center of the sleigh glowing bright. The vessel began to slowly roll out of the rising Stronghold gates and down the ramp, picking up speed as it did so. The sleigh creaked and groaned but seemed sturdy enough, at least judging by the looks of relief on the faces of the crew.

This is it. I'm really leaving!

He wondered what Tobu was doing, whether he'd discovered Ash had left yet. But there was no time to dwell on it. The sails were unfurled. With a loud *KAFWUMP*, the *Frostheart* hit the snow, white powder spraying over the sleigh like a wave, soaking Ash, who laughed at the cold shock of it. All around him was a thrum of activity. All the members of the crew were well practiced at their duties, pulling on the rigging, adjusting levers and turning dials on the enjin. Captain Nuk was at the helm, bellowing her orders and steering the tiller, tiny Master Podd at her side.

With a roar of its enjins the *Frostheart* lurched forward and dashed off and out into the wilds of the Snow Sea.

Ash hung over the side rails, wind whipping through his hair. They were moving at an incredible rate. Ash felt as though he were flying and closed his eyes at the rush of it all. The speed was intoxicating! He watched the Fira Stronghold get smaller and smaller as they left it behind,

and soon it was just a smudge on the white horizon. He allowed himself a small pang of sadness as he watched it disappear. It might have held some unhappy memories, but there had been good ones too, especially when he'd been younger. And it had been the only place Ash had ever known. The only place he had ever called home. Everything and everyone in his life was there.

Well, except for my parents.

And now he was on his way to find them! Ash's skin prickled with delight, and not a small amount of fear. There was even, maybe, the slightest, *tiniest* bit of guilt at leaving Tobu too. But that was behind him now, and who knew what lay just beyond the horizon.

Mum. Dad. At last I'm on my way. I will find you.

Ash's world had suddenly become a lot bigger.

And a lot more dangerous.

II

PATHFINDER

13

Onward
to the Horizon

The *Frostheart* tore across the Snow Sea like a shooting star. It hit a bump, and Ash was thrown right off his feet, slamming the deck hard. He'd never been on anything but still ground, and the rocking, undulating motions of the sleigh were proving quite the challenge. "You're gonna have to find your snow legs quick if you're gonna be any use around here!" said the sunstone enjineer, a man named Yorri, offering Ash a hand and laughing. His large mustache billowed in the breeze, doing an incredible impression of a mursu's tusks. His face was lined in places that showed he was quick to smile.

Ash gripped the side rail, taking in the wonder of the world that was flying by, the cold making tears stream from his eyes. There was not a cloud to be seen in the vivid blue sky, Mother Sun gleaming off the crisp white snow that stretched from horizon to horizon, a haze of light blurring the edges of the world. The Fira hunters told of how barren their territory was, how scarce resources were, but only now was Ash seeing it with his own eyes. The flat, featureless snow plains seemed to stretch on forever, with only the odd lonely pine or turquoise ice crystal breaking up the endless white.

Ash noticed that a couple of crows followed the sleigh from above.

That's strange. Two now? Ash's skin crawled, but he tried not to read too much into the ill omen. Hurtlers sped in the wake of the *Frostheart* like fish following a whale, but thankfully the sleigh was far ahead of them. This was the best view Ash had ever had of the monsters, meaning he could see them without an immediate danger of being eaten. Their pale armored skin looked rough as stone, their six eyes cold and unfathomable, heads low and unflinching as they charged relentlessly forward. A cold dread gnawed at Ash, stealing the wonder he'd experienced a moment before.

"Won't—won't they catch us?" Ash called out to a nearby crewman, who shielded his eyes to watch their pursuers.

"These ones? Not likely. We've got a head start on 'em." Ash had been hoping for a definite "*No, they will not*

catch us, Ash—*you're completely safe and have nothing to worry about*," but he supposed *not likely* would have to do.

Ash tried to take his attention away from their pursuers, looking instead at the swinging Leviathan teeth the size of daggers and the colorful flags that fluttered from the rigging. Feeling a bit more stable, he closed his eyes and let it all wash over him. Ash grinned from ear to ear. He even found a nervous thrill to the chase (thanks, mostly, to the comfortable lead they had). He gulped down the clean, fresh air untainted by the smell of hundreds of people living in a confined space. The crisp chill of it hurt his throat, but not in an unpleasant way. His heart sang out with joy, beating like a drum, chanting like his Song. So this was what it felt like to be *free*. It was incredible.

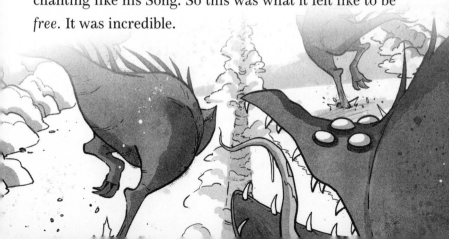

"Not thinkin' of pukin' over the side, are you, fire-boy?" came an amused voice from behind him. Ash spun round, coming face-to-face with Lunah. She was hanging upside down from the rigging, one eyebrow raised, her cloak flowing about her shoulders and threatening to cover her face.

Ash cried out.

"I'm not *that* scary, am I?" she asked, spinning from the ropes and deftly landing on the deck.

"N-no! I just . . . I didn't expect you to be so . . . so right *there*," Ash said.

"I get that a lot, don't really understand why. Probably my Drifter blood, I reckon. Always stickin' our noses into things, explorin' bein' our nature, y'know?"

"A—a Drifter?"

"You can hear me, right? Am I mumblin' or somethin'?" Lunah smiled, her tone teasing. "A Drifter. S'my people. Well, the *Frostheart* crew are my people now, but Drifters're where I come from. My folks are waitin' for me back home in the Convoy, proud as puddin' that their daughter is a Pathfinder."

"Oh," Ash replied. This was a lot of information to take in at once. He searched for something to say, not wanting to seem like an ignorant outlander. What on earth was the Convoy?

But he needn't have bothered as Lunah had apparently already moved on to the next subject.

"So why'd you decide to hop aboard the *Frostheart*? Most people'd rather eat hot embers than leave their walls."

"I—um—well, I didn't really have a choice," Ash mumbled, fiddling with the hem of his furs. "I was exiled."

"*Exiled?*" Lunah looked impressed.

"My guardian too, but I—I left him behind."

"Whoa. That's quite the list of achievements. You must be one bad customer!" She gave him a sly grin.

"It wasn't fair. I hadn't done anything wrong!" Ash protested. "Well, I mean, that's not *technically* true, but, well, it doesn't matter anyway. I want to try to find my parents. They're out there somewhere and I can only search for them on a sleigh."

"All this on account o' yer Song Weaving, I'd wager," Lunah said, nodding sagely.

"Y-yeah. I guess that's what it boils down to."

"So what can you do?"

"Do?" Ash said, confused. "Well, erm, I can forage pretty well, and shoot a bow, *kind of*, and—"

Lunah laughed. "No! I mean with yer Song Weavin'! Can you summon Leviathans? Can you make 'em do yer biddin', chomp sleighs in half 'n' stuff?!" Lunah had a huge smile as she spoke, her eyes burning with curiosity.

"Erm . . ." It felt weird being able to talk to someone so openly about Song Weaving. Truth be told, Ash didn't know if he *could* do those things, but he did know one thing, and that was that he didn't want to look bad in front of his new friend. "Yeah! I can do that. Easy!" he boasted, instantly regretting doing so when he saw her eyes light up.

"Go on then!"

"W-what?" Ash replied, knowing full well what she wanted. He was stalling for time.

"I wanna see it! Make those Hurtlers do a flip!" She pointed to the Hurtlers, racing behind the sleigh, their vicious jaws snapping, their tongues whipping saliva in long trails behind them.

Well, this was quite the situation he'd already managed to get himself into. Ash had successfully Song Woven once in his life, and he hadn't really had to think about it. It had come easily, as natural as walking, or talking even. He had just Sung his feelings; he'd . . . *talked* with the Leviathans somehow, as mad as that sounded. He couldn't imagine it went much beyond that—well, except for being able to hide signs in the sky apparently, but he didn't even know where to begin with that.

Lunah was watching him with expectant glee.

"I don't know if I should . . ." Ash began, a lifetime of being wary of Singing out loud proving hard to shrug off. Most of the crew were paying him no mind, except for the scary-looking lady who had grumbled about Ash joining the crew. *Kailen*, Ash had heard someone call her. She had short flaxen hair and narrow eyes that were in a perpetual frown, a long scar running through one, the eye now white and blind. Treelike patterns were embroidered down the length of her robes, and tattoos of tree branches ran down her arms. She was eyeing Ash with suspicion, as though she knew what he was contemplating, and she didn't like it, not one bit.

"Gooooo on!" Lunah urged. "Before the Hurtlers die of old age!"

Ash drew his shoulders back and took a deep breath. He Sang the words "*Dooooo a fliiiiiiiip,*" holding his hand out toward the Leviathans and wiggling his fingers for dramatic effect. The Hurtlers did not do a flip. Ash looked at Lunah with a hopeful smile.

She raised a skeptical brow. "Y'know, I don't believe your heart was fully in that."

She was right—Ash hadn't really tried to Song Weave. It still just felt too . . . *dangerous.*

"Look, I just don't think I should be Song Weaving whenever I feel like it," Ash began, although he would love that to have been the case. "Maybe—maybe we should respect it a bit more?"

Kailen was still glaring at him. Even though Ash wasn't facing her, he could feel the back of his neck getting hot.

"Soooo, you can't make a Leviathan bite a sleigh in half then?" Lunah asked. Ash could feel his face burning red. "Ah, it's all right," Lunah added. "My fault for bein' ignorant about Song Weavers. Least I heard of 'em, though; you clearly don't have a clue 'bout us Drifters! But stars above, how amazing would it be if you *could* control the Leviathans? The things I'd do! My enemies wouldn't stand a chance!"

"You have lots of enemies?" Ash asked.

"Well, no. Not yet. Bound to have some if I could control Leviathans, though, right? And then I'd get the beasties to *crush* them into dust!" Lunah punched a fist into her palm, a manic smile on her face.

"I . . . see," Ash said. He took a step away from her.

"Are you bothering our newest crew member with all your questions, Lunah? Don't you have some navigatin' to be navigatin'?" Captain Nuk asked, strolling over, her peg leg clunking on the deck.

"Yes, cap'n!" Lunah saluted, then she winked at Ash and leaped up into the rigging, clambering about like a squirrel.

"Don't mind her, Ash, she's just curious. Best navigator this side of the Convoy, though! She could find her way out of a blizzard with a blindfold, that one. But it's time I introduced you to the rest of the crew, wouldn't you say?"

Ash gulped. "Um, yeah, sure."

"The good vulpis up there is my right-hand man, Master Podd." She gestured at the small fox-like creature who had taken over the steering, standing atop stacked crates so that he could reach the tiller. "There are none so loyal, and none so blisteringly adorable, isn't that right, Master Podd?"

"That is correct, captain," he replied in his deep voice.

Captain Nuk led Ash into the middle of the large main deck. After a quick headcount, Ash made out a crew of eleven, not including himself. Some, including the ever-angry Kailen, were concerning themselves with the rigging, making sure the sails were catching the prevailing winds, while Yorri and his friend Yallah, both hailing from the Stronghold of Thudruk, were adjusting controls on the sunstone enjin on the upper deck. Others were busy on lookout duty, or were helping Lunah with maps and charts, using various tools and compasses Ash had never seen before. The last few were milling around, clearly off shift, playing a board game that involved carved wooden pieces.

Nuk raised her hands to her mouth and bellowed, "I SAY, CREW?! THIS POPPET HERE IS ASH! SAY 'HOW DO YOU DO, ASH?'"

"*How do you do, Ash?*" the crew said in unison, barely even raising their heads before returning to their tasks.

"And, Ash, as you may have guessed, this is the crew. Jolly good. Glad that's all over with." She placed her hands on her hips at the job well done. "Oh, and how could I forget? Please, follow me."

Ash grabbed his things and followed. They climbed the stairs to the upper deck, where the sunstone enjin

sat humming away. "Yorri? Lower the sunstone power, if you'd be so kind. Alas, the Fira had no sunstones to trade—all we have in reserve is the last shiny lovely in the hold. So steady as she goes."

"Aye aye, cap'n," he said, adjusting levers and dials. As the sleigh slowed it gave a sudden, violent shake, as though something unimaginably huge had rammed it from underneath. Captain Nuk pondered this. "Let's not lower it by *too* much, though; we must keep our lead in the race against the beasties!"

A number of hide-covered tents gathered round the warmth of the sunstone enjin, clearly the crew's sleeping quarters. Nuk led Ash to the smallest tent of them all. "Home sweet home, eh? This is your tent. Settle in and come and talk to me afterward. It's time to put you to work, my dear boy."

"T-thank you," Ash said.

"Eh, the tent was only being used to store extra kegs of grog anyway."

"No, I mean, *thank you*. For taking me on board. For not treating me like everyone else did."

Nuk smiled sadly. "You are most welcome, Ash, my boy."

Ash had one last thing he wanted to ask. He took a deep breath, trying hard to build up his courage. He'd had a question burning in the back of his mind since the *Frostheart* had pulled into the Fira Stronghold, but hadn't had the chance, or the guts, to ask it.

Now was the time.

"Do you know what happened to the Pathfinder sleigh *Trailblazer*?" The words rushed from his mouth. He was afraid of the answer now that he'd asked it. Nuk looked surprised. "It was the sleigh my mother captained. My parents were Pathfinders too. They left one day when I was very little, and all anyone will tell me is that they went on a Pathfinder run and didn't want to risk taking me . . . but they never came back."

Nuk nodded with understanding, her brow rising in sympathy. "Well, it's not unheard of for sleighs to go missing. It is a dangerous world out here. It tries its hardest to kill those that venture out into it, and unfortunately that tends to be us Pathfinders. I've heard of that sleigh, being as it was one of the few that made regular trips to the Fira before we took over the mantle. I know little of it, however."

"Oh," Ash said.

"That's not necessarily bad news," Nuk tried to reassure him. "There have been many sleighs and crews throughout history, and sleigh names can change too. The Pathfinder Council resides at Aurora, and there you will find the Pathfinder records. Perhaps when we arrive we can take a look. Master Podd will take you, I do not doubt; he never stops going on about how much he enjoys flipping through the records."

Ash gazed up at the bridge, where the vulpis stood stern and silent.

OK. Maybe this is a good thing. This doesn't mean they're dead. I—I would know. I don't know how, but I would, Ash thought, trying to reassure himself.

Captain Nuk laid a hand on his shoulder. "Your parents were brave people, Ash. It takes some guts and gusto to be a Pathfinder." She grinned at this, her mouth curling up behind her huge tusks. "And I suppose that makes you brave, or foolish too. You're one of us now, it seems, for better or for worse. I'm sure your parents would be proud."

"I'm willing to do anything to find them. To find out who I am, and where I belong," Ash said.

Nuk nodded. "Aye. I'll just bet you are."

Ash gave a brave smile, and then ducked under his tent flap.

And what he saw within nearly made him jump out of his skin.

An Unexpected
Companion

"What are *you* doing here?" Ash cried out.

There, hunched over in the tiny space with his arms and legs folded, was an extremely grumpy-looking Tobu. He was *far* too big for the tent.

"I am your guardian," he replied, as though that answered everything. "Your leaving the Fira does not release me from my duty and oath."

"But what—how—*when*—" Ash couldn't believe what he was seeing. He thought he'd left his old life behind for good! And he'd made that big dramatic show of leaving too. He felt so stupid. Clearly Tobu was going to be as hard to get rid of as the smell of fire smoke on clothes. But perhaps this wasn't such a bad thing? Tobu could prove invaluable out here in the wilds.

"The fact that you did not see me sneak aboard shows

there is still much work to be done. You will continue your lessons. You will need them more than ever now that you've so shortsightedly joined a Pathfinder crew."

Or maybe not.

"We shall remain aboard this sleigh until it arrives at Aurora," Tobu said, somehow remaining authoritative despite how squished he was in the tiny space. "But in Aurora we shall remain. You will be safe there. Pathfinders do not settle behind walls. They are forever in danger. You are not suited to that life."

Ash let out a long groan. "I can't believe you're here! I have a plan, and I can tell you right now it doesn't involve hiding behind any more walls!" He dropped his pack and weapons on his bedroll and left the tent as fast as he could.

Captain Nuk was waiting outside, looking cheerful. Yorri and his co-enjineer were looking over too, eyebrows raised at all the commotion. It seemed tent walls didn't do much to block the sound of heated discussions.

"Ah! You've been reacquainted with your yeti friend, I gather?" Nuk trilled.

"Why is he here?" Ash demanded.

Tobu emerged from the tent and drew up to his full, imposing height.

"I thought you'd be happy to see each other," Nuk said.

Both Tobu and Ash grunted at this crazy idea.

Nuk beamed. "Can you feel the love, Yorri? I think I can feel it."

Yorri laughed. "Oh, I feel it, captain."

"Well, you know what forms a bond like no other?" the captain asked. "*Working together!* Yes indeed, I'll have you two so busy you'll be inseparable by the time we reach Aurora, mark my words!"

Tobu made a dismissive gesture. "I have been giving the boy important survival lessons. They must continue. We have no time for menial work."

The whole crew ground to a halt, the general chatter and hubbub ceasing.

Lunah winced, looking up from her maps.

"*I beg your pardon?*" Captain Nuk asked, a hint of danger in her voice.

"The boy's training is more important than chores," Tobu confirmed. "Now that the secret is out about him being a Song Weaver, it is more important than ever that he is prepared for what he will face."

Captain Nuk smiled, but one eye was doing a strange twitchy thing. "Ooooh, I see. Well, that's just fine then, isn't it? I'm so glad you boys could join us for such a pleasurable cruise! What I should've said was"—in a flash her smile turned into a furious frown—"*who in a frost-bear's frostbitten frumpus do you think you are, coming aboard my sleigh and telling me what you will and won't be doing? Give me one good reason not to make you walk the plank and feed you to the Leviathans?*"

"We have a plank!?" Lunah asked, sounding surprised.

Nuk paused, looking thoughtful. "As a matter of fact, no, we don't. I have been meaning to get one, however. Master Podd, please make a note: 'Must buy a plank at the next market.'"

"Noted, captain," Master Podd called from the helm.

Nuk massaged her temples and sighed. She poked a big finger into Tobu's broad chest. "Everyone, and I mean *everyone*, works on my sleigh. There will be no free rides here, is that not correct, Master Podd?"

"There are no free rides here, captain," Master Podd called over.

Tobu looked taken aback. He was not used to being spoken to like this. Like Ash, most people were wary, if not outright terrified, of the hulking yeti. And while Captain Nuk was large, Tobu still tow-

ered over her. This did not seem to bother her one bit. She faced Tobu and wagged her finger at him as though he were a naughty child. Ash would have laughed, if Nuk hadn't been so frightening.

"The last time I checked, I was still captain on this sleigh, *Tobu*." She emphasized his name for effect, and jabbed him in the chest again. "Well? What's it to be? Are you going to play by my rules or will you be walking back to the Fira Stronghold?"

Tobu's nostrils flared. Ash could see the whites of his eyes and braced himself, ready for whatever monstrous reaction Tobu was about to unleash. The crew held their breath . . .

Finally Tobu breathed out and grumbled, "I did not mean to offend. I will work for my passage, of course."

Ash gaped.

"*Captain*," Captain Nuk reminded him.

"*Captain*," Tobu finished.

"Good!" Nuk clapped her hands together, cheerful as anything once more. "But what am I going to do with you both? A warrior and a Song Weaver. Hmm. This puts me in quite a pickle. You see, there are no attackers for you to defend us from, dear Tobu, and no Leviathans that need soothing, Ash, dear boy." Just as she said this a thunderous roar echoed across the plains. "Well, not *just yet* at least. And you can't pay your way just standing there looking all brooding and mysterious—I would hate for you two to get *bored*." She scratched her whiskered chin, deep in thought, and then snapped her fingers. "I have just the thing!"

Nuk reached into an open barrel and pulled out two dirty mops, which she shoved into Ash's and Tobu's hands.

Tobu squirmed. "You can't—surely not—"

"A mop? But—but—" Ash began, stopping when Nuk gave him another dangerous look.

"I do not think you want to go down that path, do you, Ash my dear? Not like your brute of a guardian, here, eh?"

"N-no, captain."

"Excellent! Looks like you have learned a lesson from Tobu today after all! Well, my poppets, don't let me keep you!"

Ash looked at the mop and at the size of the decks. He let out a low groan.

15

A Taste of Adventure

The next two weeks on the *Frostheart* were grueling to be sure. The Pathfinders had a shift system in place: while half the crew worked, the other half rested, to ensure the crew could recuperate while also keeping the sleigh one step ahead of the Leviathans at all times. This meant that there were actually only about six crew members doing all the work at any one time, but not one crew member slacked off. Their lives and those of their comrades depended on it after all, and to stop moving, even for a moment, could mean death.

Ash was more than up for proving himself to the crew, and threw himself entirely into his duties. He had to admit, however, that he had thought venturing out with the Pathfinders would involve a little more . . . *adventuring*, more striking out into the wild unknown and searching for his destiny, and perhaps a little less . . . dirt, grime, and soapy water. Ash bumped into Tobu, who had been letting out a low, angry grumble deep in his throat as he swabbed the decks.

It was clear Tobu wasn't having a better time of it. He held his mop like a spear and stabbed at the deck. He'd broken three mops already. Captain Nuk had gotten him to start crafting some new ones at night when his chores were meant to be over.

The matter of Ash being a Song Weaver went mostly unspoken, perhaps due to the crew deciding among themselves that the benefits of having a Song Weaver on board outweighed the risks. Kailen, however, did not seem to share that view. She stared daggers at Ash, spitting on the deck whenever Ash caught her eye (which would make his heart sink, not only due to her clear dislike of him, but also for the fact that he had just mopped the floor).

At least all the mopping allowed his mind to wander, and think up the words to a new Song he had begun to work on inside his head. Singing to Leviathans wasn't the only Singing Ash was capable of after all.

"Oh, us, yes, us, we lucky few!
Who make up the Frostheart's *valiant crew!*
Captain Nuk, she leads us brave and strong,
Master Podd watches o'er our courageous throng . . ."

It was still a work in progress, Ash would be the first to admit, and he thought better of sharing it with everyone just yet. Perhaps when he got to know them better?

When Ash wasn't cleaning the decks he would often be found helping Twinge, the sleigh's cook, to chop the roots, vegetables, and dried meats for the cooking pot in the small kitchen belowdecks. Twinge had a tendency to tell stories that meandered on and on, never seeming to have any point. "I once had to cook a meal for a crew of forty with only three knotroots and a half-rotten radish," he was telling Ash, after regaling him with the names he'd given to every single cooking utensil he owned.

"So what did you do?" Ash asked, cutting into a particularly solid hunk of dried . . . *something.*

"Oh, I just cooked 'em. Weren't much to go around,

tasted awful, but they were the only ingredients I had."

Ash had to be honest—he'd been expecting a bit more of a twist.

When Ash wasn't toiling his way through Twinge's stories he would have to help Kailen and the other crewhands, Kob and Arla, to keep the rigging in order. If Ash even so much as *whistled*, Kailen would give him a look that suggested she was preparing to lob him overboard. "We got enough problems as it is. Don't need no Singer losing their mind to the 'viathans to add to 'em," she'd snarl. Ash tried his best to not let her comments get under his skin, but it was hard. He'd been hoping he'd seen the last of this kind of hurtful words. Thankfully, aiding Lunah to take notes as she plotted the *Frostheart*'s course helped take his mind off Kailen, as did lending Yorri and Yallah a hand in trying to keep the rust off the sunstone enjin.

And then, of course, there were his continued lessons with Tobu. Archery, using empty barrels with ulk drawn on them as targets, much to Nuk's irritation. Climbing up and down the masts and rigging to the supportive cheers of Teya, the lookout, who watched from the crow's nest. And more sessions listening for the voice of the wind, and to what the snow and ground had to say. Apparently they still had nothing to share with Ash. Lunah, however, was more than happy to share how hilarious she thought this all was.

The crew seemed more concerned with Tobu than with Ash, truth be told, giving him a wide berth whenever he prowled across the deck. This seemed to suit the yeti fine; he was more than happy to sharpen his spear alone, or work on sculpting his wooden blobs (when he didn't have new mops to make) high up on the masts during the rare moments of free time they had.

Despite the hard work, Ash relished the freedom he felt among these people. He wasn't alone anymore, stuck in a small tower, with only a big grumpy yeti for company. (Well, he still had a big grumpy yeti for company, but he was freer.) He had people to talk to. He felt involved, a part of something. He had a world to roam. A world to explore, and search for answers in. Ash couldn't help but smile at these thoughts.

Lunah caught him smiling one day while Ash lounged next to her on one of his breaks. "What you grinnin' about, fire-boy?" she asked, looking up from the compass she had strapped to her forearm, using a measuring stick to compare its readings to those on her maps.

"Not much," Ash said.

Not much, but it was the world to him.

16

Whispers in the Dark

The only crew member Ash hadn't become properly acquainted with was the dark, wild-looking man who had seemed so pleased Ash was joining their voyage. Like Tobu, the man kept to himself, mingling with the rest of the crew only when he was helping with the upkeep of the sleigh's archeomek, such as the sunstone enjin or the propellers, which seemed to be his specialist job. Otherwise, he seemed to spend every moment he could at a small workbench that sat under an awning in a corner of the main deck, poring over old-looking scrolls and stone tablets, or tinkering away on ancient gadgets, all a mystery to Ash.

Ash told himself he didn't want to disturb the man, who always seemed so focused on his work, but the truth was he had been too afraid to go and talk with him. The

man gave off a strange vibe, one that felt as impenetrable as a Stronghold wall.

Ash decided to see what he could discover from the rest of the crew. "Spoke to him once," said Twinge, chopping onions, tears rolling down his cheeks. "Didn't have much to say."

"I see," said Ash.

"Spoke to him a second time."

"Yes?"

"Yeah. Still didn't say much of interest."

"Oh."

"Third time I spoke to him—"

"Yeah?" Ash's eyes lit up.

"He said nothin' worth rememberin'."

"I think I know how you felt, Twinge."

Ash decided to try Lunah.

"Why d'ya wanna know, Ash the Most Nosy?" she asked, clambering through the rigging overhead. She spent a lot of her time swinging around like a young yeti. "Is it because he's a violent murderer, who carved his way through an entire Stronghold 'n' wore their skulls as a hat 'n' used their intestines as a scarf?"

"He *did* that?" Ash asked, horrified.

"Nah. Well, I dunno. *Maybe.* I don't really know who he is. Imagine how mad it would be if he *had* done that, though!" She lowered herself to Ash's level, hanging upside down like a spider.

"Mad would be the right word," Ash said. "He's the only crewman I've not been introduced to. I just wondered why."

"Ah, well, there's yer problem," Lunah said in a manner that was clearly supposed to be mysterious, but that only succeeded in making her sound a bit crazed. "See, he's not actually part of the crew, not really. His name is Shaard. We picked him up last time we were in Aurora, moons and moons ago now. Kind of like how we picked you lot up. Guess we're pickin' up a whole load of people wantin' to find somethin' out in the wilds, hey? You're gonna outnumber us soon!"

Ash laughed, but wanted to hear more about Shaard. "So, who is he then?"

"Not sure," Lunah continued. "He's some kinda traveler-adventurer thingy. Comes from a warrior Stronghold out in the western reaches, I think. He's lookin' fer somethin' from the World Before, least that's what I heard. Every Stronghold we pull into, ol' mystery man pops out an' has a read of whatever history he can get his hands on, or listens to any story anyone's willin' to share on the World Before. Spent quite a few days listenin' to those light slingers of yours at the Fira Stronghold."

"Light bringers."

"Yeah, those. He pays his way on board by sharing his travelin' knowledge 'bout the Snow Sea an' old archeomek an' all that kinda creepy stuff. Doesn't really talk much. Real hush-hush. Cap' seems to find him useful, though, so who are we to moan?"

"Right," Ash replied, feeling like he only had more questions now. Although it was probably just his imagination, Ash couldn't shake the feeling that the mysterious man was watching him.

❤ ❗ ❥

A few days after talking to Lunah about Shaard, sleep did not come easy to Ash. Dreams of monsters and worse—of Tobu chasing him shouting "Time to train, boy!"—kept waking him up. He'd not been sleeping well at the best of times due to the fact he had to share a tent with Tobu. It was hard to relax back to back in a space only just big enough for a human being, Tobu hunched over like a giant lump, his fur making the place as hot as an armpit (and it didn't smell much better either), his big furry feet sticking out of the tent flap and letting in just enough chill to make Ash feel the worst of both worlds. Tired of being tired, frustrated with tossing and turning in his sleeping furs, Ash went outside. The night crew greeted him as he emerged from his tent, but left him to his own thoughts after that.

The scenery was beginning to change. Rocks, boulders, and snow-covered hillocks broke free from what had been featureless snow plains, paving the way toward monumental structures Ash had been told were called *mountains*, which grew closer with each passing day. There were far more trees in these parts, copses of pine rising up like watchtowers, aspen and birch adding color to an otherwise monochrome world. For someone who had only known a vast, empty space, the new world Ash

found himself in suddenly felt very cluttered indeed. But in the most wonderful, intriguing way. The stars looked as numerous as snowflakes in a snowstorm, beautiful and clear, clouds of green and red weaving their way among them in the sky. *The spirits of this land*, Ash thought, wondering what they were like. He had trouble finding the star that had lit up when he had Sung the lullaby, now unremarkable and only as bright as the others around it. Ash's life had been so hectic he'd barely been able to spare a thought to the new riddle Alderman Kindil had given him, but he'd turned it over in his head whenever he'd had a chance. The mournful calls of the Leviathans echoed far in the distance, their Song almost lost in the rushing wind. Ash felt an unexpected sadness come over him. He'd never been separated from the Leviathans' Song before, and to his surprise he found himself yearning for it.

His melancholy thoughts were broken when to his astonishment he heard another Song. A human Song. Someone was Singing on the sleigh! Ash was struck by the strangeness of it after so many years of never hearing music; how bizarre and wonderful it was to hear another person's voice.

Ash shivered, and found he couldn't tear himself away from the calming melody of the Song, which was so soothing and delicate. He looked around to find its source—and gave another shiver when he saw that it was coming from within the shadows of Shaard's workbench. Ash twiddled his fingers anxiously, but his curiosity soon got the better of him. As quiet as a snowflake he headed over.

The corner of the sleigh where Shaard worked was lit only by the warm red light of the small lantern that sat on the workbench. It took Ash a moment for his eyes to adjust. But there, among the shadows, a patch of even deeper darkness shifted in the gloom. Shaard was a slim man, but by no means weak-looking. His muscles were taut and sinewy, and his eyes seemed to glow amid the dark. He was swathed in black furs, his unruly hair draping down his face in thick strands, only just hiding his many scars. As he heard Ash approaching he finished his Song and smiled, laying down the tools he'd been using to work on his archeomek gadgets. Despite the friendly smile, there was something about the man that made Ash feel uncomfortable. Like he was wild and dangerous.

"A visitor? This is most unusual," Shaard said, amused. "And the Song Weaver himself, no less! How embarrassing—what must you think of my warbling? Indeed, what has a humble traveler like myself done to deserve such an audience?"

Ash took an uncertain step back. "Sorry, I just—I heard you singing and I—I—"

"My Song?" Shaard pondered this. "Of course, I forgot the Fira forbid music of any kind. A bit extreme, to deprive yourself of one of life's finer pleasures, wouldn't you agree?" Ash couldn't have agreed more. "But who am I to judge? We all must do what we can to survive."

As Shaard spoke Ash noticed the archeomek artifacts that hung from the workbench's awning, clinking their own tunes as the *Frostheart* moved and swayed. Most seemed like hollow, ceramic husks, often curved in shape, but some blinked with blue lights, their inner workings whirring, fidgeting, and rearranging themselves almost as if they were trying to get up and leave. They were fascinating, and oddly lifelike.

"You may find it interesting to know that the Song I was humming was actually a Fira Song once upon a time," Shaard continued, leaning back on his stool, resting against the wooden wall behind him. Ash must have looked skeptical, since Shaard laughed. "It's true! I was taught it many years ago by an old Fira friend of mine. A rousing little tune, make no mistake."

Shaard had a friend from the Fira? Ash supposed he shouldn't have been too surprised. There had been a few Fira Pathfinders throughout the years, who had left the Stronghold and not looked back. Ash felt a twinge of pride at the idea he was now one of them.

"*Hah!*" Shaard barked. He slapped the workbench with his hand. "Spirits be damned if it wasn't impressive what you did back there at the Fira Stronghold. Your Song Weaving saved us all!"

"I—I couldn't just stand back and watch. Not anymore," Ash said.

"Spoken like a true hero. Spirits know we need more of them." Ash smiled nervously. "Alas, I spend so long alone, I forget my manners. Most call me Shaard," he said, shaking Ash's hand. "That, or *the scary, quiet one over there.* I'm partial to the first myself." Ash felt his face turn red, knowing he'd had those exact thoughts. "Must've been awfully emotional, leaving your people like that?" he added.

Ash scratched the back of his head. "Erm, not—not really. They . . . they *were* my people. Once. I'm not so sure they were at the end."

"*Tsk tsk.* Their loss then, isn't that right, young adventurer?"

Ash forced out a laugh, absentmindedly reaching

for a strange archeomek object Shaard had on his workbench. It was spherical and made an ominous ticking
sound, small spheres orbiting round its circumference,
held in midair as if by magic.

"These things come from the World Before," Shaard
said, taking the object before Ash could reach it.

"Is it . . . is it magic?" Ash asked in unhidden wonder.

"I believe *magic* is just a word for something we
don't yet understand," Shaard replied.
"Archeomek has always

fascinated me. But it's a rather dull subject to those without the same interest, so don't let me bore you with it." He clicked the top of the device, the floating spheres vanishing in an instant, before he rolled it deftly down his arm, making it disappear within his furs.

Ash flushed with embarrassment, realizing he was probably being a nuisance. "S-sorry, I didn't mean to disturb you," he said, turning to leave.

"There's nothing to disturb. Nothing but my thoughts, and, believe me, I get enough time alone with them." Then he gave Ash a strange sideways look. "But you know all about that, don't you? Being alone, that is. Being looked upon with distaste and *mistrust*?"

"I guess . . ." Ash was beginning to feel uncomfortable now. "A bit."

"The life of a Song Weaver is a lonely one," Shaard said, and Ash's interest was immediately piqued again.

"How come you know so much about Song Weavers?" he asked.

Shaard gave him his wolvish grin. "I suppose you could call me a treasure hunter of sorts, though the treasure I seek is not gold or jewels, but *knowledge*." He tapped a big pile of parchment beside him, what Ash assumed were histories Shaard had gathered on his travels. "The remnants of the World Before slumber beneath the ice and snow, dreaming of the moment someone like myself may discover them and awaken the secrets only they know."

"And Song Weavers?" Ash tried again. It was hard to keep this man on track. Now Shaard looked furtive, and, leaning in, he beckoned Ash toward him.

"Between you and me, I believe Song Weavers will be the key to ending the Leviathan scourge. It'll be you and the other Weavers out there who will lead our world out of the darkness and into the light."

Ash's heart quickened. *This was big. No, it was even bigger—this was as ginormous as it got!* His belly roiled at the thrill of these words, words he'd never dreamed he'd hear about himself. To be extraordinary, to be important . . . Or maybe it was fear, *terror* at the weight of what the words meant, if true?

"H-how are you so sure?"

Shaard tapped his nose. "Call it a hunch. When you've seen all that I have, you start to notice the signs. Did you know that you, and all Song Weavers, are a remnant of the World Before? Living relics of a glorious ancient civilization. I've read that it was Song Weavers who once ruled that mighty empire. It is a crime against all human-kin that Song Weavers are feared and not embraced for what they are. They could save the world, if people would only let them. Why *wouldn't* I be fascinated with that? Why wouldn't *anyone*?"

Ash's eyes widened with excitement. *Is he right? Could we really be that . . . important?*

"So I travel the world, discovering what I can, all with the fantastical notion that I might be able to help *save the world*. Seems rather childish, I know, but I'm a romantic at heart." He flicked out a piece of gold and rolled it between his fingers before making it vanish. "And I truly hit gold when I actually get to speak to the Song Weavers themselves. Song Weavers . . . like yourself."

Ash gasped and grabbed the workbench to steady himself. "You've—you've met others?" he asked. *So there really are others.*

"Indeed I have, scattered about the Strongholds of the world." Shaard saw the look in Ash's eyes and grinned. "You're not alone, Ash. Far from it."

"I'd love to meet them," Ash whispered.

"And perhaps you will one day. I've even heard it told there's a Stronghold made up entirely of Song Weavers, if you can believe it," Shaard said with a gleam in his eye.

Ash's hands began to tremble. "I've heard the same legend," he managed to say as Shaard began searching through his scrolls. "Do you know where it is?"

"Alas, I do not," Shaard admitted, finding the scroll he had been looking for and laying it out on the work-bench for Ash to see. There, sketched out in faded ochre was a symbol. A symbol that looked a lot like a shining star. "The Song Weavers I've met call the Stronghold Sol-stice when brave enough to whisper its name. This is its sign, or so I've come to gather. And hidden it most defi-nitely is, though I intend to find it someday."

Ash gripped the table so hard he felt as though he might crush it. He could barely believe his luck in find-ing this man who was after the exact same thing as he was. Was Shaard why his parents had led him aboard the *Frostheart*? Perhaps together, Ash dared to hope, they could find the secret Stronghold?

"I'm always happy to talk Song Weaving, should you want to," Shaard said. "I'd be even keener to listen. I'm sure I could learn a lot from you."

"I'm not sure about that," Ash admitted. "I'm kind of new to all of this. But I really *would* like to hear what you know—everything—about Song Weaving, and Sol-stice, and—and all of it! If that's all right?" he added tentatively.

Shaard laughed at Ash's enthusiasm. "It would be my honor. Sadly I think it may have to wait for another time."

"Why?"

"I think our yeti friend has need of you," Shaard said, inclining his head, and Ash followed the direction indicated. There, standing in the gloom, was Tobu, arms folded, watching the two of them.

"Come away from there, boy," Tobu said. "You need to rest for training tomorrow."

But before Ash could leave, Shaard grabbed his arm. "Most people will just not appreciate the gift you have, Ash. Not like I do," he said in a rushed whisper. "People are afraid of what they don't understand. But don't let them hold you back. And *never* let them call you a monster. What's the more effective way to survive in this world—a Song that can influence a Leviathan or a pointy stick?"

Ash looked into Shaard's bright eyes and nodded. He was, after so very, very long, beyond happy to have finally found someone who understood.

17

Follow the Song

Speaking to Shaard had filled Ash with a renewed determination to find his people—so much so he was actually going to take Tobu's advice for once. He was going to *focus*. Since he'd climbed aboard the *Frostheart*, he'd been so busy getting used to life with the crew he hadn't had time to think much about the lullaby. But now he Sang the lullaby to himself every day while swabbing the decks, determined to understand what it meant:

> *"A drifting star to light the dark,*
> *To an ancient beacon, cold and stark.*
> *Guard it true, protect it well,*
> *Lest shadow break through prison's shell."*

Each time the same buzzing he'd experienced atop the watchtower filled his head, and the same sensory shift. In the clear light of day the glowing star was hidden by vivid blue sky, but he knew it was there, shining, trying to tell him something. Ash groaned, his heightened senses making the aching in his limbs all the more prominent after yet another early morning training session with Tobu.

"We have a duty to Captain Nuk that we must honor, but I also have a duty to you," Tobu had explained when Ash had asked why they needed to train so hard.

"I'm a Song Weaver now," Ash had boasted, emboldened by the importance Shaard had put on his people. "My powers will protect us. Surely all this training is useless now?"

Tobu laughed without humor. "You think you have control over that power? As your guardian it is my duty to make sure you don't get killed out here. I think it may be my greatest ever challenge."

Ash rolled his eyes at the memory, then got back to trying to solve the lullaby's riddle. *Over the horizon, to Mother Sun's light*—he had this part down, he reckoned, watching the undulating snow plains whoosh past as they headed east. It was the new part Alderman Kindil had imparted that had him stumped. *A drifting star to light the dark . . .* Was it the star that shone when he had Sung the lullaby? Was that the drifting star? Most likely. It did seem to be trying to tell him something, though what that was, he could not say. And as for the *ancient beacon, cold and stark?* He had no idea. There were so many questions; Ash didn't even know where to start.

"I have a Song like that too," said Lunah, who was hanging behind Ash. He jumped with such surprise he dropped the mop and put his foot in the bucket.

"*Spirits, Lunah! Stop doing that!*"

Lunah ignored him, cleared her throat, and began to Sing:

"There once was an old mursu at sea
Whose belly was as big as could be.
He dived for a crumb,
Fell right on his—"

"This Song isn't like that!"

"Oh no? What is it then? Some kinda Song Weaver magic spell? Are you magicking us, Ash?"

"No! Song Weaving isn't magic!" Or was it? Despite how sure he sounded, Ash flushed at how little he really knew. "I-it's just a lullaby my parents used to Sing to me when I was little. I Sing it to myself sometimes. Y'know, just to remind me of them."

"Ah. Say no more," Lunah said, looking thoughtful.

"I have a Song like that from my parents too. *There was a fat Pathfinder from*—"

"It's weird, though . . ."

"Ash, you *are* weird," Lunah replied, irked she'd been stopped mid-poetry. Then she saw the serious look on his face and relented. "Sorry. You were sayin'?"

"Sometimes I feel there's a message they left me," Ash went on, shuffling his feet. "Hidden in the Song, or . . . or guiding me or something . . ."

He didn't know why he was telling Lunah this, but he couldn't help but feel relief at actually talking about his theory with someone else. He'd been too scared to share it with Tobu, worried he would scoff at such a childish fantasy. Lunah was brave and had seen so much of the world. Maybe she could even help him with it? And . . . it would be nice to make a friend on board.

He looked at her hopefully. She was pulling a face, an eyebrow raised so high it threatened to fall off her forehead.

"You're trying to find your parents . . . based on the lyrics . . . of a *baby's lullaby*?"

Ash turned red. "Well, if you say anything like *that*, it sounds bad. And they *were* Song Weavers—so why wouldn't they use a Song to guide me? The lullaby has led me aboard this sleigh, so it can't be that ridiculous!"

Lunah grinned and put an arm round his shoulder. "Ash, you strange, *strange* person. But you can Sing to giant slobberin' monsters 'n' get 'em to sit like a good boy, so who 'm I to say what yer marvelous melodies can 'n' can't do?"

"Th-thanks. I . . . think?"

Lunah's eyes brightened. "The plot thickens! So, you gonna tell me the words or am I gonna have to guess?"

"Oh! Yeah, they—I—they're—" Ash paused. The memory of Tobu telling him not to share the lullaby flashed into his mind. Lunah folded her arms and tapped her foot impatiently. Ash grimaced. He wanted to tell her. He really did.

"I-it's kind of personal, I guess I could tell you bits of the Song. Just the bits I'm stuck on." *Which is basically all of it.* "And maybe . . . maybe you could help me try to solve the riddle?"

"OK! Tellmetellmetellme," she said, full of excitement.

"Right . . . the first bit I'm stuck on is . . . '*a drifting star.*' Do you know what that might be?"

Lunah frowned. "Ent no such thing, my friend. "Maybe a shooting star, or comet? Though you'd have to be quick to catch those."

Ash's heart sank. They weren't off to a good start.

"Really? There's no constellation or—or even just a

star called the *drifting star*?" he asked, thinking of the star that had lit up so brightly when he had Sung the lullaby.

"Nope."

"No Stronghold has that name?"

"Not that I've heard of. There *was* the Pathfinder sleigh *Comet's Tail*. But . . ."

"But . . . ?" Ash asked. *Have I joined the wrong sleigh?*

"Buuut they were wrecked by Leviathans on a run last year."

"Oh," Ash said, shoulders slumping. *Apparently not.*

"Next!" Lunah called out.

"Um . . . there's a line about '*an ancient beacon, cold and stark.*'"

"Whoa, talk about dramatic!"

Ash shrugged. "Well, can you think of any beacon like that? A watchtower or . . . torch or something?"

"Oooh . . . *treasure hunt!*" Lunah cried. "Just so happens I *do* know somethin' like that! C'mon!" She grabbed Ash's arm and tried to pull him away, but he resisted.

"Wait, what about my chores?"

Lunah looked around at the deck. "Ash, this place is cleaner than the bones of my enemies picked by vultures. Cap' won't notice we're gone, truuuust me. Chores must be patient. Treasure awaits!"

Ash couldn't fault her reasoning. "Sounds good. I haven't told you yet, but sneaking off is actually my *other* superpower." He grinned, his heart singing as he dropped his mop to follow his new friend. A friend who knew exactly what he was, but wanted to hang out with him all the same. Now, *that* was magic.

18

A Frozen Heart

The cargo hold, which spanned two levels and the entire space below the upper deck, was dark and damp. Ash squinted into the shadows, the floor rolling beneath him, wood creaking and rope complaining as it strained to hold down the small amount of cargo the *Frostheart* carried. A worryingly small amount, Ash thought, especially when Lunah led him past the sleigh's rations. There were crates of armor and amber from the Thudruk Stronghold, lanterns and weapons from the Fira, salted fish and the bones of great sea beasts from the floating mursu Strongholds of the Rus clan, but the barrels of food were disturbingly depleted.

"Is—is this going to be enough for us to get by till the next Stronghold?" Ash asked, hoping he sounded inquisitive rather than afraid.

"Maybe. Gotta tighten our belts, though, that's for sure. We were run ragged comin' this far north. Less an' less Strongholds, till we were worried we'd reached the end of civilization! Finally found the Fira, thank the stars, but slim tradin' to be had there," Lunah explained, dragging some crates aside. She turned round to face Ash, and saw the look of worry on his face. "Welcome to the life of a Pathfinder, Ash the Until Now Well Fed. But we've got through worse scrapes 'n this, believe me. Now help me move these crates!"

Together they dragged the crates aside, revealing a big metal container. Light shone brightly from within as Lunah opened it, illuminating their faces.

"*Whoa*," Ash whispered.

The container held a large spherical sunstone, shining radiant and gold. But, thought Ash, the fact that the *Frostheart* carried only one was pretty concerning as well, seeing as how the power of a sunstone did not last long.

Lunah hefted one of the stones with a smile. "This is bright 'n' stark, no question. I seen a hot one set an entire sleigh alight once!" She handed it to Ash, who took it carefully, turning it round in his hands. It was warm to the touch, and much bigger than any he'd held before.

"It's amazing," Ash said. "But the Fira have sunstones too, even if they are just shards. The lullaby told me that I needed to travel far. Why would I need to travel far for something the Fira have already? And the line is 'cold *and stark*'. . . This is definitely warm."

"Hmm, you're right. The mystery deepens." Lunah put her hand to her chin and acted like she was stroking an imaginary beard.

Ash joined her. A drifting star . . . a beacon that needed protecting . . . what did it mean? Was it even an object? Or a metaphor? Why couldn't his parents just write him a stupid note?

Lunah snapped her fingers. "There is something else, but . . ."

"But?"

She crossed the hold to its center, where the base of the mainmast rose up through the ceiling to the deck. There she pushed aside another crate, revealing something quite spectacular. An ice-blue stone, perhaps the size of a fist, sat within a specially made hollow in the mast. Like a sunstone it emanated an ethereal glow, but unlike the golden warmth of a sunstone, this was cold, like a star made of ice. Wisps of frosted air drifted from it like freezing breath. A glistening sheen of frost radiated out from it into the wood, creating circular patterns that were intersected with fernlike markings, just like frost on the smooth surface of a stone. As he looked in wonder Ash swore he could hear a gentle twinkling sound coming from within. He reached out to touch it.

"Careful!" Lunah called, but too late.

"*Ow!*" Ash cried, pulling his finger back and clenching it tight. "It's *freezing!* What—what *is it*?"

"This, my friend, is the frost-heart itself. Legend says the previous owner of this sleigh got it from another Pathfinder who got it from another Pathfinder who got it from a mysterious cloaked figure who found it in the remains of Glacia, the only Stronghold in history that even got *close* to the size of Aurora."

"What happened to it?" Ash asked, fearing he already knew the answer.

"Leviathans, o' course," Lunah said, her eyes momentarily glazing over with anger. "Meant to be a lovely place, built atop ruins from the World Before. But it was best known for the Frostspire—a ginormous lighthouse that could be seen for leagues around, its light said to come from nothin' less than a Leviathan's heart found deep within the ruins themselves!" She stuck her tongue out in mock disgust, but Ash could tell she enjoyed the story. "One guess as to what this is meant to be?"

"The Leviathan's heart . . . ?" Ash looked at it in wonder. A thought struck him. "So this was *literally* an ancient, shining beacon? Why didn't you take me to this straightaway?"

"*Because* there is no way on your Mother Sun's *back-*

side Captain Nuk will ever give it to you! It means too much to her—to all of us!"

Ash felt a flush of embarrassment. "R-right. Sorry. I didn't mean it in that way," he said. Truth be told, he wasn't sure what he was meant to do with this thing now that he'd found it, other than guard and protect it apparently—but from what? And where was this *prison* the lullaby spoke of? Who was in it?

"What does it do?" he whispered, still trying to warm his freezing-cold finger.

"Nothin', really. We think of it as the heart of the sleigh, keep it as a kinda good-luck charm, I guess. But it means the world to the Cap', an' that means it means the world to us." The frost-heart's resonance was chilling, yet calming all the same. Until—

"*Where are they?!*" came Captain Nuk's furious voice from above. "*Where are those idle good-for-nothing lay-abouts?*"

Lunah jumped, then tried to look nonchalant. "Now, earlier when I said Cap' wouldn't notice we'd slacked off . . . ? What I meant to say was: there's probably a good chance she'll notice we've slacked off. We'd better get back up there."

"R-right," Ash said, unable to take his eyes from the frost-heart. As amazing as it was, he still didn't understand what relevance it had to his parents, and if this was what the lullaby was guiding him toward at all. But he was undeniably drawn to it. The sound it made was subtle, barely audible, but captivating. It was like the most beautiful Leviathan Song he'd ever heard, but small, and far, far away, like the distant howling of a snowstorm. And if he really strained his ears, Ash thought he could *just* make out vague whispers:

"*Crows . . . harsh . . . broken . . .*"

"Lunah, can you hear that? A Song coming from the heart?"

The Song had faded again, lost to him.

"All I hear is a very angry mursu who may be about to throw us overboard. We have to go, Ash. You ent seen Cap' when she's *really* angry . . ."

Ash managed to tear himself away from the spell the frost-heart had him under.

"Yeah, we'd better get back on deck," he said, mind elsewhere. The frost-heart had mentioned crows, Ash was sure of it. Did this have something to do with those crows he'd seen? It really *was* unusual to see them this far north . . . A feeling of unease washed over him. He stole one last look at the frost-heart, before rushing up to act as though he'd been mopping the deck the whole time.

19

The World Sings

The next morning, Ash awoke abruptly to someone shaking his arm. "Mmmf—what is it?" He squinted in the darkness of the tent. He could just about make out Tobu's imposing figure crouched above him, filling the entire space.

"Come," Tobu said. He was already dressed in his armor.

"Where?" Ash asked, rubbing the sleep from his eyes.

"Your lessons," Tobu said.

"Ugh, not again . . . The sun isn't even up!" Ash protested, gripping his sleeping furs as if his life depended on it.

"We have been through this. Will the captain's chores teach you how to concentrate and focus your powers? Will scrubbing the decks enlighten you to the secrets of

the World Weave, to allow you to open your heart and
soul to the eternal wisdom of nature itself?"

"Um . . . *n-no*? But breakfast might?"

"Get up."

With considerable effort Ash shambled on deck, where
he was greeted by a terrible, grinding sound. His mind
was still acting sluggishly in the cold morning air, and
it took him a moment to realize the sunstone enjin was
not breaking down and that the awful sound was, in fact,
snoring coming from Captain Nuk's tent. He hadn't slept
well again. Instead of dreaming, his mind was racing,
trying to solve the riddle of the frost-heart, the *beacon*.
It was *important*, and yet for the life of him Ash couldn't
figure out what it meant. And what it might have to do
with *crows*, *shadows*, and a *prison* was anyone's guess.

Tobu nodded to the crew on shift but ignored Shaard,
who was still feverishly reading at his workbench. Shaard
looked up with interest at Ash and Tobu.

Those histories on the World Before must be seriously
riveting, Ash thought, *to keep him up all night.*

"Shaard knows lots about Song Weavers," said Ash,
looking over at the mysterious man. He'd much rather
have lessons from *him*. "He travels the world collecting
information on them, and he said that he would teach
me—"

"No."

Ash gave Tobu an incredulous look. "What do you mean 'no'?"

"That man is obsessed with the World Before and the unnatural relics of that accursed age. I do not trust him. The shadow he casts is longer than most." Tobu's eyes narrowed, and he huffed a warning growl in Shaard's direction. "I can teach you all you need to know."

Shaard's shadow didn't look any bigger than anyone else's to Ash, but he didn't argue.

"But what can *you* teach me about my power?" he asked. He knew Tobu was a formidable warrior, but what could he know about Song Weaving?

"Much. I chose the warrior's path hunting and defending my kin, yes, but all yeti have a close connection to the sacred energy that runs through the world," Tobu explained. "I have mentioned it before, though perhaps not by name. It is life and death. It is balance. Human-kin call it Mother Nature; we yeti call it the World Weave, and it is what we yeti dedicate our lives to understanding and defending. All things have a voice, a Song. It is a pri-mal force binding us together as one."

It felt far too early for this. Ash hadn't even had his breakfast. But he couldn't deny he was interested.

"Everything has its own way of connecting with

the World Weave. The yeti connect to it through focus and meditation. Song Weaving happens to be the way of the human-kin. Now sit," Tobu said, setting himself down on the deck in a meditative pose. Ash sat beside his guardian.

I never knew Song Weaving was a connection to nature. It's better than being called a monster-lover at least . . .

"Close your eyes," Tobu instructed. "Breathe. Focus." Ash obeyed. "Everything has a Song, from the smallest stone to the mightiest Leviathan. You must learn how to hear them all. Only then will you be able to truly communicate with the Leviathans, to express your true self through your Song. If you can connect to it, the World Weave can offer you guidance. Now be silent. *Listen.*"

I don't really understand how being quiet will help my Singing, but if it means that much to Tobu, then I'm willing to give it a go, Ash thought. *Everything has a Song? Well then, let's hear it, world!* Ash took a deep breath, imitating Tobu, and closed his eyes. He tried to clear his mind, and strained his ears to hear the Song, *any* Song. He heard the groaning of the *Frostheart*'s timbers, the creaking of the rigging above and the billowing of the sails. And then he heard . . . *wait.*

What *was* that?

Was it nature's Song?

No, he realized. It was Kob, letting out a long, drawn-out, pitch-perfect fart.

Ash burst out laughing. A growl of warning rumbled from within Tobu's chest, and Kob quickly realized he had work to do at the far end of the sleigh.

"*Concentrate,*" Tobu said. "Clear your mind. Listen to the rhythm of your heartbeat, slow and steady."

Ash took a deep breath and tried to follow Tobu's advice. He could hear the wind rushing by. The hiss of the snow as the *Frostheart* cut through it. Tobu's breathing.

He had an itch.

"I said *focus*, boy!" Tobu said, his voice getting more cross. "The Songs of the World Weave will not come to you; you must listen for *them.*"

"I'm trying! It's difficult to focus when you keep interrupting me."

Tobu sighed. "If you practiced, you would find it easier. You must shape yourself into the Weave, find the voices within. Only then can you become a part of it and join your Song with nature."

He might as well have been talking in another language for all Ash understood. Ash's frustration was quickly matching Tobu's. He scrunched up his eyes, a frown creasing his brow, and he listened. He tried to concentrate. *I'm all ears, world! Whenever you're ready . . .*

He tried to relax and focus . . . and opened one eye to take a look at Tobu, who was looking right back at him, his arms folded and a more-than-a-little-bit-exasperated look on his face.

"I once knew a boy like you," Tobu said. "He was impulsive and reckless, and wouldn't listen to advice." His voice was getting angrier. "He *always* thought he was right. Did what he wanted. And do you know what happened to him?"

"Was this boy an old student of yours by any chance?" came Shaard's wry voice, interrupting. "If you treat all of your pupils like this, I'm not surprised they turn against you."

Tobu glared daggers at Shaard. "Do not tell me how to give my lessons."

Shaard put up his hands as if in surrender. "I wouldn't dream of it." Then a sly grin slid across his face, and he seemed to turn his voice toward Ash. "Although, while you mention it, I must disagree with what you're teaching. Song Weaving is a thing of freedom and passion, of strength and power—not a thing of rules." Ash wondered if this was true. He'd certainly always felt a kind of freedom when he was Song Weaving. "How can one learn to Sing if you silence them?" Shaard asked.

"It is vital that Ash first learns control. Unrestrained passion and power burn like a raging inferno, consuming all in their path," Tobu replied, looking at Shaard with distaste.

"Exactly. Song Weaving is the best weapon we have in the fight against the Leviathans. Song Weaving should be used for the benefit of human-kin, not Singing snow shanties to trees and rocks," Shaard said.

"Leviathans are of this world, the same as we are. Song Weaving should be used to try to understand the Leviathans, not to fight them," retorted Tobu.

Ash contemplated his guardian. He'd never heard anyone speak of Leviathans in any way other than with hatred, fear, and blame. And for good reason.

Thanks to my Song, I've actually felt what Leviathans think, and there's no understanding there, only fury. Ash caught himself mid-thought. He supposed he had managed to reason with them with his Song. But surely that was due to the power of his Song, not because the Leviathans actually understood him?

Shaard laughed at Tobu's comment, shaking his head. "There are no discussions to be had with monsters. Perhaps *I* should teach Ash some lessons from now on? You could even go back to bed, Tobu—rest up for another day of swabbing the decks and sharpening your spear."

"I think not," Tobu said. "Ash has much to learn, and I will not rest until he does."

Shaard looked at Ash and shook his head with sympathy. Under his breath Ash let out a groan of despair.

20
Star Maps

"Do you *ever* stop moanin'?" Lunah asked Ash that evening as she sprawled across the deck marking notes and drawings on a large piece of tattered parchment. Ash had just completed another one of Tobu's lessons, and had been explaining his frustrations to Lunah. A thick mist blanketed the world, the warm lantern light of the sleigh reflecting orange against the ghost-white veil. The *Frostheart* was having to move slowly, just in case it were to hit any hidden obstacles or even worse: bump into any passing Leviathans. Once or twice Ash thought he could make out the distant shapes of hills and mountains, but then the gigantic shapes would move and drift away as though they were alive. Ash shook his head, telling himself it was a trick of the mist. *Nothing is that big, not even a Leviathan . . . right?*

"Waah, waah, waaah, that's all I ever hear from you!" Lunah finished.

Ash straightened up, affronted. "I'm *not* always moaning!"

"OK, *sure*. If you say so."

He was about to say that she would be moaning too if she had to spend her days swabbing the decks only to get told off in her downtime as a reward, but he realized he would only be moaning again, so held his tongue.

"What're you doing?" he asked her instead.

"Plottin' us a course to Aurora. Teya's seen Leviathans swarmin' the paths down south where we'd usually go, so I gotta find us a safer route. "Least it's helpin' me add details to my map, I suppose," she replied.

"Your map?"

"My map. All Drifters have a map," Lunah said with pride. "Drifters ent like other folk, you know; the clue's in the name. While most have found safety behind walls, us Drifters, we jus' keep on movin', an' as long as we keep movin' faster 'n the Leviathans, we'll be just fine, thanks very much. Only way to live, I'm tellin' you—different view every day, wind whippin' yer hair back, discoveries to be found over every horizon. You can strike poses like this on the prow too." She stepped forward with one leg, balling a hand into a fist, the other raised to shield her

eyes as she looked out into the endless murk. Ash had to admit she looked pretty inspiring.

"That sounds . . . *nice*," Ash said truthfully.

"Yeah, *nice* is one word for it. We were the first Path-finders there ever were! Before everyone else got in on it. Us Drifters are masters of navigation, of readin' the stars an' moon an' all that 'n' usin' them to guide our way. Tha's why we have this hair, y'see."

She gestured at her half-shaved head, and mimicked a deep, mighty voice. "'*So we always have one eye looking to the stars!*' And when us Drifters're old enough we leave the Convoy, an' set out all alone, provin' what we know 'bout navigatin' and blazin' our own trail. It's all pretty heroic stuff."

"But you're not alone; you're with the *Frostheart* crew," Ash pointed out.

The girl's smile turned to a withering scowl. "I know that! Drifters are never *alone* alone. Our Stronghold is a whole fleet of sleighs we call the Convoy, most awesome sight you ever didn't see. You need a crew, course you do. It's just we're meant to leave the Convoy behind and do a journey without *their* help. And the thing is"—here, Lunah's tone got just the tiniest bit wistful—"we're not allowed to return to the Convoy till we've discovered uncharted lands and added it to the world map."

"And you're old enough to be doing that?"

"Old enough? Probably started *too* old! My ma was only eight when she set out! Mapped a whole new pass through a humungous haunted forest far to the south. But then she beat a Murghul howler in an arm wrestle when she was my age, so it's a bit hard to compare yerself to my ma." Lunah was puffed up as proud as a pengoose.

Ash considered all he was being told and narrowed his eyes in disbelief. "Mm-hmm. Can I see your map?"

But Lunah did not seem so keen on the idea. She crumpled the map protectively.

"Uh, *no*. Work in progress, I'm afraid—not to be snooped at till it's good and ready."

"OK, OK!" he said, raising his hands.

Patchwork windows had begun to open in the thinning mist, revealing tantalizing glimpses of the sky. Lunah used the opportunity to gaze at the few stars she could see, scrawling away on the map that she still held closely to her chest. She too had quite an amazing power, thought Ash. Their world was so sprawling it felt like it could be infinite, and to be able to not lose your way by using the night sky as your guide was a powerful ability indeed.

All was calm. Ash was content to use this rare quiet moment to simply hang out, watching Lunah use her powers. As he did so he rolled his lullaby through his mind.

Suddenly realization jolted through him.

"*Lunah!*" he said excitedly.

"You're not seeing my map, Ash."

"No! Lunah, I think I've figured it out!" He grinned, heart racing. It wasn't a star at all! The answer had been right in front of him!

"How to freak out your fellow crew members? 'Cause it's workin'," she said.

"It's the line from my parents' lullaby! *A drifting star to light the dark*—Drifters! Drifters use the stars as a guide in darkness." Lunah gave him a look to suggest she didn't follow. "I think the lullaby wanted me to find a Drifter as a guide to lead me to the frost-heart and guide me using their knowledge of the stars. Lunah, I think . . . I think *you're* the drifting star! I think your navigational skills might be able to find my parents, if we can solve the rest of the riddle!" He began to Sing the lullaby out loud to make his point clearer.

And as he did the world dimmed and his senses heightened, as was normal now when he Sang the lullaby. But what was *not* normal was that instead of seeing one shining star in the sky, there was now another, glimmering beside the first. Ash thought he was seeing double, and the shock of it stopped his Singing dead, the world returning to normal.

"You all right there, Ash? I think I actually, er, *lost you* for a minute there," Lunah said, concerned.

"Before . . . whenever I Sang the lullaby that star would light up in the sky," Ash said, pointing it out. "But this time that star next to it lit up as well . . ." Lunah gave him a look. "You—you didn't see it?"

"I did not see that, no."

"Maybe . . . maybe it's like the Song-auras, and it only becomes visible when someone is Song Weaving?" Ash pondered.

"Song-auras?"

"Y'know, the misty, blue stuff that glows around the Leviathans when they Sing?"

Lunah looked baffled. "I'm gonna be honest with you, Ash, I have absolutely no idea what you're talkin' about."

"What? Glowing and flowing around, and it turns red when they're angry? You must have seen it! It happens whenever they Sing!"

"I don't see any glowy stuff, Ash. In all my time driftin', this is the first I've heard about it." Lunah was looking at Ash as though he'd lost his mind.

"I'm not going mad!" Ash insisted.

"Hey, I didn't say anythin'! You're the one talkin' about magical lights and stars winkin' at you."

"Maybe only Song Weavers can see it . . . ?" Ash said, sounding unsure.

"Yeah, maybe that's it." She mouthed the word "crazy," but Ash could see she was only joking. His mind raced, making his head hurt.

"Could it be the World Weave?" Ash whispered.

"That mystical yeti belief?"

"Y-yeah . . . Tobu said that if you can connect with the World Weave, it can act as a guide, send you signs . . . but I didn't—I wasn't sure I believed him. I've not been able to do it . . . but maybe my parents *are* strong enough to connect with the World Weave with their Song Weaving?"

Lunah thought about this. "Huh . . . Well, let's say you're right? Perhaps your parents did get the World Weave to help you, in its own strange, mystical, way-harder-than-it-needs-to-be kinda way? Maybe . . . every time you solve a part of the riddle, a star lights up in the sky to show you you've got it right? And your parents made it so only those Singin' the lullaby can see it? So you were right about having to leave the Fira, 'n' climbin' aboard the *Frostheart*, 'n' now you're right about me being the navigator? Of course *I* got the bit about the beacon. It's like a super Song Weaver star map!"

"You think so?" Ash asked, his eyes wide with wonder.

Lunah shrugged. "Believe me, I've heard weirder things in my travels. S'a guy in Aurora who swears this small bit of archeomek he found lets him talk to someone way across on the other side of the Snow Sea."

"This is incredible!" Ash laughed in awe at the secret power of the lullaby he'd been Singing all his life.

"Two stars already—this is easy!" She put her arm round Ash's shoulder. "We'll have this solved in no time!"

21

The Hunt

The *Frostheart* had come to a standstill for the first time since it left the Fira Stronghold. Hunters descended down ropes that hung from the sleigh's sides, eager to waste as little time as possible. Everyone knew that if you stayed still for too long in the wilds you became lunch.

Ash was the last to land on the snow before the sleigh's enjin roared back into life, blasting the hunting party with snow as it soared off across the plain. The *Frostheart* would make large circles around the area, trying to lure the Leviathans away from the hunt. They'd come back in a few hours to pick up the hunters—and hopefully their bountiful quarry.

This did not stop Ash from feeling like they'd been abandoned. He focused on the hunting party around him and gripped his bow to try to feel less exposed.

"A Song Weaver could prove useful on the hunt," Shaard had argued after Captain Nuk had confirmed that their supplies were running out faster than predicted, and that the crew would need to make an emergency stop to hunt for much-needed food.

"Absolutely not," Tobu had said. "The boy is not ready."

"So little faith in your own student!" Shaard had smiled his wolvish grin as he attached strange archeomek gadgets to his belt. "We might need Ash's powers if we get any unwanted attention out there."

Nuk had a think. "What say you, Ash? Mind keeping the hunters safe for me?"

Ash had gulped. He knew he wasn't ready. The faces of the crew who'd volunteered to hunt had told him they felt the same way.

But Shaard was right—what was all his training for, if he wasn't going to use his skills? *I've sent a swarm of Hurtlers away before, and I can do it again,* he had assured himself. He nodded at Nuk, nerves prickling the back of his neck.

"We're better off without him. We've done this well enough before without the help of a warbling child," Kailen had snarled.

"Kailen's right," Kob pitched in, but in a friendlier

tone. "I like the boy, but that doesn't change what he is. What if the Leviathans overwhelm him, get their claws into his mind?"

Captain Nuk pondered these words. "All of your opinions have been duly noted. Ash, do please prove them all wrong." She had smiled at Ash, who smiled back, not sure whether he should thank or curse her for believing in him.

Standing out here on the plain, the *Frostheart* growing smaller in the distance, he suspected he had the answer.

Now the hunters made their way to an outcropping of towering rocks clustered like fingers at the bottom of a large hill. The crew had spotted numerous crows circling the area, which suggested there was a good chance they'd find game. It didn't feel like a good sign to Ash, though. He was beginning to feel like the crows were watching him.

Kailen, the appointed leader of the hunt, looked to the others, who shifted with unease.

"Split into groups," she signed. "Cover more ground. Sooner find prey, sooner leave snow." Ash knew silence meant survival out in the wilds. If a hunter made a sound there was a good chance they had just become the hunted. As such, most human-kin knew sign language to use outside sleigh and walls. It had been a main topic in Light Bringer Hayze's lessons. Although Ash wasn't as confident in its use as the adults were, he could mostly understand what was being said. He particularly liked the "leave snow" part. "Ash, with Tobu and Shaard," Kailen signed, "head east. Rest of us, head west."

Ash watched as the other hunters stalked off, silent as snow. A hand came to rest on his shoulder, giving it a gentle squeeze. He turned to see Shaard, who gave him a reassuring smile. Ash smiled back and balled his hands into fists.

This is my chance to show the crew that I'm not dangerous—that I can be valuable to them! I know *I can keep everyone safe, and I'll do everything I can to make that happen,* he thought to himself.

Before long they had tracked a small herd of ulk, who were busy using their shovel-like antlers to dig through the snow in search of food. They were gathered within a large clearing bordered by tall steep rocks upon which a dozen crows perched, their beady eyes watching carefully.

"Too far," Tobu signed, dropping the snow hares he'd somehow already managed to catch and reaching for his bow. "Be patient. I'll drive toward you."

"We'll wait," Shaard signed back.

Tobu crouched low, ready to sneak into position. He hesitated, then looked back at Ash with stern eyes. "Be careful."

"I will!" Ash assured him.

"Do. Not. Sing. Not ready yet," Tobu added.

Ash frowned at this. Tobu pointed a finger at him, and Ash could do nothing but hold his hands up in submission. Apparently satisfied, Tobu nodded, and headed round the ulk to cut off their escape.

Ash and Shaard took cover behind some bushes and waited.

All was very quiet.

Ash's senses were on full alert, straining to find any hidden danger. Then he started as Shaard tapped him on the shoulder.

"Don't listen to Tobu," he signaled. "Do what is necessary. Be brave."

Ash smiled back at him and nodded. He was glad to have at least *one* person on his side.

He sensed movement ahead, but to his relief saw that it was the rest of the hunting party. They'd clearly tracked the same ulk, and were moving swiftly to encircle them, using the scattered bushes as cover. One of the hunters—Yallah, it looked like—raised her bow and took careful aim.

A crow cried out, and others quickly joined in.

What's spooked them? Ash wondered, nocking an arrow to his bow.

An ulk raised its head in alarm, its ears pricked and its nose twitching, scenting a change in the air. The others followed suit. Suddenly the crows dived from their rock perches, flocking and flying at the ulk, flapping their large wings in their faces and cawing and crying in a raucous chorus.

What is up *with these crows?* Ash thought in disbelief.

The ulk bolted.

He could see Kailen signaling for the party to fall back.

Yallah did not see.

And then—

FWOOM.

Yallah disappeared in an eruption of snow. Ash let out a gasp, and Shaard reached for his belt. As the snow cleared Ash could see the terrible serpentine shape of a Lurker clawing at the rock that Yallah had managed to leap up onto just in time. The Lurker had been lying in wait, lured to attack by the commotion above. Yallah had dropped her bow, her arm twisted into a shape that looked anything but natural. The other hunters were too far away to help.

"*KILL. HUNT. DESTROY.*"

The creature's terrible Song punched through the silence, making Ash grimace as it filled his head.

His mind raced. *I can't do nothing. I have to help her!*

"Now, Ash, now's the time!" Shaard shouted, confirming Ash's intentions.

Ash took a deep breath. He swallowed his nerves. It was one Lurker. He could do this. He had to prove himself, and what better way than by saving Yallah's life?

Ash began to Sing.

His starlight aura billowed outward and met the raging tendrils of the Lurker's aura with what felt like

a physical shudder. He shaped and formed his melody to fit that of the Lurker's, to try to find the cracks within its aura like he had with the Hurtlers back at the Fira Stronghold.

"Peace. Calm. Friends."

But this time, before his Song could have any effect, the Lurker's blood-red tendrils wrapped themselves round his aura, forcing it down and wringing the life from it. Ash's eyes widened with horrified surprise. He'd managed to calm three Hurtlers at once before—why was this Lurker so powerful? Ash felt like he was being choked! The Lurker's aura clawed its way down Ash's, and the Leviathan itself raced closer and closer toward him.

"CAUGHT. WEAK. MINE."

His head was filled with the furious screams and violence of the Lurker's Song, to the point where he felt like his skull was going to split open. The Lurker was beating him! Was it about to take over his mind? Ash's Song wriggled and struggled, but to no avail. The Lurker had him, and Ash realized it wasn't because it was too strong but because he was too *weak*. The last time he'd Song Woven, he'd unleashed the power he'd been bottling up all his life. With that surge of power gone, Ash's reserves were considerably lacking, and he couldn't seem to find the strength to fight back. His aura flickered and faded. And without Ash to calm the Lurker, the whole hunting party was in danger—they wouldn't be able to escape!

Then, with a terrible jolt, Ash was freed from the Lurker's invading Song as Tobu threw him to the side, breaking him from his Song-trance. The yeti deftly spun round in the same motion to fire an arrow at the fast-approaching Leviathan. But before he could make the shot, there was a huge explosion of blinding amber light, and arms of crackling lightning arced across the clearing. Ash and Tobu watched, stunned, as the smoke cleared, revealing the shattered, frozen body of a dead Lurker in its wake, veins of lightning fizzing around its form. Shaard held a smoking archeomek weapon in his outstretched hand, sunstone shards protruding from its top, glowing, whorl-like patterns emanating along its surface. A hungry grin was carved into his face.

"Fool!" Tobu growled. "The noise of such a thing will bring all the other Lurkers upon us!"

"They were already on their way," Shaard said, picking a trembling Ash up off the ground. "And it worked, didn't it? We're not all blessed with super-yeti abilities. Some of us have had to adapt to survive in the wilds."

"*To the high ground!*" came Kailen's voice, before Tobu could argue any more. The other hunters were climbing up a steep pinnacle of rock, helping a grimacing Yallah. Ash could see a swarm of Lurkers scrambling toward them with ferocious speed, fangs bared and jaws salivating.

"Time to move, I'd suggest," Shaard said.

All three of them ran for the pinnacle, joining the others as they clambered up the rock face. As they climbed, one of Ash's hands slipped, and he swung round wildly, barely clinging on to the surface with his other hand, the Lurkers already snapping at him mere feet below. He felt weightless for a moment as the world spun around him, then he felt a yank as Tobu hefted him up to safety. Although, from the look of anger in Tobu's eyes, Ash wasn't so sure this was the safer place to be. The hunters huddled

together on top of the high rock like the frightened herd of ulk they had been stalking, nostrils flaring and breath frantic.

They could do nothing but wait. The *Frostheart* would never make it in among the rocks, and they were going nowhere with these Lurkers snapping at their feet. Ash's body felt heavy all of a sudden. Song Weaving really took it out of him. "Hey! What are you *doing*?" Kailen called out to Shaard, the hunter who was closest to the edge.

Shaard leaned over for a better view of the snapping Lurkers and their dead companion. He wore a proud, crooked smile. "I knew I should've brought some extra rounds . . ." He laughed to the uncomfortable silence of the others.

﹀ ❧ ﹏

"Do you think they've gone?" Kob cautiously whispered after what felt like a long, long time. Mother Sun had disappeared below the horizon. The Lurkers were nowhere to be seen, but still the other hunters dared not answer.

"Why don't you go down and see?" Shaard replied finally. There was an uneasy laugh from the group, but no one moved.

The hunters shivered, almost buried under the snow that had been falling on them for the last few hours. A thin line of snot that had frozen into a green icicle dangled from Ash's nose, but he hadn't dared to move and wipe it. Finally Tobu stepped forward, shaking the snow from his fur like a dog. Picking up a stone, he threw it down to the snow below. It landed with a soft *pfft*.

The world was still.

"Nothing," Tobu grunted. The party breathed a sigh of relief.

Ash was in shock. This was just one hunting trip out into the wilds, and it had been awful. He looked at his guardian with newfound awe. *Tobu managed to walk from the World's Spine Mountains all the way to the Fira Stronghold. That journey would have taken moons, with countless hunts like this.* For the first time the true scale of this incredible feat dawned on Ash.

Tobu told me not to Sing, that I wasn't ready yet, his brain nagged, *and it looks like he was right.*

Perhaps it was time to start listening to Tobu?

Caw, a crow called, ominous and unseen—and seeming almost in agreement.

22

A Change of Plan

When the hunting party arrived back on the *Frostheart*, the rest of the crew were so relieved they didn't care that the only supplies they brought back were some measly snow hares and a few pouches of berries. On top of that, the commotion caused by the hunt must have sent signals out to other Leviathans, for soon after the *Frostheart* had picked up the hunters, they were joined by their very own procession of salivating Hurtlers hot in pursuit. It was simply too dangerous to stop the sleigh again, let alone to get off it to attempt another hunt.

"Looks like there's been a change of plans, my good fellows!" Captain Nuk announced to the crew. "Our rations are too low to get us to Aurora's Embrace, as we're all painfully aware. Instead, we shall head to Skybridge!"

"Tha's taking us leagues away from our path. An' for what?" Kailen objected.

"Simple: Skybridge is the closest Stronghold, and the best hope we have to safely resupply."

It's all those stupid crows' fault, I'm sure of it! They scared the ulk away, and brought the Lurkers straight to us! Was this what the frost-heart was trying to warn Ash about? That the crows were against him somehow? Monstrous Leviathans he'd expected, but conniving crows? He eyed the crows flying high above, apparently as determined to keep up with the *Frostheart* as the Leviathans were.

Ash's belly lurched as the sleigh changed direction. Lunah stood beside Nuk, inspecting her wrist-compass and pointing the way to Skybridge. The crew ran to and fro across the deck, altering the sails to change the *Frostheart*'s course. Ash saw Yorri begin preparations to change the sunstone within the enjin, whose power had been all but expended.

"Yorri, I wonder if you'd allow me to take a look?" Shaard asked him, stepping in front of the enjineer and taking the required equipment from his hands. "I've been hearing some concerning sounds coming from the enjin. I'd like to check if everything's in order. Why not see to your friend, and leave this to me?" he said, indicating Yallah, who sat on the steps to the upper deck, broken arm in a sling.

"You sure?" Yorri asked. "No one knows the *Frostheart*'s enjin better 'n me . . ."

"Trust me. It's what I do."

Yorri seemed reluctant, but Shaard's smile was very convincing. He nodded and strode over to his wounded friend.

Ash took the opportunity to approach Shaard. "Thank you for saving us from that Lurker," Ash said to him. "He would never say it, but I'm sure Tobu was glad you were there too."

Shaard looked dubious. "I'm not so sure. But your thanks are most welcome, young Song Weaver. The wilds are a dangerous place, and I'm sure the time will come when you will do the same for me." He'd taken a spherical archeomek case from Yorri that contained, Ash saw on closer inspection, a bright, powerful new sunstone. "Come, lad!" Shaard said to Ash. "Let me show you how to change a sunstone!"

The stone in the enjin was now nearly black as flint, warm red veins streaking across its surface, fading from existence like the cooling of embers in a hearth.

Shaard loaded the new sunstone casing into the sleigh's enjin by pulling on levers and opening rusted compartments. He was fast, so as not to leave the enjin without power for too long. He then ejected the old stone, tossing the metallic casing that contained it from hand to hand.

"Phew, still hot! Hot!" He put his hands on either side of the object and turned them in opposite directions, the archeomek clicking open and the sunstone within dropping into a barrel of ice water. "Stones get hot as flame when the life is sucked out of 'em!" The water hissed and breathed out steam as the drained sunstone fizzled into its depths.

Ash gasped in delight. It was spectacular to watch.

"Think I'll keep this, though," Shaard said, looking at the archeomek casing with a grin. "These things can withstand the most extreme temperatures, which is always useful for research. Least, if you research the type of things *I* research . . ." Shaard revealed the scorch marks running along his leather gauntlet, giving Ash a wink.

Not for the first time Ash was tempted to tell Shaard about the lullaby. Shaard knew so much about how the world worked and its history, Ash was sure he would know what to make of the lullaby's riddles. But there was something just a little too hungry about Shaard's expression, and just like the previous times, Ash thought better of it.

"I-I'd better go and find Tobu. He'll be wondering what happened to me."

"Aye, off you go, lad!" Shaard laughed. "And, Ash?" Ash stopped in his tracks to look at the suddenly serious face of the archeomek tinkerer. "I really do want to help you, you know. I know you want to find the Song Weaver Stronghold as much as I do. If you ever recall something your parents said to you, a clue they may have left behind, anything at all . . . well, I could try to help."

Ash stood awkwardly on the deck, biting his lip and gripping the hem of his sleeve. It was like Shaard had read his mind! And that thought wasn't very pleasant.

He gave a slow nod before rushing off to his tent.

23

A Teacher and His Student

To Ash's surprise the tent was empty. Even though it was his break, Tobu must have been off somewhere helping the rest of the crew.

So Ash sat in the tent and tried to enjoy having a few moments to himself, warm, cozy, and (relatively) safe. He dug into his pack and found what he was looking for. He passed the two pieces of his ocarina between his fingers, sorrow pulling at his insides. It was useless in this state, unable to be played, but he couldn't bring himself to get rid of it. He matched the broken windway to the main body, trying to figure out a way to fix it. As he did he tried to focus on happier thoughts, like how he'd figured out what, or rather, *who*, the "*drifting star*" was. He still didn't understand the relevance of the frost-heart, though, or why it needed protecting, but it felt like he was making some progress.

But his mind was elsewhere, and he was not as excited as he'd thought he would be. Tobu's words, warning Ash of the dangers of the wilds and how unprepared he was for them, echoed in his mind, and now he saw the truth in them. He had thought his Song Weaving would help keep them safe out on the Snow Sea, but the Lurker had proved powerful and merciless, and he realized that he still had much to learn if he wanted to stay alive.

So when Tobu finally came back to their tent, carrying a large pile of wooden arrow shafts and a sack of feathers, Ash was all questions.

"What do you hear when you listen to the World Weave?" Ash asked Tobu, sitting cross-legged and alert, ready to learn.

Tobu, who had begun to fletch the arrow shafts with sinew, looked surprised by the question. He lowered himself to face Ash and met his eyes.

"I hear . . . the world's sorrow," Tobu answered. "I hear it crying out for help. For balance. For the hateful corruption that has so long infected it to be healed."

Ash blanched at these heavy words.

The yeti closed his eyes and took a deep breath. "But I also hear . . . the wind. It Sings a Song of pure joy at its freedom. I . . . hear the ice chime its excitement at being,

thrilled to exist before it melts back into water. I hear the
water roaring and rushing, pulsing with energetic life. I
hear the earth below it hum with a deep, mighty rumble,
reminding me that wherever I am, whatever I am doing,
I am never truly lost, for the world, all of it, is where I
belong."

Ash blinked. He'd never heard Tobu be so open, let
alone share anything so beautiful. The yeti took another
deep breath and opened his eyes. He reached for a feather
and cut it in half with his knife.

"It sounds similar to when I listen to the Leviathans'
Song," Ash said carefully, realizing it was true. "And

when . . . when I Sing back to them . . . our Song seems to connect us. I know it's . . . *wrong*, but it's true. I feel safe. Almost at home." He paused. "So long as they're not roaring and trying kill us, that is," he added sheepishly.

Tobu looked thoughtful at this, as though an idea had suddenly struck him, his eyes lingering on the broken ocarina in Ash's hands.

"With training and perseverance you will master your power," he said.

"I wish we could actually train my Song Weaving, instead of . . . well, just sitting around, *listening*."

"Just because you are not Singing does not mean you're not learning. Before you can Song Weave success-fully, you have to show restraint and control. You cannot rush headfirst into such power. Those who do are the ones who darken the Song Weaver name."

"I do want to show restraint and control."

"I eagerly await seeing it."

Ash swore to himself that he would. The quiet drew on, Tobu winding the sinew the only sound to be heard. Ash became conscious that he was just sitting there star-ing at his ocarina. It felt strange, after all these weeks of hard work, to be doing nothing. He reached for the pile of arrow shafts and began to help Tobu fletch them.

"Shaard seems to know so much about Song Weaving.

Do you think . . . do you think that maybe you should give him another chance? I need all the help I can get," Ash ventured, feeling brave. He wanted to take advantage of finding Tobu in such a reflective, gentle mood. "I know you don't like him, but he says he wants to help me find more Song Weavers—maybe even find my parents—and maybe . . . maybe you'd like him if you tried . . ."

"A Hurtler can look like it's smiling before it has your head in its jaws," Tobu replied, eyes distant and mouth snarling with distaste. "Trust me, boy. I've met people like him before. You'd do best to stay away from the likes of him."

Ash sighed. *Keep chipping away; he'll understand . . . one of these days*, Ash assured himself. An awkward silence dragged on. Ash pulled too hard on the sinew, crushing the fletch he had been trying to tie to the shaft. He cursed at his carelessness. Tobu paused momentarily, looking as though he was about to say something, before apparently deciding against it. On the silence stretched.

"What are the yeti lands like?" Ash asked after a while, surprising even himself with his boldness.

"*Cold*. And harsh," Tobu said without glancing up.

Ash nodded. *Yep*. Given that the land had produced Tobu, this was pretty much what he'd imagined.

"But they are beautiful," Tobu added. "The World's

Spine Mountains look blue, or purple, depending on the light. They are cold, but not so featureless as the Fira lands. Deep forests and tall grasses defy the snows, herds of bovores roam the lands, stalked by mountain cats, while the skies above almost ripple with the beating of birds' wings. And stone statues stand guard over the mountain passes, carved by yeti craftsmen. The mountains truly are a place of life."

Ash wished he could see it, but he knew he never would. The yeti did not allow human-kin to enter their lands.

"Do you miss it? You must miss them—the rest of the yeti, I mean?" Ash asked. "I don't really miss the Fira, but I do miss my parents. Or, at least, the *idea* of them. I would love to have a family." Ash was about to reach for the pieces of his ocarina, but he stopped himself, knowing full well the pieces would not stick.

Tobu watched him, his brows for once not fixed in a frown. "Clinging to a painful past will only poison the present," he said softly. "But the future is still there to be made."

Ash smiled. These were the most comforting words he had ever heard from Tobu.

Another silence drew in.

"I didn't know you had been a teacher before," Ash

said after a while. Tobu gave him with a puzzled look. "You—you mentioned before when . . . you were teaching me about the World Weave on deck. About a boy, who wouldn't listen to you? And something bad happened to him."

Tobu lifted his chin in acknowledgment, but remained quiet.

Ash studied his face with a side glance, too afraid to look him right in the eye. He was surprised to see sadness there, memories of past pain.

"He was my son," Tobu said at last.

Ash's breath caught in his throat. *Tobu—a father?* He couldn't even begin to imagine it.

"What . . . what happened?"

The yeti was silent for a long while. "Some things are best left in the past," he said, throwing an arrow down and leaving the tent.

24

Scavenger's Nest

The ruined spires jutted out from the snow like giant freeze-fly nests, black against the white sky. Once they must have been masterfully crafted buildings, inlaid with intricate designs, whorled patterns carved deep into the stone, but now they were decaying skeletons, rusted and glistening with frost. Statues of once revered gods and heroes crumbled away, wearing cloaks of snow and growing beards of icicles. Whoever had built such a wondrous place could not have been human-kin surely— the scale and detail of the architecture was beyond Ash's understanding. Even as mere echoes of what they once were, the smallest ruins still towered above the *Frost-heart's* highest sail.

Delicate flakes of snow danced and whirled about the stone-still figure of Ash as the *Frostheart* darted among ruins of the World Before. For once the thought of his cozy, warm bedding was not on his mind. Well, that was a lie, but it certainly wasn't at the forefront at least. Not this time.

He could hear the wind howling through the cracks and chasms of the monumental ruins. He could hear birds calling, a different Song from the snowgulls that nestled around the Fira lands. He could hear the crew busy at work readying the sleigh to dock at Skybridge.

Fwooooosssssshhhh came a rhythmic sound from close behind him.

Ash heard his tent flap being pulled aside, and the sound of someone—Tobu—stepping out into the crisp morning air. He heard him stride across the main deck.

And then Ash thought he could hear Tobu's jaw drop in astonishment. At least, he liked to think that's what happened once Tobu had spotted him sitting cross-legged high up on the mainmast's crossbar. Lunah was hanging upside down behind him, swinging back and forth, making a f*wooooosssssshh* sound with her mouth each swing. Ash's eyes were closed, his chest rising and falling with controlled breathing, his brow twitching slightly with concentration. Without making a sound Tobu climbed up to them and crouched on his haunches, watching the scene with a raised brow.

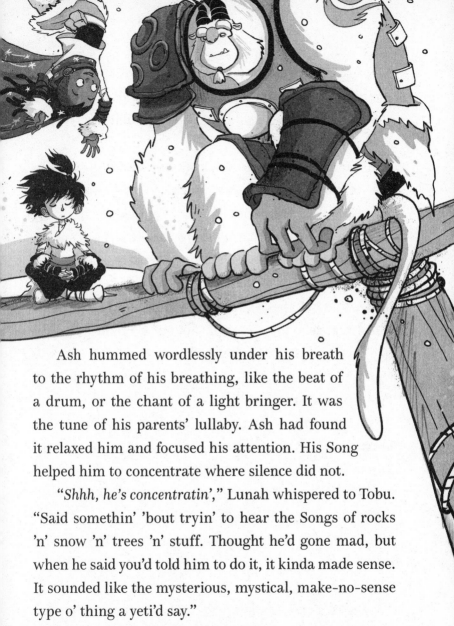

Ash hummed wordlessly under his breath
to the rhythm of his breathing, like the beat of
a drum, or the chant of a light bringer. It was
the tune of his parents' lullaby. Ash had found
it relaxed him and focused his attention. His Song
helped him to concentrate where silence did not.

"*Shhh, he's concentratin'*," Lunah whispered to Tobu.
"Said somethin' 'bout tryin' to hear the Songs of rocks
'n' snow 'n' trees 'n' stuff. Thought he'd gone mad, but
when he said you'd told him to do it, it kinda made sense.
It sounded like the mysterious, mystical, make-no-sense
type o' thing a yeti'd say."

Ash was sure he could feel Tobu's muscles tense in

surprise. Ash tried not to get too happy, too proud at the thought of Tobu realizing he was trying to listen to the World Weave, trying to improve his abilities without having been forced to.

And it must've been working, because unless it was his imagination, Ash was convinced he could almost sense Tobu's mouth twitch a little. Tremble, even.

Little by little he sensed it growing into a full smile.

"And the sound you're making?" Tobu asked Lunah.

"Oh! That's a Lunah spesh, that is," she said with pride. "Found the sound of the waves at the Broken Coast real relaxin', y'know? Thought it might help fire-boy focus. Stars know it's makin' me sleepy . . ." She continued to make the sound. "*Fwoooooossssssshhhh. Fwoooooossssssshhhh.*"

"Ash is lucky to have a companion as wise as you, Lunah," Tobu said, folding his arms, unable to hide the humor in his voice.

"Doubt he could've even climbed up this high without my help, to be honest."

"Hey!" Ash said, the insult finally breaking his concentration.

Lunah stuck out her tongue.

The two children laughed, and even Tobu gave what could have been a huff of amusement.

None of them noticed Shaard below them on deck, preparing himself for docking—gathering his research journal and some pieces of archeomek he suspected the vulpis would be interested in trading for . . . and listening very carefully to the children high above. In particular to the Song Ash had been humming.

Hefting his pack onto his shoulders, Shaard allowed himself an extremely satisfied smile . . .

➤ ❗ ⟨

The Skybridge Stronghold was built atop the huge stone base of a mighty tower, high enough so that the Leviathans could not reach it. The *Frostheart* raced up the slope that led to the main gates, and the snapping, snarling Hurtlers who had followed them for so long smashed against the scrap-metal barricade with a thunderous *CLANG* as the gate closed behind the sleigh. The *Frostheart* was out of their reach, at least for now.

Ash ran to the side of the sleigh to catch his first proper glimpse of Skybridge. He'd heard stories of the vulpis who lived there, although Master Podd was the only one he'd ever actually met. Vulpis were small and nimble enough to not attract the attention of the Leviathans (for the most part), and as such made great scavengers and archeomekologists, digging deep under the snows and into the ruins left behind by the World Before, reaching places the larger races could not. Any ancient archeomek or sunstones that were not used in the construction of their strange contraptions were then bartered to Path-finders, who in turn traded with the Strongholds.

Ash could only gawk in awe. The first thing to catch his eye was the dizzying height of the ancient tower above them, reaching so high it seemed to scrape the clouds themselves. Massive protrusions stuck out from its top, crumbling away into nothing. It looked like it might once have been a bridge, but one so lofty and massive it must have been raised by magic. He narrowed his eyes at the sight of large black birds circling its heights.

Crows. Again!

Windmills, wooden cranes, and intricate pulley sys-tems lifting heavy scrap littered the tower like spindly arms extending from a stone giant. Ash couldn't keep still, astounded at the sheer scale of what he was seeing. This was a sight he'd remember for as long as he lived. Then his eyes traveled down to the vulpis village that sat at the base of the tower.

It was a mess of structures made from scavenged scraps, crude rope and leather bindings linking them together, all held aloft by irregular wooden supports. Everything seemed to have a practical function; nothing

was made for beauty. Large wheels and grinding gears spun and clanked, strange machines shuddered and belched out smoke like bonfires. The whole place looked unnatural. The Fira could use only what the land had to offer, but the vulpis, and the World Before, shaped the land themselves.

The whole scene was nothing short of mind-blowing.

Ash sensed Tobu shifting, uncomfortable in such a place, and despite his wonder Ash could empathize. The place scared him a little too. On his other side, however, Shaard took a deep, exaggerated breath of the bitter smoke-filled air and sighed with satisfaction. "Breathe it in, Ash! That's the smell of *progress*."

❧ ❦

Once docked, the crew brought out the meager supplies they were able to spare from the cargo hold, carrying them down the gangplank toward the waiting vulpis. All, that is, except for Shaard, who had nearly left a dust-cloud he'd moved so fast to discover Skybridge's ancient secrets. Tobu was hefting three large crates, seven barrels, and a little clay pot upon his shoulders. "Kindly watch those bulging muscles of yours, Tobu. You'll take some-one's eye out if you're not careful!" Captain Nuk chortled, lifting a couple of barrels herself.

"What's *in* this?" Ash gasped through gritted teeth, sweat trickling down his back as he struggled toward the makeshift dock with a crate.

Yorri grinned, a barrel under each arm. "Come along, lad, lifting and carrying's half the fun of being a Pathfinder. You're gonna have to get used to it!"

Ash's legs trembled, his knees knocking together. He'd never lifted something so heavy!

"Look out below!" Lunah called, running atop a row of rolling barrels, surfing them down the gangplank toward the small vulpis who was making a list of the items on a long scroll. "Need a little help, fire-boy?" she asked Ash as she rolled by.

"Is there a *Leviathan* in here or something?" Ash puffed, dropping the crate with a loud crash. He peeked through a hole in the crate and narrowed his eyes. "*Redroots*," he growled. "My archenemy. Of course . . ." He slumped down to the floor, back against the box as he caught his breath, before heading back into the *Frostheart*'s hull. He'd been hoping to impress the others with his incredible strength, but was now just thankful no one else was in the hold to witness his great struggle with the next crate he tried to lift. He was making his way to a much smaller and altogether more tempting box when he heard a sound that stopped him in his tracks. It was subtle, like a distant chime or a sorrowful sigh. Looking about the hold, half expecting to find Lunah hiding and preparing to make him jump, Ash confirmed he was alone. The crew were moving about on deck, sliding barrels down the gangplank toward the docks.

Did I imagine it?

But no, there it was again. The sound was quiet, almost just a whisper in his head. With a chill Ash turned to face the frost-heart. There it glowed, its cold radiating in the relative warmth of the hold. With trepidation Ash approached the mysterious object. He was sure of it now. He could definitely make out a Song, so distant and delicate, but there on the edge of his hearing.

He looked about the hold. Still alone. Closing his eyes, Ash reached out a hand and touched it to the cold frost-coated mastpole that the frost-heart was embedded within. Its chill hurt to the touch. Ash recalled all he'd learned throughout Tobu's numerous lessons. He breathed in . . . and out.

I can do this, but not in silence. I'm going to do it my way.

He thought of what Tobu had said about the World Weave, how similar it had sounded to the connection he had with the Leviathans. He focused his attention entirely on the frost-heart and its whispers, and Sang the lullaby under his breath to the rhythm of his heart, the flow of the words helping to concentrate his mind and block out any distractions. He felt his starlight aura stretch out from his fingers into the mast and up into the frost-heart. He tried to cling to the heart's distant Song. To his amazement he felt his aura entangle with the Song that had so far slipped his grasp. He coaxed it forward. *"What are you saying? What are you trying to tell me?"*

The Song grew clearer in his mind, growing in volume and meaning. It had all the character of a Leviathan's Song, but . . . *greater,* if that was possible. *Deeper.* An intelligence that still lived within the heart, a wisdom so deep that Ash suspected there might be no bottom to it, that it was as ancient as the world itself. Despite the frost-heart's freezing nature, Ash felt as though he'd been caught up in a warm embrace, nuzzled by an invisible creature that had been waiting an eternity to find him and was overjoyed to be there with him at last. *What kind of creature did this heart once belong to? And how is it still alive?*

> *"Crows will call, harsh and broken,*
> *Offering you friendship's token . . ."*

He gasped and let go of the mast, his hand trembling. His fingers burned, coated in glistening frost. But despite this Ash couldn't help smiling. He'd heard the message,

clear as crystal. His heart leaped for joy. The comfort and
happiness he felt when he was Song Weaving had been
magnified a hundredfold though the frost-heart's Song.
He felt like he'd met with a long-lost friend he'd forgotten
he'd ever had. And at last it had actually worked! He'd
listened, and he'd heard. Though he couldn't quite believe
it, the frost-heart, *the beacon,* had given him the next
riddle in the lullaby. *So the crows are offering me friendship, not trying to hinder me? You could've fooled me!* He
didn't understand what it meant, not yet, but he was
determined to find out.

25

At the Top of the World

Ash could barely contain his excitement, and was desperate to tell Lunah what he'd discovered, but it would have to wait. He came back up onto the deck to find Captain Nuk negotiating with the vulpis.

"Two sunstones!" Nuk exclaimed to the leader of the Stronghold, a small bearded vulpis bedecked in glittering archeomek that dangled from his clothes. Unlike the ever composed Master Podd, these vulpis were jittery, their ears twitching and their hands constantly fidgeting. "For what we're bringing you, I demand at least four, and even then you're robbing me blind. Master Podd would be the first to tell you!"

"I would indeed," Master Podd agreed, standing at her side.

Ash wasn't surprised to see such haggling. Pathfinders were merchants before anything else, and were always looking for the best deal. Survival had a price, and Ash was learning this lesson fast.

"The olden shinies you have on your deck, then we make deal," said the Skybridge leader, who sat atop a clanking construction that walked around on metal legs like an ulk. As awesome as the contraption was, Ash couldn't help but feel repulsed by it. It looked entirely unnatural, and its jerky, heavy movements were, to be quite honest, creepy. He felt that at any moment it could gain a mind of its own and come twitching toward him.

"*Ah*. Shaard's archeomek," Nuk said. "I'm afraid it does not belong to me. A valiant effort, but it is not mine to give."

"Then only two," said the leader, before whipping his head to one side, having spotted something. "*What's that?*" he called, and pointed frantically.

The other vulpis jerked their heads in the same direction. "*A thing!*" they said as one, some diving into the snow headfirst in search of something Ash could not see.

The leader's tail swished. "It's no thing," he decided after consideration, looking back to Nuk. He held out his paw. "Sweeten deal."

Nuk harrumphed and reached into a pouch at her belt, pulling out a talisman made of the strange ceramic from the World Before. The leader snatched it from her hand and bit it with his sharp, pointy teeth. Apparently satisfied he gave a nod.

"Have deal."

"Indeed?" Master Podd asked.

The leader nodded. "Two sunstones and scrap-box."

"*Scrap?* I said four sunstones, not the ancient rubbish you don't want!" Nuk bellowed.

"Scrap or no deal," the leader said, before spotting something else. "*What's that?*" He stared intently at an empty spot, before shaking his head. "It's no thing. *Unless?*"

"*A shiny?*" his comrades called, leaping into the snow that had gathered atop the ruins.

Nuk groaned. "I thought I had a special understanding with the vulpis," she said, surrounded by vulpis bottoms sticking out of the snow, tails swishing to and fro. "I suppose our relationship is truly one of a kind, wouldn't you agree, Master Podd?"

"I would indeed, captain," he said, composed as ever.

Later on, Ash took a moment from his task of brushing tar into the cracks in the *Frostheart*'s hull to watch the clunking scrap-built hulks the vulpis used to dig into the ruins, the large insect-like shovel-arms throwing debris behind them like a fox digging under the snow for food. The vulpis scurried about their machines with frantic furor, and the whole operation seemed as spectacular to Ash as any Leviathan he'd seen.

BRAAK, cried a crow, making him jump. It perched atop one of the nearby wooden lifts used to transport heavy loot up and down the ruins.

"I don't know how to speak Crow," Ash said to the bird, glaring at it.

"Talkin' to yer new friends, fire-boy?" Lunah asked, a huge grin (and a few splodges of tar) on her face. Ash had told her about the crow verse the frost-heart had Sung to him, and she found it funnier than Ash could understand. "*Caw, caw, craw caw!*" Lunah imitated, flapping her arms. "I believe that's the polite way to greet someone in Crow."

"Very funny," Ash said. Another crow landed next to the first. "I think they're trying to tell me something, but, like always, I don't understand what that is."

"Well then, why don't we follow 'em an' find out?" Lunah said, dropping her brush and grabbing Ash's arm, leading him toward the lift. "You ent gonna get anywhere tryin' to talk to 'em!"

"We can't leave our posts again after the last time! Captain Nuk was furious!" Ash spluttered, but only because he felt like he should protest. Really, he wanted to follow the crows as much as Lunah.

"C'moooon, Ash! You ent ever gonna discover the mysteries of your singy-doo-da by tarrin' hulls! *Follow the crows! Follow the crows!*" Lunah chanted.

She was right, of course, and it was always hard to resist a chant.

"OK. You win. My 'sneaking-away' skills are getting a bit rusty anyway, right?" Ash grinned. "And I think I have an idea . . ."

ㅡ ㅣ ㅡ

The pair stepped back and admired their handiwork. They'd dipped a mop into the tar, so its strands had turned black, and wrapped another with dark cloth. They'd then tied some other pieces of scrap across the mops to act like arms, and had dressed the makeshift figures in furs. From a distance, with the cold air bringing tears to your eyes, they could almost pass for Ash and Lunah.

Lunah looked at Ash with pride.

"You learn fast, Ash. There's hope for you yet. Let's go!" she said, leading him back to the lift. "Coast is clear!" she whispered. Lunah hopped aboard the lift, the crows squawking in protest and flying up toward the tower's summit.

"Are you sure it's safe?"

"Ent nothin' better 'n vulpis mek!" she said. Ash wasn't convinced. "Cross my heart, Ash. Look, this is my serious face," said Lunah with a smile the size of a sleigh. "Don't tell me you're *scared*?"

"No, I just . . . No, of course not!" Ash hesitated, then climbed aboard, the rope that held the lift creaking ominously. "I hope you know what you're doing!"

"Always!" Lunah said, smiling and pulling down on the rope to raise the lift. It began its climb up the side of the tower in the same direction the crows had flown. Ash lay flat on the platform, clinging tight to the edge with sweaty hands. He'd never been so high, and even though he was petrified, he had to admit that the view was breathtaking. Mother Sun bathed the world in her light, the ice flats surrounding the ruins glistening like crystal. Ancient structures emerged from the ice like breaching Leviathans, pale blue and hazy with distance. Lunah whistled in appreciation as she hoisted them ever higher.

"It's nice not being the baby on the sleigh anymore," Lunah teased.

"I-I'm not a baby, I just . . . just like the view from down there, that's all."

"*Uh-huh.*" Lunah laughed, then she went quiet for a time. "Still, nice to have someone to muck about with, y'know? Dunno if the rest of the crew woulda followed me onto this lift, s'far too dangerous."

"*What?*" Ash shrieked.

"S'good to have a friend on board around my age is all I'm sayin', Ash, Conqueror of Heights."

Despite his fear, Ash smiled from ear to ear. "Thank you! I like *being* around, Lunah! I've never really had many friends before. Because of . . . well, y'know . . . So . . . thank you."

She smiled back, the two of them enjoying a comfortable silence as the platform rose higher and higher. They passed many stepped levels of the tower, and Ash couldn't help but notice the remains of old dwellings littering their surfaces. Animal skins glittered with ice, half-buried under the snow, the branches that had once been the support beams of the homes splintered and broken. Crows took wing from the ledges, circling up and around the lift.

"Did this place used to be a human-kin Stronghold?" he asked.

"Hasn't been for many winters now, but, yeah, once."

"What happened to it?"

"Same thing happens to most Strongholds after long enough. I heard Leviathans smashed through the gates. The people had to flee up here to get away, too scared of the ghosts within to go inside the ruins. They were trapped. Surrounded, couldn't hunt or get supplies. The Wraiths came 'n' finished the job the Leviathans'd started once the coast was clear. Poor Skybridgers were too weak to fight back. Place was empty fer winters, 'fore the vulpis moved in."

Ash blanched. He thought of the same fate befalling the Fira Stronghold, and all those he knew there, and it was a thought he almost couldn't bear. He tried not to think about it in case by doing so he somehow made such an awful thing happen.

A cloud hid Mother Sun, shrouding the land in cold shadow. Snow began to fall.

"Who *are* the Wraiths? Does anyone know?" Ash asked.

"Not so much *who*, more like *what*," said Lunah, her expression grim. "Some say they're the souls o' dead Pathfinders trapped in this world, ridin' black war sleighs an' seekin' vengeance for lives cut cruelly short. Others say they're dark spirits sent from the depths of the underworld, who ride Leviathans as steeds and steal the souls of the livin' back to their nightmare realm. What-ever they are, the only thing that's certain is that you should steer far and clear. No one, and I mean *no one*, survives a close encounter with 'em."

A shiver ran through Ash.

"Anyway," said Lunah far too brightly, "'nuff of all this downer-talk. We're here to find whatcha lullaby was goin' on about, ent we?"

"R-right," Ash said, before reciting the riddle.

"Crows will call, harsh and broken,
Offering you friendship's token . . ."

The lift came to a stop at the top of the tower, a dozen crows circling above the wooden supports that held the lift. "Well, the crows're certainly callin', harsh 'n' bro-ken," Lunah said.

Ash swallowed hard. It truly felt as though they were high enough to reach Mother Sun. The lift swayed in the wind, hanging a few feet from the tower's edge.

"Yer gonna have to jump over," Lunah said.

"W-what? No!" Ash's legs had turned to water, and he dared not look down.

"Well, it's either that or stay on this lift! It's easy, a quick leap an' you'll be on solid ground. It's better 'n stayin' on this shaky thing!" She spoke undeniable truth.

Ash took a deep breath, mustered all the courage he could find, and leaped across the gap, his eyes shut tight. He landed safely, gasping with relief. "See! Easy!" Lunah smiled, and at that precise moment one end of the rope holding the lift snapped, sending Lunah hurtling down the side of the tower.

Ash cried out in shock, rushing to look over the edge. His head spun with vertigo as he came face-to-face with the dizzying drop below.

Ash thanked the spirits when he saw Lunah a ways down clinging to the frayed rope, the wooden lift and looted relics it had carried tumbling down the mind-boggling drop below her. "That's shoddy workmanship, that is!" she called to him, somehow still able to laugh. A knot in the rope had jammed in the pulley system, catching it before it fell, but who knew how long Lunah could hang from it.

"What—what are we gonna *do?*" Ash called down.

"There's a doorway down here!" she shouted, her voice almost stolen by the howling wind. "I'll meet you inside!"

"*Are you crazy?*" Ash cried, finding his answer when she swung from the rope to the ledge before her.

"See you inside!" came her voice, though she was lost from Ash's sight. He had never met someone as brave, or absolutely *nuts*, as Lunah.

He scrambled away from the edge, the gusting wind making his belly lurch and his body feel weightless enough to be blown over.

I'm gonna be sick, please don't let me be sick . . .

Just then, a crow çawed.

Braaak.

Ash turned round slowly. He had been too busy shaking like a leaf to notice the bird that sat on a stone block that rested beside a large ominous hole leading inside the ruins.

Braaaak, the crow screamed again.

Another crow dropped from the sky to join it.

Braaaak. Braaaak.

There were more of them now. Four. Each crow looking at Ash intently with its glinting black eyes. They seemed to be waiting for him, gathered at the entrance

to the ruins. Objects hung from the doorway, little birds woven from twigs, crow skulls and black feathers hanging from sinew threads swaying gently in the wind, the bones clicking together.

Tak. Tak.

A shiver ran down Ash's spine. There was no way of going back now.

The entrance was dark. It seemed to grow larger as he stared into its shadows. Steeling his nerves, Ash made his way inside.

26

Cry of the Black Bird

Ash could barely see a thing. He could just make out the shapes of more hanging bones and feathers. Though he couldn't see much, he could hear something. The sound of harsh squalling crows. He reached for the cold, clammy wall and felt his way inside.

What am I doing *here?* he thought, a creeping dread building up inside him. *What was that?!* He jumped, feeling something brush his leg, but it was too dark to see. He took a cautious step into a chamber, a change in the air telling him it was tall and wide. As his eyes became accustomed to the darkness he realized he was surrounded by strange objects. Pots and jugs cluttered the floor, and jars of strange liquids and bizarre objects lined the alcoves set into the walls. The woven birds, crow bones, and feathers trailed down in the hundreds from the high ceiling like cobwebs. Ash began to breathe hard, the shadows shifting and warping in the darkness until he realized they weren't shadows at all, but hundreds upon hundreds of crows. In an almighty chorus they began to call out as one, a strangled, ululating cacophony, disturbing to behold and disorienting Ash's senses. The floor was slick with their droppings, and the smell of them singed his nostrils. He could barely hear himself think through all the noise.

What is this place?

Then, to Ash's horror, something arose from amid the mass of ragged black shapes. A giant crow, its feathers tousled and scruffy, its head large and dark as shadow. Ash trembled in fear. Was this some kind of dark magic? He should never have come here without Lunah!

The creature turned to face him . . . and he realized with a shock it wasn't a monster bird at all, but a person clothed in tattered black rags, the face hidden in the darkness of a large deep hood. Crows perched on the figure's shoulders, cawing into its ear as though whispering dark secrets.

"*Weaver,*" it said.

The voice was female and it sent shivers down Ash's spine.

"Y-yes?" Ash squeaked.

It took him a moment to realize that the words had not been spoken. The figure was Singing, if the sound could be called such a thing. Her Song was a harsh, strained whisper, like a blade being dragged through ice, broken and jagged, like crows crying out as they feasted on the dead.

"*Journey. Answers. Seek. FOUND.*"

Her Song was somehow forming into words inside his head, just like when he heard the emotions of the Leviathans. He had no idea *human-kin* could do this!

"Who—who *are* you?" Ash replied, too scared to start Song Weaving himself.

"*Crows. Sing. Tell. Speak. DANGER.*" The crows shrieked and flowed around the figure like thick black smoke. The next instant, she was gone.

"Wait! Where are you going?" Ash whirled round, his skin prickling with fear.

"*HIDDEN.*"

Ash spun round again, staggering back as he discovered the figure standing right before him. "It was *you! You* sent the crows to watch me! But how did you find me?"

"*Echoes. In. World Weave,*" she Sang.

"But—but how did you know I'd come here? We—we weren't supposed to . . ."

"*Friends. Help. Twist. Fate.*" She raised her arms and gestured at the crows, who called out in agreement. Ash gritted his teeth in sudden understanding, although he had no idea how she'd actually done it.

"The crows that scared the ulk away during the hunt . . . ? You were *leading* me here? You knew we'd have to come to Skybridge for supplies if we had none! But . . . but *why*?"

"*DANGER. Hidden. Within.*" She took a step toward him, Ash doing his best to keep his distance. "*BEWARE.*"

"I don't understand!"

"*Beware. Outcast. Hated. FEARED. Talons. Sink. Deeper.*" She made her own hand into the shape of a claw to underline her point.

"The outcast . . . who do you mean?"

"*OUTCAST. Evil. Seeks. DEVOURER.*"

The crows clouded over her once more. Then they flocked in front of Ash, a flurry of feathers and sharp talons, and Ash yelled out in shock, his arms raised to protect his face.

The dark figure rushed forward and grabbed his wrists with cold, clammy hands, faster than he could re-coil. "*Outcast. Walks. Shadow path. Despair. BETRAYER.*"

"Outcast—do you mean *me*?" The crows' calls hurt his eardrums; it was hard to think.

"*Outcast. Not. Fira!*"

With cold realization Ash felt as though he could hear a message hidden within the crow Song, much like with the frost-heart. He struggled to focus, but he was too terrified to concentrate on it. "*HEED. CROWS. HEED!*"

the figure Sang. He could feel her urgency, her desperation for him to understand.

"*Ash?*" came Lunah's voice close by.

The figure spun round with a hiss. "*FEAR. BEWARE. OUTCAST,*" she shrieked before dissolving into the shadows.

Ash was left alone, a feeling of cold dread trickling down his spine.

"There you are. I thought I'd never find you! Did you even try to look for me, you big scrumpalump?" Lunah entered the chamber. "*Whoa.* What is *this* place? It *stinks!*"

Ash was too shaken, too lost in thought to answer. *Who* was *that? And what did she mean?* Was she saying he should fear someone, or that he should fear himself?

"Ash? Helloooooo, Ash? Are you there?" Lunah saw the hollow look on Ash's face, the whiteness of his skin. "You all right? It looks like you've seen a ghost!"

Ash gulped. He had a horrible feeling that Lunah might be right.

27

Nothing's Changed

"A *ghost*?" Lunah asked, raising an eyebrow, feeling her way down the dark spiral staircase that led through the center of the tower. "Well, they do say these ruins are haunted . . ."

Ash had been so affected by his encounter with the crow-lady he'd barely even registered the fact they'd been climbing down the dank, cold stairwell for ages, spiraling round and round. It would've made him dizzy, had he already not been so disoriented. Eventually their path became illuminated, flaming torches lining the walls, lighting the space for the vulpis miners who worked down there, who now watched the children pass with startled curiosity.

"What human-childs doing here?" one asked.

"Sorry, took a wrong turning!" Lunah said, casual as ever.

"Or . . . or maybe she was a witch?" Ash said, still thinking of the crow-witch. "She was flying all over the place, Song Weaving straight into my mind. It was . . . impressive, but really scary. I'm telling you, there was something . . . *strange* about her. And I think she was trying to tell me the next part of the lullaby, but I didn't understand it. I mean, this must be why my parents wanted me to find her, but it doesn't seem to fit the Song. *Beware the outcast*. Maybe . . . maybe I heard her wrong? But she disappeared before I could ask her . . ."

"You sure it wasn't just a vulpis tangled up in some old rags? They do that, sometimes, you know. Or, more likely yet: you didn't just imagine it? Fear does weird stuff, an' I saw you clingin' to that lift like it was your ma!"

"I didn't imagine it, Lunah," Ash insisted. "I think she was a Song Weaver. But her Song wasn't like mine; it was . . . it was *scarier*."

"You obviously haven't heard yourself Sing, have you?" Lunah joked.

"Lunah!"

"Look, I dunno what to tell you. Let's get ourselves

out of this endless stairwell an' maybe then we can have a little think, eh?"

"Or maybe it was a warning?" Ash said, oblivious to Lunah's suggestion, the crow-witch's Song still echoing in his mind.

FEAR. BEWARE. OUTCAST. But whom was she talking about?

As the two children emerged from the ancient tower, squinting and covered in dust, they found Captain Nuk and Tobu waiting for them. The mop replicas were clutched in their hands, and neither looked best pleased.

"An' I thought we'd just got back to safety," Lunah muttered to Ash under her breath.

"Do you know what?" Nuk said, scowling. Ash did not know what, and he suspected he didn't really want to. "I think I may leave you both here. I'd wager these mops will do far more work than either of you lay-abouts." Ash noticed that behind Nuk, at the edge of the Stronghold, the vulpis were leaping up and down and barking in a fluster about something, the other Pathfinders trying to calm them down.

"Imagine meeting like this, Cap'!" Lunah said with mock astonishment. "You won't believe it, but it's actually a really funny story."

"Oh, is that so?" Nuk asked. Ash could sense danger brewing.

"*Just* so," Lunah replied. "Tell 'er, Ash."

"I . . . no, we just . . . um, what it was, was, we just, um, had to check this stairwell, for safety, you know, but, yes, it looks all good to us. Not a problem here, so we can get straight back to work now!"

"Mm-hmm. And why, may I ask, are you covered in bird poo, Ash?" Nuk asked.

But as Ash gaped at the white muck that was splattered across his shoulders, the vulpis leader rushed over. "What is meaning of this?" he yelled, tugging on Captain Nuk's arm, leading her and the others to the precipice where the agitated vulpis were jittering around. "Deal is off! Deal is off!" he cried.

"Now, now," Nuk said. "I'm not sure what you're getting so worked up about, but I'm sure there's a reasonable explanation . . ." The leader huffed and pointed down over the edge of the ruin. Following his paw, the Pathfinders looked over and saw a swarm of Lurkers writhing around in a frenzy far below. Scattered around them, among their claws and in their jaws, were the shattered remains of sunstones and a broken wooden lift. Ash and Lunah gulped.

"*Please* tell me this had nothing to do with you two," Nuk muttered to Lunah out of the corner of her mouth, over the angry barks and squeals of the vulpis.

"You'll be proud to know that it most definitely did not," Lunah lied.

"Vulpis saw children messing with lift. Broke it! Precious shinies—lost! Tooth-nasties ripping and shredding!" the vulpis leader cried, tugging his ears back in despair. His comrades scurried about, ears twitching and fangs bared. "Deal off, deal off!"

"No need to be so hasty!" Nuk spoke in her most apologetic voice. "I'm sure we can work something out—"

"You break, you buy!" the leader insisted.

"It wasn't our fault; it was your shabby lift!" Lunah argued. "It nearly killed us!"

Ash didn't feel like arguing. He felt terrible. He knew the *Frostheart* had nothing to spare, and how desperate they were for the supplies the vulpis could provide. Had he and Lunah ruined everything?

"Once more, you display a lack of judgment, boy," Tobu grumbled at Ash. "You disappoint me."

"No! I was following the World Weave, just like you said I should, going where it guided me!"

"By breaking a lift?" Tobu wasn't buying it.

"I—I can fix this!" Ash said, desperate to make things right. "I can clear the Lurkers away with my Song, and then we can collect the sunstone shards!" He wasn't sure he had the power to do so, but he had to try to help.

"Ash, *no!*" Tobu ordered. But it was too late. The vulpis had stopped their protests and were now staring at Ash with wide eyes.

"*Song?*" the leader said.

Nuk held Ash back with one arm. "Ash, my boy! I know you're a budding young musician, and we all *adore* the rousing snow shanties you perform for us, but perhaps now's not the time for that, wouldn't you agree?" She raised her eyebrows and widened her eyes as if she was trying to tell Ash something unspoken.

His mouth opened and closed like a fish. *What was going on?*

The vulpis cocked their heads to the side, and the *Frostheart* crew shifted nervously, trying too hard to look unconcerned.

"Lunah, kindly take Ash away, won't you? I think Yorri could do with your help preparing the *Frostheart* to set sail," Nuk said, speaking much faster than normal.

"Aye aye, captain!" Lunah said, beginning to lead Ash away.

"*Song Weaver?*" a vulpis questioned Captain Nuk.

"You bring a Song Weaver here? Not welcome! Must go! You all must go!" said another.

"*You can't Sing in front of these guys, Ash! You'll blow yer cover!*" Lunah whispered in Ash's ear as she led him away.

"My cover? What are you talking—"

Before Ash could finish his sentence, Kailen tore him from Lunah's grasp, her teeth gritted and her eyes burning with fury. "What do you think you're doing?!" she hissed. "You've ruined us all!"

Ash followed her gaze.

"*Out!*" the vulpis were barking at Captain Nuk. "*Get out! Not welcome!*"

"This has all been a great misunderstanding! We'll be laughing about it over a deal-sealing drink tonight, just you wait," Nuk assured them.

"No deal! No drink! You bring danger to us! *Get out!"*

Kailen growled in fury, pulling Ash away from the crowd so that they could talk without being overheard. "You've ruined this deal, and I will *not* let you put the crew in any more danger with your warblin'."

Ash's shock was replaced with annoyance, and he ripped himself from her grip. "I would never do anything to hurt them! How does *not* getting rid of the Leviathans put us in any *less* danger?"

"No, she's right," Lunah said in a small voice.

"What?"

"Like it or not, people don't trust Song Weavers, Ash. The vulpis've seen the *Frostheart* carries a Song Weaver, and word could spread. People'll avoid us. We won't be able to trade, an' that means we won't be able to survive."

Ash felt sick. *So that's the truth of it,* he thought. *Nothing's changed, not really. Everyone still thinks I'm a monster.*

"I'm sorry, Ash, I really am, but it's just the way it is," Lunah said. She reached a hand out to his shoulder, but he pulled away. He felt embarrassed enough.

"The *Frostheart* is the only place I've ever felt welcome. I'd do anything to keep it safe," he said.

"Thing is, you're *not* welcome, Song Weaver. Your kind *never* is. You'll *never* be one of us," Kailen said.

Ash went cold. He felt like his insides had been frozen by the Ice Crone herself.

"Hey! *Too far!*" Lunah yelled. "That's not true. Don't listen to her, Ash! Cap' would be havin' a fit if she heard you speak like that, Kailen!"

How do I keep doing this? I—I ruin everything and take those I care about down with me, Ash thought in despair. *If ever there was an outcast who was a danger to others, who should be feared, it's me! The crow-witch was right.*

"You want to help, Ash?" Kailen asked, ignoring Lunah. "Then leave the *Frostheart*. Singing to Leviathans will only put us in danger. You may have the others fooled, but not me. I catch you Singin' out here again, and you'll regret it. Be sure of that."

28

Shadows of the Past

The pebble Ash had thrown in frustration flew over the ramparts, tumbling down and clacking off the ancient stone. Ash lost sight of it, but thought that maybe he heard it skip off the ice far, far below. He was keeping out of the way of the *Frostheart* crew, especially Captain Nuk, whom Ash could almost hear thinking up a way to teach Lunah and him a lesson, and he didn't want to be around when inspiration finally struck. He watched as a caravan of squat mekanical vulpis sleighs chugged off into the Snow Sea, black smoke trailing behind them. These were not the elegant streamlined sleighs typical of the Pathfinders, these were clunking and brutal, pieced together in a patchwork of rusted scrap.

Probably off scouting for someone they can actually trade with, someone without a Song Weaver to dirty the deal.

"Why does everyone hate me?" he said aloud, squeezing his eyes tight and grinding his teeth in frustration.

"I'd call it *jealousy* myself," came a voice, startling Ash. He hadn't seen Shaard leaning on the wall nearby, hands resting behind his head. He grinned his wolvish grin as always. "You have the power to overcome the very thing that every other person in this world lives in fear of. They want what you have, but know, deep down, that they will never have it."

"Maybe," Ash said. "But I just want to be normal."

"Don't ever say that!" Shaard demanded, springing up off the wall, light as a feather. His furs billowed behind him as he strode forward, giving Ash a hard look. "I have something to show you, Ash. Quickly now—we don't have much time."

Compelled, Ash let Shaard lead him into the dark heart of the ancient tower. They eventually came to a stop at a huge wall painting that stretched as high and wide as the *Frostheart*. It was jaw-dropping to look at. "Listen to me, Ash. The Leviathans make the Strongholders scattered and weak," Shaard said. "But if I've learned anything in all my years of searching, it's that the Leviathans make Song Weavers *strong*."

He gestured at the painting. "In my travels, far to the west, I came across a ruin untouched by vulpis or human-kin. Within its depths I learned of things beyond imagining." The chill in the air seemed to get colder as Ash gazed up at the mural. It looked like a huge village from the World Before, a village many times the size of the Fira Stronghold. Towering above it was a monstrosity unlike anything Ash had ever seen. It seemed to reach up to the thunderous sky, lightning raining down upon the land. Appendages like tree roots spilled from its mass, piercing through buildings and swatting aside what looked like warriors armed with the ancient, terrible weaponry from the World Before as though they were nothing more than annoying insects. It was the eyes, though, the six pitiless eyes Ash had seen so many times before on Lurkers and Hurtlers that told him this was some kind of Leviathan. He felt his mouth fall open, his skin crawling at the mere idea of such a thing. It must have been an exaggeration. Surely nothing like this could *actually* exist?

"Leviathans are the greatest predators this world has ever known. Nothing can match their strength. But who can influence that strength? Who can guide, who can *control* such a power?"

"Song Weavers . . ." Ash whispered, a chill going down his spine at the thought of Weaving with such a monster.

Shaard smiled. "That's right. The *only* things in this world more powerful than the Leviathans are the Song Weavers themselves. You have great power within you, Ash, and you should never wish to be any less." Ash's mind was in a whirlwind. What Shaard was

suggesting—the idea of that kind of power terrified Ash. But it intrigued him too.

What if I could control Leviathans? Then I could really help the Frostheart, really prove to them that I am a valuable member of the crew.

"But . . . but none of this matters," Ash said. "What I did with the Hurtlers back at the Fira . . . it was a fluke. The Lurker that attacked Yallah . . . I was helpless against it. I don't have a clue what I'm doing . . . There's no way I'd be able to Weave with something . . . something like *that.*"

Shaard nodded, thoughtful.

"Perhaps. But maybe you have your friend Tobu to thank for that. His lessons are getting you nowhere fast, in spite of how hard he works you. I've begun to suspect that the yeti is scuttling your abilities on purpose. He's scared you'll become more powerful than him—like all the others, he's *jealous* of your power."

Ash stepped away from Shaard with indignation. "Tobu would never do that!" he said.

Shaard gave a small smile. "Perhaps not. But the Song Weaving technique you use can only soothe the Leviathans, which is all well and good behind the safety of walls. But it won't win us any wars—and this *is* a war, make no mistake. You need to fight, Ash. There is more than one Song Weaving technique. I've heard it told, even seen it with my own eyes. Mighty Song Weavers, commanding power beyond any Song you have Sung, wielding Leviathans like *weapons*." Shaard's eyes gleamed with a sudden fervor. "You could be great, Ash, just like your father."

"My . . . my father?" Ash asked, confused.

Shaard looked up at the gigantic mural, his eyes distant, lost in memory, his smile soft for once instead of hungry.

"The night we first spoke, I mentioned that I once had a friend from the Fira. His name was Ferno." Shaard chuckled to himself. "We were very close. Saved each other's lives a few times, though I don't doubt he saved me more than I saved him. Ferno was a proud Song Weaver." Ash gasped, but Shaard continued. "I knew he had a son, a son who lived far up north, though I didn't put two and two together at first. Not until I heard you hum that tune up on the mast while you were training, that *lullaby*. Your father used to hum that same tune, *all the ruddy time*, humming away to himself. I knew it then, Ash, without a doubt in my mind." Time felt like it was moving in slow motion. The ground disappeared below Ash's feet; it felt like he was flying, high, high above the world.

"Ferno was your father, Ash."

29

A Debt to Pay

Ash's head spun. The world had just been turned upside down. His father—*Ferno*—truly *had* been a Song Weaver! And the man standing next to him, right *there*, had been friends with him!

"Th-this is *incredible*!" Ash blurted. Joy bubbled out of him like a geyser. "I can't believe—I never knew—is there—do you—do you know where he is?" His thoughts were racing so fast he could barely string a sentence together.

Shaard smiled sadly as he began to lead Ash out of the ruins by the shoulder. The vulpis miners had spotted them and were getting agitated, but Ash barely even saw them.

"I'm afraid not," Shaard answered as they walked. "But he'll be out there somewhere—he was far too stubborn to die. We parted ways some time ago, and I've not been able to find him since, though not through lack of trying. I believe he has gone to Solstice, and there is no place in all the world I would like to find more. Your father was born there, you see; least that's what he told me. Always wanted to keep the location a secret, though. I understand, of course. I've seen how the world treats Song Weavers." He looked at Ash with sympathy. "Ferno believed, just like you and me, that Song Weavers deserved better in the world, that they could lead the Strongholds to true freedom, if only they were given a chance. He was a man who knew injustice when he saw it, and would do anything to see wrongs put right."

Ash nodded, thrilled his father was the man he'd always hoped he'd be. He was disappointed Shaard didn't know where his father was, of course, but unable to get over the sheer joy of discovering some information about him.

All the signs are pointing toward the Song Weaver Stronghold! I knew it!

Shaard looked wistful. "Ahhh, aye, there aren't many like ol' Ferno. Strong, brave, knew how to have a good time. Your parents found me one day when I was at my most desperate in the wilds, and took me aboard the *Trailblazer*. I'll forever be in their debt for that—and if

I can help reunite them with their son . . . well. Part of that debt would be repaid."

"You knew my mother too?" It was almost too much to take in. Ash and Shaard emerged from the tower, the blazing sun warming Ash's goose-pimpled skin.

"I did. Though your mother . . . I reckon she never did approve of the mischief I would get your father into. Not that I blame her." Shaard grinned, then saw the somber expression on Ash's face. "Your parents loved you, Ash. Leaving you behind must have hurt them more than they could say. They would have been desperate to get back to you. Seems they must have run into some serious trouble along the way. Believe me when I say I'd like to find them as much as you would. And I think we can, Ash, using that Song your father left behind for you." He started to explain. "Ferno always thought of these kinds of things. He always planned ahead, no matter how desperate things became. I believe he has hidden a map within the lullaby, a map that uses the World Weave to guide the one who Sings it!"

"I—I know!" Ash buzzed with excitement.

It was Shaard's turn to look shocked now. "You *know*?! You've been using the map?"

Ash smiled and nodded. "I've been trying to at least! But I've kind of hit a snag . . ."

Shaard looked flabbergasted, but his grin quickly returned, his turquoise eyes burning bright. He started laughing, and ruffled Ash's hair. "You absolute hero, Ash! You've done it! As if there was any doubt. You must tell me the lullaby! I can help you; no, I *must* help you! It'd be my honor!"

The relief of telling Shaard the truth lifted Ash's heart. *Shaard can help now! Working together, we can't fail!*

"I could get us out of here right now!" Shaard hissed, his mind clearly racing. "Captain Nuk will not change her course, nor jeopardize her crew, but I would go to the ends of the world to find Solstice! We could do this together, Ash!"

"What? Without the *Frostheart*?" Ash froze. "*But why?* I don't—"

Shaard interrupted him sharply. "The *Frostheart* races toward failure. The vulpis won't trade with them. But they'll still trade with me. Just so happens I have a few trinkets up my sleeve, which could buy us a nice small ride . . ."

"No! We can't leave them like this!" Ash protested. "They're in trouble!"

Shaard took hold of Ash's shoulders, his grip strong, his eyes wild. "Why not? They don't care about you;

they showed you their true colors today. I know it's hard. They've been good to you, good to us both, but the Pathfinders know what they're doing. Surely you have a greater responsibility to your people, to find them, to help them. Ash, you're *so* close!"

Ash was tempted. He felt guilty admitting it, but it was true. But that didn't stop the doubt niggling away at him.

Ash *liked* the *Frostheart* crew, despite what they thought of him. He still wanted to prove that he was one of them, a true member of the crew. He had never really belonged anywhere, but for the weeks he'd been aboard the *Frostheart* he'd felt a connection he'd not had anywhere else. He considered them friends, and wanted nothing more than for them to see him as the same.

"I can't," Ash said at last. "I can't leave them now. I want to find my parents and Solstice, I really do, but I can't abandon my friends when they need us."

Anger flashed across Shaard's face—but only for a second. It was so quick Ash almost wondered if he'd imagined it.

"Of course. You're quite right. You'll forgive me, I hope? I got overexcited, that's all. I'll follow you, Ash, and together we shall solve the riddle of the lullaby. And perhaps we can convince Captain Nuk to follow wherever it may lead."

Ash smiled in thanks. "I'm sure they'll come round and see the worth of Song Weavers."

For once Shaard's grin did not seem genuine. Together they made their way back to the waiting *Frostheart*.

30

A Gift

Despite Shaard's amazing revelations about Ash's family, things were looking grim indeed. Ash gripped the sleigh's side rail and watched the ruins of Skybridge vanish swiftly behind them, as Captain Nuk ordered the sunstone enjin to be pushed harder. She'd weighed the risks and decided it was better to race back to Aurora before their supplies ran out. They'd just have to hope the last sunstone they had would be enough to get them there.

The entire crew were now on quarter rations. Ash's belly rumbled and cramped. He had never been so hungry, and he'd lived through the Great Hunger the Fira Stronghold had experienced six winters before.

He also suspected his roiling belly might have something to do with Shaard, who gave him a knowing look whenever he caught his eye, and he'd asked to hear the lullaby again and again since they'd left Skybridge. But Ash had made excuses. He couldn't help being concerned by Shaard's suggestion about leaving the *Frostheart*. It was a tough decision, however, as when it came to the lullaby Ash was stumped. A third star had begun blazing in the sky when he Sang it, confirming he had been right in assuming the crow-witch was the "friend" the crows had been leading him to. But the new line she had given him, *Fear, Beware, Outcast*, made no sense to him at all. Had he misunderstood her? *Some token of friendship! All she did was scare me half to death.*

He also didn't want to talk to Lunah about it. Things were a bit awkward between them since the incident with the vulpis, and she had been short with him. She was hungry, Ash supposed. And the reduced rations were his fault after all.

"Ash, my boy!" Captain Nuk's booming voice rang out, bringing him out from his gloomy thoughts. She came to stand beside him and watch the world pass by. "How are you doing? Are you still happy to be aboard the *Frostheart*?"

"I am," Ash answered.

"Despite the last few days?" Nuk asked, her voice kind, but questioning.

"Well . . . n-not the last few days, no. But it is nice to talk to you now. I don't think anyone else wants to at the moment. Especially Tobu, and he's not much for talk at the best of times."

"We all have our own ways of showing how we feel, Ash. Look at Master Podd—I can barely get the man to shut up!"

Master Podd's ears pricked at the mention of his name. He was standing upon some piled boxes, steering the sleigh through the increasingly rocky terrain. "Indeed, captain," he said.

Nuk laughed and shook her head. "No, I don't think this whole 'guardian' business comes naturally to Tobu, but he takes it as seriously as everything else he does. And deep down in that ice-cold heart of his I suspect there is the

smallest, tiniest sliver of affection for you." She gave him a wry smile.

Ash was unconvinced. "He doesn't believe in me, or trust that I can control my powers."

"Or," Nuk mused, "perhaps he sees something more in you, and expects more as such?"

"You think so?"

Nuk shrugged. "Anything's possible, is it not?" They stood together in silence, gazing out at the snow-capped peaks that surrounded them. Then Nuk noticed Kailen giving Ash the usual evil eye from across the deck, grumbling under her breath.

"Something more interesting than your job over here, Kailen?" Nuk yelled at her. Kailen dipped her head and got on with her duties. "That lummox doesn't much like anyone, truth be told. But she would do anything for the *Frostheart*, and that's a fact. That scar across her eye? She got that leaping atop a Lurker and wrestling with the writhing wurm long enough to give the rest of us time to board the *Frostheart*."

"She *did* that?" Ash asked in wonder.

"Aye. And you should've seen the *other* guy." Nuk looked Ash in the eye, her features warm and kind. "She'll learn that you're one of us soon enough. But you must give her time. And we're not used to having a Song

Weaver aboard. We're having to learn how this works as much as you are."

Ash nodded, not knowing what else to say, but feeling hopeful at Nuk's words.

"Thank you," he said at last.

Captain Nuk laid a hand on his shoulder, smiling, her small eyes nearly disappearing amid her leathery wrinkles. "You're welcome, Ash. Now, if I were you, I would go and face the music—no pun intended!—with that yeti guardian of yours."

And with a gulp and a sigh Ash set off to do exactly that.

"Oh, and Ash?" Nuk called out before he got too far. "I believe the latrine needs a good clean after that."

"Y-yes, captain," Ash said, his stomach churning.

As he dragged his heels toward his tent Ash thought on what Nuk had said about Tobu really caring for him. Could she be right? But what if Shaard was right, and Tobu was trying to hold him back? It did seem to add up. He was so confused.

Ash was not surprised to find Tobu waiting for him at their tent. Ash groaned and prepared himself for a telling off. But the yeti surprised him.

"You are frustrated with your Song Weaving progress," Tobu said, more statement than question. "And while I trust you will come to see the reason for my gradual approach, I understand it has left you feeling confused and discouraged. Which in turn makes you behave in a . . . *brash* manner." Tobu's eye twitched. "This . . . is my failing."

At first Ash thought he'd misheard. Tobu was admitting he was wrong?

"So. Here," Tobu said, handing something to Ash. He took it with care. To his utter surprise it was an ocarina. Brand-new and unbroken. "It should have been obvious to me from the beginning, but perhaps I was too blinded by tradition," Tobu continued. "I have faced challenges before, World Weave knows. I have been in raging battles, and faced true tests of my strength and endurance. But I was beginning to think training you might be the challenge that finally defeated me.

"But then I saw you up on the mast, the morning we arrived at Skybridge. Using your Song to focus. To listen to what I had been teaching you. I saw that it was not laziness that hindered you, but my method. You need encouragement and support, as well as trial and grit. You need to know that you're progressing, and I must do better to express this to you."

"So you . . . made this for me?" Ash managed to say. He put the ocarina to his lips and played a little tune.

Spirits, did it feel good to play again. The familiar sensation of safety and warmth enveloped him. The ocarina was quite crude, but it worked. And it was by far the nicest gift he had ever been given.

"Tobu, I—I don't know what to say—" Ash's throat was scratchy, and he could feel tears stinging his eyes. He dashed in and grabbed the yeti round his waist, giving him a hug. "Thank you, Tobu. Thank you!" he said, speaking into his warm fur. Startled, and not used to affection, Tobu seemed at a loss. "I want to make you proud. I want to do well," Ash was saying.

Composing himself, Tobu began to reach down to return the hug, but hesitated and then apparently thought better of it. Clearing his throat, he patted Ash on the head, and then pulled him away, looking him in the eyes. "I know," Tobu said, allowing himself a smile.

But then, breaking the calm: "*Sleighs, dead ahead!*" shouted Teya's voice from up in the crow's nest.

31
Cut Off

The startled crew ran to the port side to catch a glimpse at what Teya was pointing out.

"Pathfinders?" Yorri asked, hopeful.

"This far out? What kind of idiotic Pathfinder crew would do that?" Kob replied.

"You mean, besides us?" Kailen said.

"Stars above, let 'em have some food to spare!" said Lunah. Ash squinted and could just make out the shapes of the sleighs, dark smudges against the hazy white.

There were lots of them. A whole fleet by the looks of things, heading toward them like a wall of sleighs. Something about the sight made him very uneasy.

Captain Nuk was straining her eyes too. The whole crew had fallen silent, tension clogging the air.

"*Turn the sleigh about!*" Nuk ordered suddenly. "*Due east. Turn it now!*"

The crew scrambled into action, pulling at the rigging, and Ash joined them, fear gripping his throat. *What was happening?*

Nuk yanked hard on the tiller, and the *Frostheart* swiftly turned to the starboard side.

"*Wraiths!*" Teya called. "I count ten of 'em!"

The fear tugging at Ash became full-blown terror. Despite all the horrifying stories he'd heard of the Wraiths, he'd never dreamed he'd actually come face-to-face with the terrible raiders. His knees shook and buckled. A rope slipped from his hand as he began to tremble.

"Somersaulting sea lions," Captain Nuk cursed.

"They're spreading out—trying to pincer us!" Teya warned. "We're gonna get surrounded if we're not quick!"

"They're cuttin' off our route, Cap'!" Lunah had run to Nuk, maps in hand. "And the path round the Frost Finger Mountains is hundreds of miles; we'll never make it with our supplies!" Kailen shot an angry glance Ash's way at this. "Ent no other Stronghold this far out," Lunah said, then gestured at the encroaching Wraiths. "We have to go through 'em, else we won't survive the journey!"

The crew listened with grave faces.

"Blast it all, you're right," Nuk agreed. "Of course you are. Brace yourselves, dear fellows, things are about to get a tad tumultuous!"

"*Wait!*" Shaard called out. "What about Shade's Chasm?"

The crew rippled with unease as the *Frostheart* sped across the snows, the black Wraith sleighs getting closer every moment.

"Stand a better chance against that lot than makin' a run through the chasm," Kailen spat.

"Are you so sure? The chasm cuts through the mountains. We could still make it to Aurora with our rations, and we won't have to go up against a fleet of Wraiths! What's more, I've heard tales of the Isolai Stronghold, which watches over the lands not far from the chasm's other side. We could even be resupplied before we reach Aurora's Embrace!"

"The *Isolai*?" Kailen mocked. "Ent no such thing."

"Kailen's right, Shaard," agreed Nuk. "The Isolai whereabouts are unknown, if indeed they are still out here at all."

"I have heard too many tales about the Isolai for them to be mere legend. I strongly suggest we try to run the chasm. Even the Wraiths aren't likely to follow us through there. It could be our salvation, the difference between life and death!"

"Ent like we're gonna stand a much better chance against that," Yorri said, nodding toward the oncoming fleet, as impenetrable-looking as the mountains to the east.

The crew went silent. Kailen spat on the deck and Yallah made a sign to her gods.

Nuk growled and massaged her forehead in thought.

Ash cleared his throat. "What's—what's Shade's Chasm?" He was almost afraid to get an answer.

"'Tis a haunted place, cursed by the vengeful spirits of those who die within," Twinge began, lowering his voice and looking around as if to make sure the coast was clear. "And that's a *lot* of spirits," he finished.

The crew shuddered.

"It's full of Leviathans! *Gargants*, no less," Yallah added.

"It's *actually* a frozen river that's cut a long, narrow ravine through the mountains," Lunah said, looking worried. "Once you go in, you'd better be quick 'n' fast, 'cause there's no escape but out the other end. It's a perfect ambush spot fer monsters to crunch yer bones and spit out yer gristle."

Ash swallowed hard. The smile that was always on Shaard's face twitched a little. Even Tobu looked concerned.

"I—I will get us through," Ash said, though he felt like he was floating above his body, hearing himself say it.

The crew gasped.

"Ash, no—" Lunah began.

"Like you did back on the hunt?" Kailen sneered.

"What other choice do we have?" Ash said, getting angry. It felt good to be taking control of his destiny, even if that destiny was to charge headfirst into a horrible death. "You know we won't last a minute against that many Wraith sleighs! At least with my Song Weaving there's a *chance*—"

"Lurkers and Hurtlers are one thing, boy, but Gargants are well beyond you," Tobu butted in. "You've never even seen one before, let alone tried to Weave with one."

The crew mumbled with apprehension. Captain Nuk was still deep in thought, weighing her options. She watched the oncoming fleet, the ragged black vessels like gaping jaws preparing to swallow the *Frostheart* whole.

"I just want to make things right," Ash said in a small voice. "And I've been practicing."

"He has!" called Lunah. "I've seen him. I believe in you, Ash!"

"Valkyries above!" Nuk said. "Enough ghost stories, you lot. You've got furs to keep you from the chill, you've got spears 'n' arrows to keep you safe, and you have the best blasted crew that ever ran the paths at your backs. If there was ever a sleigh that could make it through Shade's Chasm, it'll be the *Frostheart*. Right—you have your orders. Set sail for Shade's Chasm!"

"Aye aye, captain!" cried the crew as one.

"That's the spirit! Trust me when I say we'll all look back on this safe in Aurora, and we'll have a good ol' laugh!"

And perhaps she was right. But at that moment laughter was the last thing on the crew's mind. Ash aided the others in turning the sleigh round, a determined fire in his belly. Shaard gave him an approving glance as he rushed to help, and Lunah punched Ash on the shoulder as she passed. He'd never felt more determined. The *Frostheart*'s safety was in his hands. It was time to show them all what he could do.

"I'm not scared," Ash said to himself.

But even he knew that was a lie.

SONG WEAVER

32

Shade's Chasm

The Frost Finger Mountains rose like jagged, rotten teeth, black against the grim gray sky beyond. Shade's Chasm was even darker still, a rugged cut that gouged through the mountains like a wound. Tendrils of icy mist slithered from the ravine's mouth, and the skeletons of wrecked sleighs littered the ice outside like bones.

So far Shaard's plan seemed to be working. The Wraith fleet had come to a halt a ways from the chasm opening, blocking the *Frostheart*'s escape, but seemingly no longer in pursuit. The *Frostheart* crew stood at the sides of the sleigh, weapons in hand, glaring at the towering cliffs in fearful silence. Ash's heart thumped. He gripped the side rail so hard his knuckles hurt.

"Deep breaths, boy," said Tobu, standing by his side,

an arrow nocked to his bow. "Stay calm. Stay focused."

Ash nodded and tried to slow his breathing.

The *Frostheart* began to make its way into the chasm mouth, slower now, much slower, so as not to stir any unwanted attention within. The sheer cliffs loomed high above as though they were clasping shut over the sleigh. The wan light refracted off the ice and colored everything in an indigo gloom, as if the sleigh were traveling deep underwater. It was a claustrophobic, stifling place. Ash felt as though he should hold his breath for fear of drowning, though his breath came out in ragged misting heaves, despite his trying to slow it down. Loud cracks echoed between the walls, the frozen river protesting under the *Frostheart*'s weight. The ice-passage seemed to hum and Sing with a Song of its own, as if the very ice spirits themselves were announcing their arrival.

"There's no such thing as ghosts," Tobu told Ash, never once taking his eyes off the narrow passage ahead.

There he goes reading my mind again, Ash thought. Shaard stood alone at the prow of the sleigh, a dark shadow against the luminous ice-blue walls of the gorge. Although Shaard looked out with concentration, Ash noted that he still wore his usual wolvish grin. What could he possibly find to smile about in this situation?

The *Frostheart* wove its way through the snaking chasm. The shadows grew deeper. You would never have known it was day, except for the thin sliver of white that wound its way high above their heads, like a river in the sky.

Teya began signaling from atop the crow's nest. Following her gestures, the rest of the crew could just about make out the dim shapes of something amid the dark blue murk ahead.

"A vulpis caravan," Lunah whispered at Ash's side.

As the *Frostheart* came alongside the contraptions the crew gasped in horror.

The tops of sleighs were sticking out of a huge tear in the ice, and Ash recognized them as those he had watched leave Skybridge. Freezing water lapped at the scrap-built sides, the rest of the vehicles lost below in the deep darkness. Archeomek and barrels floated on the water. The vulpis were nowhere to be seen.

"Good gracious," said Captain Nuk breathlessly. "Why did they come through here? What were they *thinking*?"

A deep, loud, mournful howl reverberated through the passage.

Another echoed out in answer.

What is that?! Ash thought, fear threatening to overwhelm him.

Lunah signed to the captain. She seemed to be saying that there were no survivors from the vulpis sleigh.

Nuk nodded grimly. "I'll get us through this," she signed back.

Steering the *Frostheart* round the sunken sleighs, she pushed steadily forward. The entire crew seemed to be holding their breath. All was quiet except for the ghostly whispers of the wind. Ash could hear his heart pounding in his ears.

Teya peered into the gloom from the crow's nest, but there was nothing to be seen.

The sleigh slid forward.

The rigging creaked.

Ash dared look over the edge. Only ice, and the dark depths below.

Suddenly the weight of the vessel caused the ice to let out a loud crack, which echoed throughout the gorge like thunder. The entire crew grimaced. But all was soon quiet again. Nothing moved.

Then a low, haunting wail filled the air. It vibrated through Ash's bones. He looked up at Tobu for reassurance, but Tobu was gazing over the side, his face dark with concern. The rest of the crew were the same. They stood alert, the whites of their eyes showing, ready to spring into action.

"*Steady . . .* " Captain Nuk whispered.

Dark shapes appeared under the ice.

Large shapes.

So large Ash had no doubt they could pull the *Frostheart* down with ease. He felt so helpless, looking over the edge in silence. He itched to do something, *anything*, other than just stand and watch whatever these things were stalk the sleigh.

Ash concentrated, straining all his senses. He cleared his throat, ready to Song Weave.

The shapes drew closer to the surface . . . and began to Sing. It started tentatively at first, but the Song quickly rose in volume, a wail like the wind howling through a mountain pass.

"*HUNT. CATCH. KILL.*"

Ash sensed the emotions, the *intentions*, of the Leviathans thrumming within the howls.

"*HUMANS. HATE. CHASE. DESTROY.*"

The beasts sensed there was something above them.

The ice let out another bone-splitting echo under the sleigh. The crew winced in what felt like slow motion. And then the world exploded.

Ice blasted up around them, churned into large tumbling boulders. Dorsal fins the size of sleigh sails and scarred rough hides emerged from the depths. Multiple

eyes, white as bone, rose high above the deck and gazed at the crew hungrily.

Three of the biggest Leviathans Ash had ever seen were now gliding alongside the *Frostheart*, carving their way through the solid ice as if it were slush, their bellowing calls rumbling through the timber and shaking Ash's ribs. The volume of their Song was so intense it felt like he had been struck round the head with the force of it.

"*Gargants, port and starboard!*" Teya shouted from the crow's nest, as if anyone hadn't noticed. Yorri sped the sleigh up, attempting to get a lead on the Leviathans.

"Ash, dear boy?" Nuk called from the tiller. "I'd appreciate it if you started Singing something soothing, if it's all the same to you?"

"Y-yes, captain!" Ash stammered, but having seen the true scale of what he was up against, he felt like doing anything but.

If I mess this up, it's all over. No second chances. So no pressure, Ash. Only everything ever riding on this . . .

"Breathe," Tobu called to him, bow trained on the gargantuan beasts. Ash thought back to all he'd learned from Tobu, trying to clear his head from the distractions around him.

He opened his mouth to Sing . . . but managed only a dry croak as his voice caught in his throat. His mind raced, sour bile rising up instead of Song. *All I've ever wanted to do is Sing, and when I finally get the chance all I do is choke!* He tried to concentrate and listen to the World Weave like Tobu had taught him, but he couldn't slow his racing thoughts down.

Clear your mind. Listen to the rhythm of your heartbeat, slow and steady. For once Ash found comfort in remembering Tobu's advice. Trembling like a little squink exposed outside it's bolt-hole, Ash approached the prow of the sleigh and closed his eyes.

You can do this. You can do this.

He started to Sing. He tried his best to forget where he was, and the fact that there were Leviathans larger than sleighs looking at him as though he were dinner.

His starlight aura whirled round him like stars caught in a breeze, which helped calm him. The aura fluttered out toward the colossal shapes of the Gargants' Song-aura, which pulsed out like waves in the ocean. They dwarfed the Song-auras of Hurtlers and Lurkers. Ash's aura danced around it, whispering calming words and soothing thoughts.

"Peace. Let us pass. We mean no harm."

Misted visions of his parents' faces came to Ash as he Sang, giving him strength.

But as soon as his aura began to weave within the waves, the Gargants let out a bellow of rage. Large membranes of skin on their flanks vibrated like drums, enhancing the sound. The roar was louder than anything Ash had heard in his life.

It was like falling into deep freezing water: shocking and biting, stealing his breath away. It was utterly overwhelming. Ash was caught completely by surprise. His Song faltered, his swirling Song-aura extinguished like a candle. Immediately the Gargants' Song began to attack *him*. The Gargants let out a mountain-shaking wail, ice cracking all around them at its volume. Ash felt like his head was being bashed between two gongs. The rest of the crew fell to their knees, clutching their ears in agony. But Ash was determined.

I have to get us through this! I need to show the others that my power can be used for good. I can get the Frost-heart through the chasm safely, I know it!

Ash gritted his teeth and Sang even louder, keeping his heartbeat steady, Singing to its regular rhythm.

"*Good! Slow! Steady!*" Tobu shouted. Ash dived and dodged his Song-aura through the Gargant attack, weaving it up and round, flowing through it like a needle sewing thread. He scrambled for the calm clarity he'd felt when he'd heard the frost-heart in his mind, trying to replicate it. He pulled his innermost desires along through the current.

"*BE CALM! PEACE! WE MEAN NO HARM!*"

In response the Gargants let out a low bellow, and Ash was thrilled to see their auras were fading to a moody purple, no longer blood-red. They were annoyed—but they weren't attacking. *I'm doing it!* Ash thought. *I'm really doing it!*

"Jolly good show, Ash!" called Captain Nuk. "Keep it up, dear boy!"

But in his joy at doing something right Ash hadn't realized that there was something very wrong . . .

At first it was barely audible amid the rest of the din. A niggling buzz in the back of his mind.

He tried to ignore it, tried to focus on his own Song. But the buzzing grew louder and louder, pushing back against Ash like an invisible force. Ash knew it wasn't the Gargants.

It was a different Song, one Ash had never heard before. It sounded like a terrible cloud of droning insects swarming around him, buzzing about his head and crawling into his ears.

What is *that?*

The Gargants heard it too. They began to become angry again, their auras returning to a vicious red.

Ash screwed his face up, trying to push the droning sound out of his mind. *GO AWAY!* he screamed in his head, disrupting his own Song—but it was no use. The droning got louder and louder, until it was all he could hear. He tried to force his Song through it—"*Calm,*" he Sang to the Gargants, to himself, "*please be calm*"—but he didn't believe in his Song, not any longer. All Tobu's lessons flew to the wayside. How could he keep the Gargants calm when his own mind was spinning and churning due to the drone, the endless, awful drone?

Ash cried out suddenly, grasping his head, the buzzing tearing through his skull. It was agonizing. Tobu caught him before he fell to the deck, throwing his bow aside to free his hands.

"I-it's too powerful," Ash stammered, realizing there was blood leaking from his nose. His vision spun, his head felt like it had been turned upside down. "GET IT OUT! GET IT OUT OF MY HEAD!" he screamed. The pain was unbearable; he could barely think.

"What's going on over there?" Nuk yelled.

"He's losing it. The boy's losing it!" Kailen cried out. "Just like I said, the beasts're taking him! Keep the boy pinned down, 'less you want him to put an arrow in your back!"

"Calm down, Kailen!" Nuk ordered. The world fell silent for a brief, disorienting moment, before a roar louder than comprehension filled the chasm. Ice cracked, the Frostheart's mast splintered, and an avalanche of snow crashed down from the cliffs at the power of the Gargants' Song. Nuk pushed hard to the port side, skidding the sleigh out of the way of the avalanche, the crew clasping their ears and crying out at the bone-shaking sound.

Ash's mind spun, the droning buzz reverberating

through his head. He couldn't understand the words, if there were any at all, but deep down in his soul, he understood the meaning. It was urging, no, *demanding* bloodshed and carnage from the Gargants. Ash's belly roiled with nausea. He'd never experienced such hatred.

"We need to get out of here—" Nuk began, before the core of the sleigh shook as a Gargant rammed into it, its huge weight nearly toppling the whole thing over. "We need to get out of here *now!*"

Yorri pulled down on an enjin lever and the *Frostheart* thrust forward, just as the giant maw of a Gargant chomped down, missing the stern by a hand's breadth.

The droning no longer hurt now that Ash had stopped trying to fight it, but it was still there, hidden underneath the echoes of the Gargants' Song blast. Ash looked at Tobu, trying to find reassurance in his usually stone-calm face, but saw only the same confusion he felt.

Lunah had rushed over to help, but skidded to a stop, eyes wide at what she saw ahead. "*To the front!*" she shouted over the howling ruckus. There, emerging from the blue mist and heading straight toward the *Frostheart*, were three black sleighs. They were jagged and sharp, like wrecked vessels that had not been told they were too damaged to go on sailing. They had black sails, ripped and billowing, crude red markings defacing the cloth. Skulls and bones decorated their edges; blades and spikes glistened on their sides. They were things from a terrible tale, a horrible nightmare.

"*Wraiths!*" Lunah screamed. *"It's the Wraiths!"*

"By Aurora . . ." Nuk cursed under her breath, before shouting, *"All hands, we need to move now!"*

Ash managed to stand, trembling, as the dark ragged shapes raced toward them.

"Go—help the others!" he croaked at Tobu, pushing him away.

The droning sound filled the chasm.

The Wraiths were here,
and they were coming for
the *Frostheart.*

33

Ambush

In a heartbeat Nuk shoved all her weight into the tiller. Ash stumbled in the opposite direction, trying to steady his legs against the deck. The *Frostheart* sheered hard to the side of the encroaching Wraith sleighs, narrowly avoiding being trapped. As they shot past, the smell of dank rotting wood filled Ash's nostrils. The black sleighs were smaller than the *Frostheart* but much faster. They were built for combat, their jagged edges made for rending and tearing rather than for transporting goods. They wheeled round to face the same direction as the *Frostheart*, and sped after it like arrows, the bellowing Gargants giving chase in their wake. The ravine walls loomed above the sleighs, barely allowing any room to maneuver.

"*More power!*" Nuk shouted, "*and man the ruddy weapons!*"

Yorri grunted as he pulled the levers of the enjin, which grew brighter, humming louder. Kob ran to the port-side bolt-thrower while Master Podd manned the one to starboard. They opened fire on the Wraiths as Lunah and Twinge hurried to reload the bolts. Tobu fired his arrows at the Gargants, with Kailen and the rest of the crew following his lead, but the arrows clacked harmlessly off their ice-hard hides.

The Gargants unleashed another barrage of sound, using their Song as a weapon. Ice shattered and crashed down, smashing through the frozen river and soaking the deck of the *Frostheart* with freezing water. Ash covered his head with his arms, chunks of ice raining down on him like hail. Wiping the blood from his nose, he gripped the side of the prow, trying his hardest to keep Song Weaving, to try to stall the Gargants, but his heart was so full of fear he could barely focus. The gusting snow that had started to fall burned his eyes and stung his face.

Between the rushing wind, the war cries of the Gargants, and the endless, terrible droning sound, he could barely even hear his own voice.

A black sleigh launched a harpoon, which slammed

into the rock face to the left of the *Frostheart*. Master Podd fired his bolt-thrower back at the sleigh, ripping a hole through its hull. A Gargant burst from the frozen river in between the two vessels, creating a wave of water that sent the *Frostheart* tilting to the side. The Gargant nearly tore through the sleigh's deck, arrows thwicking into its hide.

Ash thought he was going to be sick. *Come on, Ash. Focus.*

Another harpoon ripped through the *Frostheart*'s hull, tearing right through the deck a hair's breadth from Ash's feet. "*Spirits!*" he cursed. Wicked-sharp prongs burst out of the harpoon point and clasped themselves into the wood. A black sleigh had snagged the *Frostheart*.

The crew nearly fell to the deck as the entire vessel lurched, pulled back by its attacker. The sunstone enjin roared ever louder in protest—or was it the Gargants that were roaring? There was so much noise Ash could barely think. A Gargant rammed the side of the hull, the entire sleigh groaning from the force of it.

"*They'll pull us over!*" Tobu yelled, unsheathing his hunting dagger. "*To me!*" He launched himself from the main deck to the prow and began hacking away at the rope attached to the harpoon, Kailen and the others joining him.

The ragged, tattered figures of Wraiths brandishing spears and calling out war cries motioned to the ropes. They were going to try to board the *Frostheart*! Ash ran to aid Tobu and the others, pulling his dagger from his belt.

"*I need you singing, Ash!*" Nuk called out as she tried to steer between more tumbling ice, face strained with pain as the Gargants roared another deafening howl. "*Shut these ruddy beasts up!*"

"*S'one over here!*" Lunah shouted while hefting another bolt. "*Come get 'im, Ash!*"

The cold, merciless eyes of a Gargant rose above the deck, the ice turning into crumbling slush as it tore forward. It studied Ash, weighing him, deciding how best to swat this annoying fly.

Ash's Song became a gurgled yelp as he was thrown from his feet, Nuk pulling hard on the tiller to avoid the Gargant as it tried to ram them. The *Frostheart* jolted again as a black sleigh rammed them from the other side, splinters of the hull exploding up into the air.

"*One thing at a time, you blasted corpse-walkers!*" Nuk cursed out loud.

Another noise joined the already mighty cacophony. *Thok. Thok. Thokthokthok.* Ash saw that the sound belonged to arrows. They were piercing the masts and deck, ripping holes in the sails and tearing through the tents.

One thudded right into the railing by Ash's hand. The point oozed green foul-smelling liquid. Looking up, he could see the ghostly black-swathed figures of the Wraiths on the other sleighs aiming their bows. Shaard stood at the starboard-side rail, shaking his head angrily at the Wraiths, throwing his arms up and cursing them with incredibly rude gestures in a language Ash did not understand. Ash ducked just before an arrow skewered his head.

Tobu and the others had succeeded in chopping through the harpoon rope, the *Frostheart* surging free once more. In one smooth motion Tobu threw his dagger to the deck and whipped up his bow. In the next breath he was firing back at the Wraiths. He scored a direct hit, a black-robed figure dropping to the ground as the arrow struck home. Tobu leaped over an arrow heading for his feet and fired back while still in the air, another arrow whooshing past his white fur. Ash watched with his mouth agape.

The Wraiths' arrows were making a pincushion of the *Frostheart*. Even Tobu had to take cover behind the sleigh's raised sides. Ash took note and did the same. His voice was croaking, his throat dry and sore, but he closed his eyes and still he tried to Sing on.

Suddenly something twisted him round. *They've got*

me, Ash panicked. He opened his eyes to find Shaard looking back at him, eyes wild with excitement.

"Now's the time, Ash!" he yelled over the noise.

"What?"

"Tobu's tactics won't help here—you need to be aggressive! You have to *force* your way through, Ash, like a spear thrust to the heart. Grip and bend the Gargants' Song instead of weaving and dancing with it. Take charge. *Dominate.*"

Ash frowned. The idea sounded wrong, like it was the opposite of what Song Weaving should be.

Shaard saw his hesitation. "It's the only way you'll break through, Ash. It's a far more powerful technique than your own!" He looked him square in the eyes. It was a calm, reassuring gaze of trust and belief. "You're thinking too hard, lad. Remember that this is natural to you! No one's going to stop you now."

Maybe he was right. He had to try. Ash nodded, and saw a giant Gargant preparing to ram the sleigh once more. Ash began Song Weaving at the top of his lungs. Once again the Gargants' Song filled his mind. But this time he stabbed his Song-aura at the tidal wave of the Gargants' auras, which whipped around him, threatening to swallow him whole.

Ash wove his Song the other way.

Up, down, left, right, trying to find a chink in the monsters' defenses.

There. That was it! He'd found it!

A tiny but significant hole in the Gargants' aura.

Ash steeled his nerves . . . and forced his Song-aura through the crack, putting as much power and fury behind it as he could.

"*DESTROY, FIGHT, DEFEAT!*" his emotions screamed. And the moment they did his aura changed. It felt different—it even *looked* different. His usual blazing white-blue Song-aura had become purple-black marks of nothing, dark voids scorching through the natural world. His voice changed too. Instead of the bright, soothing sounds he'd made before, his Song now came out harsh and guttural, like the roar of a warrior as they swung their ax for the killing blow. Ash recoiled in disgust, pulling himself out of the Song Weave as fast as he could. This new way of Singing felt horribly wrong. *Unnatural.*

But his Song had had an effect. The Gargant fell back from the *Frostheart*, looking dizzy and confused. With an earth-trembling grumble it turned into the path of an oncoming Wraith sleigh, which tried to swerve out of its way but couldn't move fast enough. With an almighty *crash* the sleigh collided with the monstrous beast and skidded, spinning round and round until it came to a stop, nothing more than motionless wreckage.

The Pathfinders cheered and whooped for Ash, hoping the Gargant would turn its attention on the Wraith sleigh. Instead, the Gargant dived under the ice and continued its chase of the *Frostheart*.

"Why aren't the Gargants attacking the Wraiths?" Lunah cried out.

"They're too focused on us!" Twinge shouted, fixing another bolt the size of his forearm into the thrower. "Reminds me of this time when—"

"*Twinge, so help me, I will come down there and throw you over the side if you start telling a story!*" Nuk roared. "We need to get the beasts to notice the other sleighs!"

She shoved the tiller in the opposite direction as far as it would go, the entire sleigh skidding round to face the way it had come. The force of the spin threw everyone standing to the deck, Master Podd and Kob gripping on to the mounted bolt-throwers for dear life. "*Hang on!*" Captain Nuk shouted a bit too late. "Yorri, more power! I have an idea!"

34

Breaking Point

Yorri looked worried about the enjin. "We'll run outta juice if I keep pushin' her!" he yelled.

"There's no use in having power if we're all dead! Do as I say!" Nuk commanded.

Yorri pulled the levers. The sunstone shone even brighter, its humming rising above the chaos of the battle.

The *Frostheart* surged forward again, directly toward a black sleigh that had been hot on their tail. With a thunderous crash a Gargant tore through the ice behind the *Frostheart*, its horrifyingly large maw gaping wide to bite the sleigh in two. The black sleigh swerved out of the *Frostheart*'s way, the *Frostheart* clipping its stern, wood splintering off both sleighs with a deafening *crunch*.

For a heartbeat Ash was close enough to see onto the enemy's deck. It was crawling with black-clad creatures, their faces disfigured and monstrous, gnarled and rough like tree roots. Twisted horns protruded from their heads, blood-red paint smeared across their lifeless faces. The stories were true! Whatever they were, they were not human-kin. Ash shivered in horror.

"*See how you like a Gargant to the face!*" Nuk shouted as they passed. She'd led the chasing Gargant right to the Wraith sleigh. There wasn't enough time for the Wraiths to move out of the way. The *Frostheart* crew held their breath, anticipating the moment the monster ripped through their pursuers . . .

But the moment never came.

The Gargant dived under the black sleigh just in time, sending a wave of icy water careering over it, but doing no harm other than that. The beast burst from the frozen river on the other side of the Wraiths, continuing its chase of the *Frostheart*.

The crew couldn't believe what they were seeing.

"Well, that was . . . *unexpected*," Nuk said. Ash could tell panic was clawing at her courage. She spun the *Frostheart* round, once again changing the sleigh's direction, weaving back and forth to avoid the roaring monster, its jaws so close to the sleigh that its rancid saliva was raining down on the deck.

"*What now?*" Lunah shouted.

"*I'm working on it!*" Nuk yelled back.

Just then, one of the Gargant's long tentacle-like feelers whipped out and coiled round Lunah. With a gasp she was wrenched off the deck.

"*Shoot it!*" a wide-eyed Kailen shouted. She leaped onto the side rail and began firing arrows at the monster with furious precision. But then another feeler drew up behind her, and Ash watched in horror as it snatched her feet from under her and pulled her screaming from the sleigh. Tobu and Teya rained arrows upon the Gargant, but they weren't having enough of an effect.

The feelers brought the thrashing Lunah and Kailen above the monster's gaping maw. They were done for! *Unless . . .*

Ash felt Shaard stir at his side. "Take control—*force* the Gargant to let them go!"

"I—I can't!" Ash was exhausted. "I can't keep that kind of force up!" His Song Weaving always took a toll, and against such an enemy Ash's muscles cramped, his head ached, and his throat burned like fire.

"I know you can," said Shaard, lowering himself to face him. "You must. It's the only way to save your friends!"

He was right. Breathless, Ash dug deep. His voice came out in a croak, his throat raw, his body trembling.

He searched desperately again for the crack in the Gargants' auras, which threatened to wash his Song away. He found it. He poured the dark, spherical voids of his new Song-aura into the crack, and thought of the *Frostheart* crew, of Lunah, and the terrible danger they were in.

Rage obligingly boiled up inside Ash. True—this wasn't the slow, calm technique Tobu had taught him. This was more, this was *better*, this was brutal and fast. Ash felt his blood boil with renewed might and surged with hidden strength he hadn't even known he had. He would smash aside anything that threatened them. *Nothing* would stand against him. He would stomp out this pathetic Gargant Song!

"DON'T YOU DARE HURT MY FRIENDS!"

The Gargant shuddered and, in that split second, Ash was able to overpower it. The dark tendrils of his aura wrapped round the Gargant's and began to strangle it, cutting off the beast's Song. Ash tightened his grip, harder and harder, fury boiling up from deep within and rushing out into his voice like a scream. *How dare these monsters try to hurt Lunah!* The Gargant recoiled and struggled, desperate to be free, but it was no use—Ash's Song had it in an inescapable grip. The creature whined in fear, and Ash buzzed with the intoxicating power he had over the Leviathan. His skin tingled and fizzed, his heart racing.

Such control! Such power!

"*Now . . . RELEASE MY FRIENDS!*"

The Gargant threw Lunah and Kailen into the air. They crumpled into the *Frostheart*'s sails high above and crashed hard into the rigging, which they managed to grab with their scrabbling hands.

Shaard shook his shoulder in celebration, laughing.
"I knew you could do it, lad!"

Ash laughed back in relief, but as the new Song left
his lips he felt caught in a dark icy grip that would not
let go. It felt like it came from his very core, pooling out
and stretching as far as his fingers and toes. He tried
to break free, but try as he might he could not escape.
It was drowning him, choking him like he'd choked the
Gargant's aura.

Just as panic threatened to overwhelm him, a new
Song came to him through all the chaos.

It was delicate and gentle, and yet somehow, for that
moment, it was all he could hear.

It warmed his body. It reached out for him, and
pulled him out of the shadow.

His head began to clear, and Ash felt like himself
once more. Shaking his head, Ash realized he knew the
Song. It was that of the frost-heart, coming from belowdecks. It was helping him, healing him . . . and Ash
clung on to it with everything he had.

"*Thank you . . .*" he managed to Sing back.

But as he came round, the sounds of the chase exploded back into Ash's senses. The battle wasn't over yet.

The remaining black sleighs gathered together like

a spear point thrust directly toward the poor battered *Frostheart* that sped before them.

"*I need more power!*" Nuk shouted.

But Yorri didn't answer. He lay still and silent, face down on the enjin he so loved, an arrow protruding from his back.

Ash's belly gave a sickening lurch.

"No . . ." Captain Nuk whispered. "No, no, no, no . . ."

Tobu saw what was going on, and realizing that there was no one controlling the enjin leaped down to help. But before he could reach it, an arrow thunked into his left shoulder. He growled and hit the deck hard.

"*Tobu!*" Ash cried, trying to run to his aid but instead falling to the deck like a rock. Now that he'd stopped Singing, he had no strength left.

With gritted teeth Tobu dragged himself up and pulled the lever as far as it would go. The sunstone shone so bright it looked as if it would burst into flames. Tobu fell to the deck as the sleigh burst forward, faster than ever. The roar of the propellers was deafening; the deck rattled and shook.

Can the sleigh even hold together? Ash fretted, gripping on to the side rails for dear life. *I need to help Tobu!* The rigging and sails creaked and strained with the sleigh's speed. Still they raced away from their incoming attackers.

"*Hang on!*" Nuk shouted over the intense roar. Not that the crew had any other choice.

The Gargants burst from the ice ahead of the *Frostheart*, forming an impenetrable wall. They stretched across the chasm—there was nowhere to go! They were trapped, and Captain Nuk was playing chicken with Gargants, which may as well have been a solid mountain.

Closer.

Closer.

The *Frostheart* was heading directly for them!

What is she doing?

At the very last moment Nuk slammed the tiller to the left, sending the sleigh careering to the right. With an earsplitting *crunch* the *Frostheart* used a rock as a ramp and mounted the ice wall with its starboard side. Wood splintered, shattered, and tore off in a rain of ruin. The entire crew were thrown to the port side, the sleigh skidding along, shuddering violently and shaking Ash's bones. *Chuh-chuh-chuh-chuh* went the runners, fracturing against the solid ice, giant chunks of it raining down and tearing holes through the hull. Ash realized he'd bitten his tongue, a warm, salty-sour taste filling his mouth. He gripped on to the rigging like he would

never let go, his stomach rising up into his throat. They squeezed past the Gargants, the top of the mast snapping off as it clipped the closest one's hide. The Gargants were unable to turn fast enough. It felt like the *Frostheart* was about to be torn apart at any moment.

Nuk rammed the tiller in the opposite direction.

All went quiet. It felt like they were flying. Ash's feet had certainly left the deck.

For a heartbeat it seemed almost peaceful.

And then . . . *KU-RUNCH!* The *Frostheart* hit the snow with a crushing jolt and burst forward, hanging together at the seams.

The black sleighs had to swerve to a stop before they collided with the Gargants teeming ahead of them. But the Gargants were moving too fast, with no room for correction. With an almighty *CRASH* they collided, the Wraith sleighs splintering into pieces, the Gargants a tangled mess on top of them.

Captain Nuk had done it! They were in the clear!

With a swish of snow the *Frostheart* shot out of the ravine, the mournful howling of the Gargants cursing their escape.

35

Forge Fires in the Sky

The *Frostheart* crawled through the rugged mountainous landscape like a wounded animal. It needed help, and fast. It was terribly damaged, and the sunstone that was giving it life was incredibly low on power, its once bright glow dimming like a cooling ember. If it wasn't replaced soon, the *Frostheart* would be dead in the snow, and then so would its crew.

The Pathfinders were on edge, battered and bruised, with many simply slumping on to the deck in exhaustion. But they had passed through Shade's Chasm and had lived to tell the tale. There was a grim satisfaction to be had.

Kailen caught Ash's eye and recognized the look of fear there. She hesitated, and then approached. Ash prepared himself for a barrage of unpleasantness. But she surprised him.

"Worry not, Ash. The *Frostheart* is a hardy vessel— she's got us through worse scrapes than this. And there's no better captain to see us through than Captain Nuk." Kailen nodded, as if to reassure herself as much as Ash. "And . . . thank you," she added. Ash crinkled his brow in confusion. "Thank you for saving Lunah. And . . . and me. I owe you one." With that she quickly turned away back to her duties, red-faced and flustered.

Ash was flabbergasted, but there was no time to dwell on it. He rushed over to the healing tent, where the sleigh's healer, Arla, had taken Tobu to treat his wound.

"Tobu, how are you doing?" Ash asked. Tobu, who sat upright on a narrow bed, didn't answer. Instead he

pulled the arrow from his shoulder with a small grunt.

"I told you not to do that!" Arla scolded. "I don't know how best to treat a wound like this. The poison is unknown to me, as is the antidote it requires."

"The poison is wolversbane, if ever I saw it," Shaard said as he ducked into the large tent. "The Wraiths coat all their weapons in the stuff, a nasty little poison indeed. Fast-acting, horrifically painful, kills a person in minutes." Ash gasped in horror. "Fortunately the yeti are rather resistant to the stuff, though if left untreated it'll take even them down in time. I happen to have learned the antidote on my travels, if you'd allow me?"

Arla stepped aside to let Shaard get to work, but Tobu pulled his shoulder away, growling in protest.

"Now is not the time, Tobu!" Ash scolded. "Shaard is trying to help!"

"Like he tried to help you in Shade's Chasm? The Song he taught you is unnatural. It caused my tail to twitch and my fur to stand on end. Don't ever allow yourself to succumb to rage, boy—it will ruin you. Hate breeds hate."

"Oh, and you're suddenly an expert on Song Weaving, are you?" Shaard laughed. "I wish you'd said—I would've had a scholarly discussion with you sooner!"

"Please, Tobu, don't be so stubborn!" Ash pleaded. "You're badly hurt."

Tobu tried to get up, but grimaced with pain as he moved his shoulder. The wound looked raw, veins of black poison leaking out in a snowflake shape. Realizing Ash was right, Tobu yielded and slumped back down to the litter. Shaard turned to consult Arla about the herbs and ointments he needed and proceeded to make a foul-smelling salve that he lathered over Tobu's wound before bandaging it up.

"You see? That wasn't so bad, was it?" he commented.

Tobu said nothing as he got up and, pushing past Shaard, strode toward his tent. Ash had been worried at first, but watching him go he saw that Tobu seemed as strong as ever. Perhaps he really was as invincible as he looked. He allowed himself a breath of relief.

Most of them had made it.

But there was something they needed to attend to before they could start celebrating.

❧ ❧ ❧

The world had never seemed so peaceful. Snow drifted gently from the peach-colored haze that was the afternoon sky, the surrounding mountains and pines simplified to silhouettes of pink and purple. It was one of the very rare instances the *Frostheart* had slowed to a stop out on the snow. Ash had gotten so used to the

constant movement of the sleigh, the stillness felt un-
settling. And the *Frostheart* felt incredibly exposed and
alone out here in the frozen wilderness. Still, there were
no Leviathans to be seen. Though of course that meant
nothing.

Yallah began to chant the farewell dirge of her
Stronghold, Thudruk, the very same that Yorri had hailed
from. Instead of being sorrowful, as Ash had expected,
it was energetic and happy. "In Thudruk the words are
telling the spirits of Yorri's exploits, celebrating his life
and bravery," Twinge explained to Ash as they watched
the ceremony. "While we may weep, the spirits should
rejoice, for they have gained a hero at their campfire, another strong arm in their smelting forges."

A lump formed in Ash's throat. He had liked Yorri.
Yorri had always been kind to him, right from the first
moment he had climbed aboard the *Frostheart*.

The crew gathered quietly in a circle, heads bowed in
sorrow as Yallah chanted before Yorri's body, which had
been wrapped in cloth and surrounded with kindling.
Only a few sniffles and cries could be heard.

"Here lies our friend, Yorri," Yallah declared in the
common tongue, her chant finished. "We loved him in
life. But now we must send him to the forge fires in the
sky. Spirits welcome him, and love him as we did."

"He was a good man," Captain Nuk said sadly. "And he shall be dearly, dearly missed."

Then the crew worked quickly, using ropes to lower the platform Yorri's body lay upon down to the snow below. Kailen dipped an arrow into a barrel of tar and passed the arrowhead through the flames of a torch, as with a rumble, the *Frostheart* began moving again, leaving Yorri behind. The crew turned their backs, Ash following their lead. He heard the twang of a bowstring and knew that Kailen had fired it at the platform. Yallah let out an animalistic howl as the platform lit up with flame, marking Yorri's passage between worlds.

Ash looked over to Lunah, who was wiping her eyes, her cheeks flushed. She avoided his gaze. He turned his head away too, looking back to the now raging fire that was Yorri's funeral pyre, thinking about all they had lost. He clenched his hands into fists.

If I hadn't tried to calm the Gargants, if I'd just Sung Shaard's powerful Song earlier, maybe . . . maybe I could have saved him.

He stole a glance at Shaard, who gave him a meaningful look, as though thinking the exact same thing.

36

The Lost Stronghold

"Sleigh approaching, captain! Dead ahead!" called Teya from up high.

"Not again," lamented Lunah.

But this sleigh wasn't a large sunstone-powered vessel like the Pathfinder sleighs, nor was it a sleek vicious-looking war sleigh like the Wraiths had ridden. It was small and simple, pulled along by two ulk. Ribbons of white and purple cloth fluttered behind it in the wind. One of the two drivers was waving to the *Frostheart*.

The Pathfinders moved to grab their bows, but Nuk raised her fist, stopping them. "Bludgering bandahoots," she said, beaming. "It's a scout sleigh. That means there's an unmapped Stronghold nearby. Aurora knows we need one, the state we're in!"

"It's the Isolai, I'm sure of it," Shaard said, grinning.

"The ribbons, the ulk sleigh, the location, it all matches the stories I've heard. We should follow them. They'll help us, I have no doubt."

"Not so fast," Kailen said. "Let's think about this. How does a Stronghold survive hidden from the aid of the Pathfinders? If they've deliberately isolated themselves from the reach of Aurora, I doubt they even *want* to be found."

"I heard stories they were cannibals!" Twinge began. "I heard they—"

"Not now, thank you, Twinge," Nuk interrupted.

"Campfire tales," Shaard said. "The Fira survive all the way out in the middle of nowhere, and no one tells tales of their man-eating habits."

"They do like redroot, though, that's pretty weird," Twinge commented.

Ash started to disagree, to defend the Fira, and then thought better of it. Redroot was pretty weird.

"What other choice do we have?" Shaard asked Nuk. "You could avoid them, but the likelihood of the *Frostheart* making it more than a few leagues in this state is a fool's hope at best."

The crew began to protest, but Nuk raised her hand to silence them. "Shaard is right. It is too great a risk to carry on as we are. My poor pup isn't going to glide for much longer in this state, are you, my beauty?" she asked, stroking the tiller of the *Frostheart* tenderly. "No you're not, no indeed! But don't worry, Mother's going to take care of you!"

But it was clear most were uneasy about the captain's decision. And their unease wasn't lessened as the small sleigh led the *Frostheart* to what at first looked like a forest, the dark points of trees stark against the white of the snow. As they got closer Ash saw that they weren't trees at all. They were the skeletons of hundreds upon hundreds of sleighs. The small sleigh led the large one into the mass of torn timbers. Splintered wood and rotting masts stuck out of the snow like tree trunks, and torn sails flapped in the wind like thick foliage.

"It's a sleigh graveyard," Ash whispered.

"I've heard tales, though I didn't believe 'em," said Lunah, who had come to look by Ash's side. "Scavengers that pick at the wreckages of the poor souls who tried to make the run through Shade's Chasm. A smart idea to bring them back and pile them up here, though. Leviathans wouldn't find it easy to get through these ruins. But I always thought no one'd be crazy enough to live so close to Shade's Chasm." They watched the sleigh that was leading them, brows creased and eyes narrowed. "Guess I was wrong."

"Welcome to the Stronghold of the Isolai!" announced a tall Isolai man, arms wide open in greeting as the *Frostheart* crew cautiously descended the gangplank. The Isolai people huddled behind him, eyeing the newcomers with suspicion. "I am Temu, Song Searcher and leader of the Isolai people."

The scout sleigh had led the *Frostheart* to a Stronghold that was quite unlike anything any of them had ever seen before. The Isolai lived in houses built from sleigh ruins, a mishmash of different Stronghold styles and materials, with streets made of intersecting walkways raised high above the snow below. It was hard to make out what was a dwelling and what was wreckage, for they were pretty much the same thing.

"A most heartfelt thanks for guiding us to safety. We were in dire straits out there, and I fear we would not have survived long without your help," Nuk said. "I am Captain Nuk of the *Frostheart*, this fine vessel here." The foremast crashed down upon the deck as she said it, the sail crumpling into a messy pile. "*Ahem*. This here is my fearless crew. We have archeomek to trade, as well as goods from the Fira Stronghold, including a rather delicious-looking crate of redroot."

The gathered Isolai groaned and pulled faces at this.

Nuk continued. "We've had . . . well, a few run-ins with Leviathans and Wraiths on our journey. We made it through Shade's Chasm, but only just. Any help repairing our sleigh and looking to our injured would be greatly appreciated."

"Of course!" said the Song Searcher.

He was dressed in very strange clothing. Scrap enjin gears had been sewn onto his cowl to look like eyes, and he was wrapped in sleigh sailcloth that hid his human-kin shape, with protrusions stitched to his cloak to resemble extra limbs. Peering closely, Ash thought he looked a bit like some kind of Leviathan. "We don't often receive visitors—it is wonderful to have you here! I must ask, though, how it is you made it through Shade's Chasm in one piece? I can't say I remember the last time the Leviathans deemed anyone worthy enough to pass through alive . . ."

The *Frostheart* crew gazed from one to the other, careful not to allow their eyes to dwell for too long upon Ash.

"You just happen to be looking at one of the finest Pathfinder crews in the Snow Sea," Captain Nuk said. "Wraiths and Leviathans never stood a chance at catching us, and that's a fact, is that not so, Master Podd?"

"It is so," Master Podd agreed.

Temu raised an eyebrow. "We know what happens in the chasm. We live in the wreckages the Gargants leave behind. It is not a place for human-kin. It intrigues me that you have accomplished what so many others have not. You will have to tell us your secrets."

Nuk had just opened her mouth to answer when Shaard butted in: "There is no secret to hide here. We

are honored to have a great Song Weaver among us!"
And he pointed straight at Ash.

The crew and gathered crowd gasped. Ash sensed
the Pathfinders preparing for things to get messy, Tobu
growling as he reached for the spear at his back.

"Why, you insubordinate little—" Captain Nuk began, clasping her hands into mighty fists.

"Why would you even say that?" Lunah said, giving
Shaard a shove.

"Because they asked," Shaard replied, returning Lunah's hard look with a smile. "And given what Ash just
did for the *Frostheart*, he should no longer feel ashamed
of his wonderful powers."

Ash looked sheepish, but he couldn't help feeling a
tiny flare of pride too.

"A *Song Weaver* . . . I suspected as much," whispered
Temu.

Well, here we go . . . Ash prepared himself for the in-
evitable rush of scorn, fear, and insults.

"We are *honored* to have you among us, great Song
Weaver!" Temu cried with a huge smile. "This is a mo-
mentous occasion!"

"It—it *is*?" Ash asked, more confused than ever.

"Indeed, a gift from the Leviathans themselves!"

"The . . . *Leviathans*?"

"A Song Weaver has come before us!" Temu announced to the Isolai, turning. "Truly, we are blessed!"

The crowd let out a huge cheer, nothing but joy on their faces. No fear. No mistrust. The *Frostheart* crew exchanged glances. This was all very strange . . .

Ash looked at Shaard, who was beaming. And—befuddled as he was—Ash found the corners of his mouth begin to creep up into a smile too.

37

Searching for a Song

After their bizarre welcome, the Pathfinders immediately set about preparing to trade and, more important, to repair the *Frostheart*, which looked to be a few hours away from falling to pieces altogether. The Isolai had an abundance of scrap that they were happy to trade to the Pathfinders in exchange for some of the rarer, more useless items the crew had picked up far out in the wilds, such as a mummified hand clutching a mysterious object (no one could prize open the hand to see what it actually was) and a drinking horn made from a broken mursu tusk that had been engraved with a coded message no one could decipher. Shaard had disappeared into the Stronghold with Song Searcher Temu, off on his usual mission to uncover the history of the World Before, while Tobu had been ordered by Arła (and then by Nuk, after his many protests) to rest in the healing tent aboard the *Frostheart*.

Ash took a moment from hauling planks of wood up to the *Frostheart* to breathe the crisp air in relief.

Relief that they had made it this far.

Relief that his Song Weaving had actually helped them do it.

Relief that he had been lucky enough to find the *Frostheart* at all. To think he could've been trudging through the wilds on foot right now, if he'd even managed to survive that long!

The only thing niggling at him was Tobu. Ash couldn't help but think that if Tobu hadn't been so stubbornly mistrustful of Shaard, maybe they could *both* have helped Ash learn about Song Weaving, and he'd have much better control over his powers by now.

"Drop what you're doing, Pathfinder!" came a loud voice.

Ash spun round in alarm, only to see Lunah's grinning face.

"Cap's released us all from our duties today. A special treat for our 'valiant efforts within Shade's Chasm,' she says, and I ent arguing with that. What say we get outta here an' explore this Stronghold that ent meant to exist? I have to take some notes for my map!" she said, waving her rolled-up parchment. "And, you never know, we might find out something new about that lullaby of yours. Feels like we've been stumbling on clues wherever we've landed so far!"

"Sounds great!" said Ash. And it really did.

❧ ❧ ❧

Unfortunately the Isolai Stronghold was more like a maze than a village. "We've been here before, right?" Lunah asked.

"No, I think we were over there," Ash said, pointing to the other side of a long bridge.

"Nah, we've definitely seen this house. Look at the markings! It's an old Ensera Stronghold sleigh—I remember it from before!"

"But there's an old Ensera sleigh-house over that side too."

"Yeesh, you could really lure yer enemies to this place an' they'd never find their way out!" Lunah remarked, then scratched her chin in thought. "Hmm, that's not a bad idea actually. Really need to get to work on finding those enemies . . ."

While walking up stairs and along bridges through the Stronghold's many streets, in circles more often than not, they took in all the sights, sounds and smells the Isolai had to offer.

There was the ulk pen.

The high gardens.

The wooden figurehead from a wrecked sleigh.

It was such a sizable Stronghold it even had a market! Ash had to wonder how they managed to support such a big place.

His mind felt like it was doing roly-polies and somersaults and trying to climb inside out all at the same time, and he did not mind one bit. It was so exciting to see a new place so different from the Stronghold he had known all his life, yet more familiar than the baffling mek-built Skybridge. The Isolai all wore clothing made from materials scrounged from the wreckages, extra eyes painted onto their faces, bodies sporting sailcloth and monsterlike headwear.

"It's like they're *trying* to look like the Leviathans," Ash noted.

"They look pretty intimidating. *I like it.* Look at the claws on that one!" Lunah pointed at an Isolai girl on the platform above who wore long sharpened bones attached to her sleeves. Lunah cupped her hands and shouted, "Girl, your spiky claws look amazing!"

The girl looked surprised, then smiled nervously and bowed. "Thank you!" she said.

"You realize you could totally stab someone with those?" Lunah asked eagerly.

The girl suddenly looked quite uncomfortable. "Erm . . . I suppose? I hadn't really thought about that."

"Ah, well, good thing I bumped into you then!"

"I just—just thought they looked nice," she mumbled.

"Come on, you," Ash said, steering Lunah away. "It's usually *my* job to scare the locals, not yours."

They made their way round a corner, where they found Kailen and a red-eyed Yallah grimly watching a group of Isolai gathered round a tall structure made of wood and fabric adorned with talismans and ribbons. To their surprise they realized it had been constructed to resemble a Gargant. At its base the Isolai were on their hands and knees, bowing and worshipping. At the structure's center sat a captivating object. It looked like a large crystal made of ice reflecting a cold blue light.

Lunah gasped. "A Leviathan's heart . . . just like the frost-heart."

"I don't think so," Ash said.

"How d'ya know?"

"This one has no Song," he said, listening carefully. His arm prickled with goose pimples as he remembered the way the frost-heart had Sung to him, and how it had pulled him out of the shadow he'd felt himself falling into in Shade's Chasm.

Close behind the idol, Isolai were taking turns to climb a platform that extended over one of the Stronghold's many walls. One by one, they called out to the Snow Sea in harsh guttural voices that echoed across the plains, then a young woman stepped forward.

"I . . . I think they're trying to Song Weave," Ash whispered in wonder, recognizing the sound as a rough imitation of a Leviathan Song.

The low belly-shaking rumble of a Gargant reached them from far off in the distance.

The Isolai woman who had just called out burst into tears of happiness, facing her friends with a smile. "They answer my Song!" she squealed.

The others gathered round her, giving her hugs and clapping her on the back. "You have been blessed! They have chosen you to become a Song Weaver—they will lend you their Voice!" the crowd cooed.

Ash may not have known much about Song Weaving, but he did know that was not how it worked. *Why would they even try?*

He didn't know how he should feel, watching this strange ritual.

Apparently Kailen did. She spat on the ground with her usual delicacy. "Disrespectful is what it is," she said. "They know we just lost one of our own out there, yet they treat the cursed monsters like heroes."

"They're not monsters," said an Isolai villager, who had overheard her. "They are divine."

"Think you might've spent too long dancin' around in the snow, Isolai," Kailen snarled in reply.

"Kailen," Yallah cautioned.

Some Isolai warriors armed with spears were approaching.

"We didn't ask you to come here," a warrior grunted. "We are happy here, enlightened and in the Leviathans' favor. You don't like it, you can leave."

"If only I could," Kailen said. "A stupidity like this could be contagious."

The warrior shoved Kailen hard for this comment. "Ignorance!" he snarled. "You Pathfinders all act big and mighty, but when it comes to it you're all just frightened children, running clueless in the snow."

Kailen charged toward him, teeth bared and fists raised. Luckily Yallah and Lunah were there to hold her back.

"Stop it! We need their help!" Lunah hissed to her.

"Glad you're not on the map—you don't deserve

Pathfinder help!" Kailen spat at the warrior as she allowed Yallah to lead her away.

"We don't need you," he called after Kailen. "We have all we need. It is you outsiders whom I feel sorry for."

Ash and Lunah shared a glance, breathing out in relief at a narrowly averted scrap.

Ash, on the other hand, had never met such friendly people. Everywhere he went the Isolai smiled and waved, and even went so far as to bow and cheer as he walked by.

"Bless you, Song Weaver!" they would call out. "May the Leviathans forever smile upon you!"

Ash was even given free food at the market. "Thank you!" he said, munching some savory dumplings the merchant had handed to him.

"Anything for the Song Weaver!" the merchant said with a big smile. "You're from the Fira Stronghold, are you not?" he asked. "I think I have some redroot around here that I scavenged long ago, if you'd like some?"

"No!" Ash said, perhaps a bit too quickly. "No, thank you."

The merchant shrugged. He seemed a bit disappointed not to be able to get rid of his stock. "I thought all Fira liked redroot."

Lunah reached for a dumpling, but the merchant moved the platter out of her reach. "These are not for Pathfinders. Only for the Song Weaver."

Lunah clicked her tongue, which was impressive considering her mouth was still full of the food she'd helped herself to from Ash's stash. "Oi really wanted dose dumplin's," she said as they walked on. "Gud t'ave s'm proper 'ood after weeks o' rations!" Flecks of spit flew from her mouth as she spoke.

"It feels . . . weird having everyone being nice to me," Ash said as another store owner filled his hands with roasted chestnuts.

Lunah swallowed, wiping her mouth with the back of her hand. "You think too much, Ash! Enjoy it while you can. I know I certainly will!" she said, helping herself to as many of the chestnuts as she could fit into the cradle of her arms. "People'll go back to hatin' your guts before you know it!"

"Don't get me wrong, it's amazing! I've never felt so . . . so *welcome*. It just feels a bit odd is all."

As evening drew in, they paused again in front of another strange sight—a lively, colorful dance the Isolai were performing. The dancers all had extravagant Leviathan costumes on, their ribbons and talismans rattling and jingling as they paced around to the rhythm of the drums. They skipped round huge sculptures that had been carved from sleigh wood shaped into the forms of Lurkers, Hurtlers, Gargants, and Leviathans Ash had never even seen before.

An Isolai dancer dropped out of the dance as the

others began spinning round in a circle. She approached Ash and Lunah with a smile. "Are you enjoying our dance, Song Weaver?" she asked.

Lunah grinned. "We are!"

The dancer ignored her, not taking her eyes off Ash.

"It's—it's great." Ash nodded. And it really was, he supposed, if a bit strange.

"You do us great honor to say so. All of our dances represent a part of the great Saga of the Leviathans. This part shows the Time of Fury, when the Leviathans stopped loving and protecting us, and became enraged with the sins of the people of the World Before. It is chaotic and hectic, to represent the rage the great Leviathans felt then, and to this very day."

The dance was indeed hectic. The drums thrummed at a frantic pace, the dancers writhing and leaping around like a whirlwind. It was powerful to watch, but there was no denying that worshipping Leviathans felt very unnatural to Ash.

"How can you worship the Leviathans?" Lunah asked the dancer, seeming to read Ash's thoughts. "It seems pretty odd, considering they try to kill us all the time."

The dancer smiled, but Ash was sure he saw a flash of annoyance behind her eyes.

"The question is: How could we *not*? The Leviathans are beautiful yet powerful; they are terrible in their fury and yet Sing the softest Songs. They rule this world undeniably. If we were to seek forgiveness from them, then perhaps we could find peace once more."

"Huh. I'm not so sure it's workin'. I've traveled far and wide, and no matter where I go the Leviathans don't seem to be in too much of a forgivin' mood."

"We have found that treating them with the respect and reverence they are due, and offering them gifts of our devotion every year, has kept our Stronghold safe. We have not been attacked in living memory," the dancer answered, confident and calm.

Ash thought it probably had more to do with how well hidden and well defended their Stronghold was, but he kept that to himself.

The children sat and watched the dance for a bit longer. Now the Leviathan dancers were gathered round a solitary dancer who Ash guessed represented the people of the world. She looked so small, so vulnerable compared to the other dancers. The Leviathans swarmed around her and hid her from view as she fell to her knees, her arms raised in a futile attempt to protect herself. It was like she was being consumed.

Ash jumped as a black crow called out into the night. *Crows again?*

Ash turned his head to see where the cry had come from—and for a second he could have sworn he saw a shadowy feathered figure, staring at him from a perch up high. *The crow-witch!* He blinked. But the figure, if there had ever been one, had vanished.

I'm just imagining things . . .

But all the same a chill ran down his spine.

38

Anger Is Your Spear

The next day Ash awoke early stretched out like a star, savoring the opportunity while Tobu was still resting in the healing tent.

He'd been thinking hard overnight. He yearned to become a powerful Song Weaver, and he knew he needed help understanding his powers. Shaard wanted to help, and the technique he'd taught him had been the only one to really work. It had saved Lunah and Kailen back in Shade's Chasm, but its cold, relentless power scared him.

Tobu wanted Ash to be patient, to learn what he considered to be the "proper" technique, spending days upon days in silence, listening, with no Singing whatsoever. Ash still struggled to understand the purpose of this. Sure, it had enabled him to hear the frost-heart, but what else had it achieved? In the meantime people were *dying.* And the Isolai had shown him that Song Weaving could be celebrated, if only people understood its worth.

So, he'd made a decision.

Ash wandered down the gangplank, the deep blue of the sky turning a watery yellow with the arrival of Mother Sun. He found Shaard talking to an excited Song Searcher Temu on the docks below.

"Young Song Weaver!" Shaard greeted Ash as he approached. "So early—I'd have thought you'd take this rare opportunity to rest?"

"I—I can't," Ash admitted. "I've been thinking. I'll never find my parents without learning more about Song Weaving—and how to protect myself and my friends. There's so much I don't know . . . so . . ." He took a deep breath. "Tobu's lessons aren't working. I want you to take over my lessons!"

Shaard smiled at Temu, who grinned back.

"Why, that's all you had to say," Shaard answered.

"It'd be an honor to watch, Song Weaver, if I may?" Temu said. "My people and I dream of one day being able to follow in your sacred footsteps, to learn your incredible skills. To be able to talk with the Leviathans—to hear what they want from us—I believe it would be the greatest of gifts!"

"That makes two of us," Ash said in a quiet voice. A

pang of guilt stabbed his belly. He couldn't help feeling like he'd betrayed Tobu by turning his back on his teachings.

"So! First things first, you must forget all that Tobu has taught you," Shaard said as the lesson began. "I have learned from Song Weaving masters, who could bury Tobu with their wisdom and knowledge. You do not need to be calm to Song Weave. You need to be passionate. Anger, fury—they are fuel to your power. Please, Sing for me, if you would be so kind."

Ash began to Sing. His starlight aura flowed round him, and he was happy to see the return of his starlight blizzard.

"There! You see! Your Song is far too gentle. It needs

to become a spear. You are a fighter now, Ash—your aura is your weapon."

Ash tried to follow Shaard's advice. He thought of how the Fira had outcast him, his friends betraying him. He thought of Tobu's harsh guardianship, and of how mistrusting Kailen had been, how the vulpis had refused to deal with the Pathfinders. He thought of how weak and helpless he had felt in front of the Wraiths . . . of Yorri's fate. And, most of all, he thought about his missing parents, the way they'd abandoned him. Left him on his own in a world that hated him, with nothing more than a stupid lullaby that led him nowhere.

Immediately the light of his Song-aura bled into darkness like ash from a fire.

"That's right! That's it, Ash! You're—" Shaard began, but before he could finish, a white blur rushed forward and hoisted him up by his neck.

The attack snapped Ash straight out of his Song-trance, and a familiar shape came into focus.

"*I've warned you for the last time!*" Tobu roared, his eyes ablaze with fury. He held Shaard high off the ground with ease. Shaard struggled for breath, grasping for release from Tobu's immovable strength.

"Tobu! *Put him down!*" Ash pleaded, horrified by Tobu's fierce reaction.

"What—what are you g-going to do, T-T-Tobu?" Shaard choked. "What w-was it you were s-s-saying to Ash about restraint and s-s-self-control?"

Tobu snarled but loosened his grip, though he did not drop him.

"Am I in the middle of something here?" Song Searcher Temu asked nervously.

"You say I need to learn how to control my powers, Tobu, and you're right," Ash pleaded. "But I've tried it your way, and I feel like I'm getting nowhere . . . What else can I do?"

"Mastery does not come overnight," Tobu replied. "Anything worth learning takes time and patience. The Gargant that seized Kailen and Lunah was beyond you, and it was only through dark means that you were able to *force* it to do your bidding. That is not the path anyone with a conscience would walk."

"You're wrong!" Shaard choked out. "Ash has unimaginable skill locked within; all he needs is someone to have faith enough to let those powers thrive . . . All you do is smother him!"

"I definitely feel like I'm in the middle of something here," Temu said.

"*Liar!*" Tobu roared, throwing Shaard to the ground.

"*Tobu!*" Ash shouted in shock. He noticed the band-

age covering Tobu's left shoulder was soaked in blood.

"I'm—I'm just going to step away from this—leave you lot to it," Temu said, walking hastily away.

"You see, Ash, he's dangerous," Shaard said, picking himself up and rubbing his neck. "Why would he react this way if he knew I was wrong? Who is he really? He's never said, has he? In all my travels I have met only one other lone yeti. If they are exiled, it is for something heinous indeed. So what about you, Tobu? Why were you made an outcast?"

Outcast.

Suddenly the words of the crow-witch came flooding back to Ash. *FEAR. BEWARE. OUTCAST.*

It all fits together, Ash thought in horror, the crow-witch's Song scratching at his thoughts. *Maybe Shaard was right all along—maybe Tobu has been holding me back? Maybe the lullaby has been trying to lead me to Shaard, to protect me from Tobu?*

"*Enough!*" Tobu shouted. He reached out as if to grab Shaard again, but instead winced and put a hand to his shoulder, his wound clearly hurting him.

"No, it's not enough. He's right, Tobu," Ash said. "Who *are* you? What happened to you—and to your son?"

Tobu looked at Ash, and Ash was surprised to see that his face was full of shame. But all he would say was "I am your guardian. It is my duty to protect you."

Yet another nonanswer! It infuriated Ash.

"Duty this, duty that! Don't you ever think for yourself?!" Ash spat.

Now it was Tobu's turn to look taken aback.

"Ash can make his own choices," agreed Shaard. "He's been told what to do all his life by people who don't know any better. I think it high time he received more . . . *enlightened* lessons from someone who knows what they're talking about. From someone who can support his cleverness and talent."

A fire flared in Tobu's eyes. "Do not tell me what the boy is or isn't. I know his qualities better than you ever will!"

Ash felt anger boiling within his belly. "Only because you were made to! If Alderman Kindil hadn't made you my guardian, you wouldn't be here! You never believed in me, and nothing I ever do is good enough for you! Well, I didn't ask you to come along, and I never asked you to protect me."

"It's not always about what you want," Tobu said. "It's about what you need. You can't survive on your own—with *him*."

Now Ash was really cross. "You say I don't know how to survive on my own? Well, that's a *lie*. It's all I've *ever* done!" Ash took a deep breath. "I can manage just fine without you. In fact, I release you of your duty, Tobu. You're free to go."

Tobu's eyes narrowed. "You don't get to decide that."

And then Ash's anger overflowed. All the hurt and fear and rage he'd been channeling into his Song just moments before spilled out into the open. "I don't care how it works! I don't want to listen to you anymore! I. DON'T. WANT. YOU. HERE!"

For a brief second Tobu's unwavering calm and control vanished. Suddenly this giant fearsome warrior looked small and vulnerable.

But only for a second. The emotionless mask that Tobu wore returned as swiftly as it had left. He clenched his fists and nodded. "So be it. I am only sorry that I failed you. But know this: that man is dangerous." Tobu inclined his head toward Shaard. "I know you are not in the habit of doing so, but if you follow only one piece of my advice, let it be this: do not be so easily led into the darkness."

With that Tobu turned and, slouching over on his wounded left side, walked across the docks into the confusion of the Isolai village.

Ash watched his guardian walk out of his life. The only guardian who had not given up on him. The only guardian Ash had been the one to give up on.

He was just beginning to feel the stirs of regret and panic, when suddenly a terrible cry rose up from the *Frostheart*.

"Bouncing barnacles! It's *gone*!"

39

Farewell Feast

"Someone's taken it!" Captain Nuk cried out from the hold. Ash and Shaard ran belowdecks to see what all the commotion was about, where they found the rest of the crew (minus Tobu, Ash noticed with a pang) gathered round the captain. "The ruddy thing's been taken!"

"What's gone?" asked Teya.

"The frost-heart! The *Frostheart*'s frost-heart. Blast it all!"

The crew gasped and Kailen growled.

"Who would've taken it?" Lunah asked.

"Damned if I know, but if I find them, I'll wring their neck!" Nuk said, clambering up the ladder to the main deck.

Ash and Lunah shared a glance as the others followed their captain, thinking of the imitation heart set within the Isolai idol.

"You don't think it could be our yeti friend?" Shaard proposed.

"No!" Ash replied. "He might be a lot of things, but Tobu is no thief!"

Shaard didn't seem convinced, but shrugged and followed the others. Ash took a closer look at the hollow depression that had once held the frost-heart, ice-melt trickling down the mast, and noticed the black feathers that lay scattered about its base. Then, with a tremor of suspicion tickling the back of his neck, he raced to join the others.

➤ ❧ ✦

"There's only so many insults we can take," Captain Nuk said to Song Searcher Temu at the entrance to his sleigh-house. The Isolai warriors had their spears at the ready, and Kailen, swinging her arms wildly and cursing, was being held back by Kob. "We have tried to be reasonable, but this has crossed the line."

Temu held up his hands placatingly, sweat dripping at his brow. "I wish I could help, but we do not know where your 'frost-heart' has gone. I have not seen nor heard of it!"

"*Liar!* You lunatics had a fake in that stupid idol of yours!" frothed Kailen. "Bet you'd like nothin' more than to steal the real deal!"

"Our Leviathan heart is sacred to us and has been within the Stronghold for many generations," Temu replied.

"As was *ours*."

"Stop it, all of you!" Ash called out. "I think I know who stole it!"

Everyone turned to look at him.

"I . . . met someone, back in Skybridge," Ash began. "A . . . a witch covered in crow feathers."

Shaard looked concerned.

"*Ash . . .* no!" Lunah said, slapping her palm to her forehead.

"I don't know how, but I think she may have followed me here . . . and I think she's taken the frost-heart. I found these at the mast's base . . ." Ash held up the black feathers, to the bafflement of the crowd.

"Proves nothin'. Just looks like ruddy feathers to me!" Kailen said.

"Well, whoever the thief is, I swear we will find them!" Temu assured, thankful for the shift in blame. "You shall not leave without your precious frost-heart!"

"You can be sure of it," Nuk threatened. "And the

Council will hear of the way we've been treated, you can be sure of that too."

Temu spread his hands magnanimously. "I know there has been some . . . *friction* between our people, but it pains me to think of you leaving under these circumstances. Our ways are strange to outsiders, but we beg your forgiveness and understanding. A feast shall be thrown in your honor tonight, and we pray we can show you proper Isolai hospitality to help to heal any wounds or ill will caused during your visit . . ."

The Pathfinders grumbled, giving each other worried looks. But then again, they did love a good party.

"Fine," barked Nuk. "But we'll be leaving first thing tomorrow—with our frost-heart!"

"Of course," said Temu smoothly, wearing the smallest of smiles.

➤ ❙ ❮

The Isolai were true to their word and laid out a grand feast for the Pathfinders. The *Frostheart* still needed repairs, but they'd done as much as the Isolai Stronghold could offer. The runners had been mended and attached with fresh sliders, the sails had been patched up, and the enjin had been installed with a brand-new sunstone. The *Frostheart* was fit to ride—just.

The entire village had gathered to feast. They sat round huge long tables in a large hall comprising three overturned sleigh hulls. There was more food than Ash had ever seen in his life: roasted ulk, hare stew, smoked fish, maple and spruce shoots in spices, jams made from all kinds of berries, and many vegetables and fruits that had been grown in the high gardens. The Isolai seemed to do well for themselves hidden from danger and scavenging from the fallen. Dancers hopped and sprang round an open, burning hearth, once again reenacting the story of the Leviathans. Ash thought back to when he'd wished the Fira would play music at their festivals, and about how much happier it would've made the people. But instead of the joy he'd hoped to feel, the scene

of the dancing wannabe Leviathans before him only offered a creeping sense of unease.

He looked at the meat before him and crinkled his nose, remembering the strange hunt he'd seen earlier that day. Ash had watched as some ulk were released into the mazelike pathways that ran through the ruins below and around the Stronghold. Dressed as Hurtlers, the hunters gave their quarry a head start, and then they ran into the maze after them, chasing down the ulk one by one to the raucous cheers of the villagers watching from above. Ash had found it pretty barbaric. The Fira had always treated the animals they hunted with respect, offering prayers of thanks to their spirits once they had been killed. This had been more like a spectacle or some weird game.

Now Ash barely noticed the celebrations around him, he was so deep in thought. He twizzled one of the small sculptures Tobu had left behind in their small tent. He had improved. This blob had the most number of blobs protruding from it yet. There was a danger of it actually looking like something . . . perhaps even like a small yeti, Ash thought with a lump in his throat. No one had seen Tobu since the confrontation that morning, and even though Ash thought he'd probably done the right thing in sending him away, he was still worried about him.

"Heeeey, nice sculpture!" Lunah said, leaning in and pausing from stuffing her face just long enough to speak. Ash closed his hands over the blob and hid it in his furs. "Helloooo? I'm lookin' for this scruffy ragamuffin called Ash. Have you seen 'im?" Lunah said, waving her hands in front of his eyes.

"I–I'm sorry. I've got a lot on my mind," he mumbled.

Lunah swung herself upside down from a nearby lantern rope as though it was the most natural thing in the world. And with Lunah it kind of was.

"Fair enough. You figure out any more of that lullaby of yours?"

"Haven't really had a chance to think about it, what with all the fleeing for our lives we've been doing since we found the last clue," Ash replied.

"Ah, you'll never get anythin' done if you're waitin' for a moment where you won't be fleeing for your life with us!" She laughed, but Ash wasn't in the mood.

"Where do you think your family are right now?" he asked.

He hadn't told Lunah—or anyone—that Shaard had known his parents. He was still processing the information himself. He'd turned it over and over in his head, picking at it like a scab, trying to decide how he felt about it, wondering whether it really was too good to be true.

Lunah shrugged, avoiding Ash's gaze. "Dunno. Convoy's always roamin'. The end of my quest'll be to find 'em—'s part of the challenge."

"So where do you think?"

"Probably south of Aurora, near the Dancing Waters?"

The Dancing Waters. He could only imagine what that was. Ash hoped he survived long enough to see all the amazing sights he'd learned about since joining the *Frostheart*.

"It's warmer there. Well, not *freezin'* at least," Lunah went on. "Good huntin' too. Not many Leviathans. Convoy won't stay there for long, though—discovery's in our blood. My ma is an all-round adventurer-hero, 'n' my pa and big sister taught me all I know 'bout navigatin'. Even gave me this for my tenth winter." Lunah tapped her finger on the compass strapped to her wrist, and beamed with pride.

"Do you miss them?" Ash asked quietly.

Lunah snapped out of her happy thoughts and shook her head firmly.

"Course not, I'm a Drifter! We don't miss people— we just live for the adventure!"

But Ash wasn't convinced. "You're allowed to miss them. I miss my parents, and I never really knew them."

Ash thought he'd caught Lunah's determined expression softening for a heartbeat. It was the first time Ash had seen her look vulnerable. But it was gone before he could tell if he'd imagined it or not. "Yikes, how long have you been hanging upside down for?" he joked, trying to break the tension.

"Ah, wow, I dunno. Too long probably. I feel a bit sick." She stuck her tongue out to show this and used the ropes to flip herself the right way up at the table. "Hey, why don't we put that new pipe of yours to use? It can't be worse than your Singin', right?"

"What, my ocarina? Play a Song?" Ash said, suddenly flustered. "I don't know if I—I can't—"

"Play us a Song! Play us a Song!" Lunah chanted.

"Yes, go on, lad," chipped in Yallah, who was seated on his other side. "Either you do, or I start Singing, and, believe me, nobody needs to hear that."

"Y'see, Ash? The crowd demands it! Play! Play! Play!" Lunah crowed.

"I dunno . . ." Ash felt his face growing hot. But Lunah was using her magically persuasive power of chanting a word over and over, and he felt himself cracking. "OK, I'll try . . ."

Pulling out his new ocarina, he began to play, dipping and weaving his melody to the rhythm of the Isolai drums. The comfort and joy of the music gave him a sudden flash of inspiration. "I—I *have* made up a Song," he paused to say. "About the crew. It's . . . it's pretty stupid, but, well, I finished it today." Then, before he could change his mind, he took a deep breath and began.

"Oh, us, yes, us, we lucky few!
Who make up the Frostheart's valiant crew!
Captain Nuk, she leads us brave and strong.
Master Podd watches o'er our courageous throng.
Kailen's mouth curses and keeps the deck damp.
Twinge's tales like a sleigh that can't get up a ramp.
Teya and Kob get the sleigh moving day after day.
Shaard's knowledge and skill helps keep it this way.
Lunah, she watches, she plots, and she maps.
Ensuring the sleigh avoids Leviathan traps.
Arla, the healer, will stitch you up good.

And Yallah so wise, and as sturdy as wood.
Happy memories of Yorri, despite our great pain.
A hero to all, in our hearts he'll remain.
That's us, yes, that's right, oh yes, yes, it's true.
That's all of us, the brave Frostheart's *crew!"*

"That was lovely, Ash," Yallah said gently, once Ash was done. "It's not finished, though."

"Isn't it?" Ash asked, confused.

"No. It's missing you and Tobu. Wouldn't be the whole crew without you guys."

The memory of Tobu's shocked, wounded face flashed in Ash's mind. Guilt roiled up inside him.

"Speakin' of yer guardian, where is the great hunk-agrump?" Nuk slurred. She looked at Master Podd for an answer, but he was facedown on the table, having an adorable little snore after accepting (and clearly losing) an ill-advised grog-drinking challenge.

Ash stared into the stew bowl that lay before him on the table as though it held the courage he sought.

"I don't know," he mumbled. "I—I sent him away. I freed him of his oath to be my guardian."

Nuk looked surprised, and Lunah pulled a face. *"Why?"*

"I need to learn how to Song Weave, and all he did was put me through pointless exercises. Plus nothing I did was ever good enough for him!"

"Oh, boohoo for you, Ash," said Lunah. "Grow up! He may be hard on you, but it's only 'cause he doesn't want you to *die*."

"You sound a lot like him," Ash grumbled. "You haven't heard what Tobu did to get exiled in the first place—"

"Oh? And?"

"He—well—he—OK, I don't *actually* know, but Shaard agrees he's bad news. And the crow-witch said he wasn't to be trusted!"

Lunah rolled her eyes. "Not this again . . ."

"They both warned me about him. We don't know anything about his past—he could be dangerous!"

"You don't know anythin' 'bout Shaard or the freaky bird-lady either! Did you ever stop to think about that?"

She had a point. Ash really didn't know much about Shaard at all, and he knew even less about the strange crow-witch.

"At least Shaard gets what I'm going through. At least he can *actually* teach me how to Song Weave, unlike Tobu."

Lunah made a *kuh* sound as she looked down at the table, annoyance darkening her features. "Ever since I left the Convoy, the *Frostheart*'s been my family. That includes you, Ash. Least I thought so. An' I thought Tobu was a part of that family too?"

Ash felt awful, like something was crushing his insides in a terrible grip.

"Look, I'm sorry . . ." he began.

"No, you're not. You only care about yourself. Well, now you've turned away the yeti who always had your back. Good for you. I'm sure Shaard will be really happy to have you all to himself."

Ash felt like he'd been slapped across the face. He could find nothing to say.

Luckily for him Song Searcher Temu chose that moment to raise a toast to Ash and the Pathfinders. "May your visit bring the favor of the Leviathans for years to come!" he announced.

The crowd banged their cups in acknowledgment and drank deeply, Ash miserably following suit. The drink was delicious, making the guilt he felt all the harder to swallow. Ash suddenly felt completely worn out. He just wanted to go to bed—and noticed that the rest of the crew seemed to feel the same.

Lunah had her head in her arms, flat against the table. Kailen was also asleep on her stool, her head resting on Twinge's large shoulder. Twinge also seemed to be nodding off.

Strange, Ash thought, his brain feeling as thick as stew. He lurched forward and caught hold of the table to steady himself. *A lot's been going on. I can't think straight. I—I just need some rest.* He tried to leave the table, but succeeded only in stumbling. The world was spinning. His limbs felt as heavy as stone.

Something was wrong. *Very wrong.*

With a thump Ash found himself with his head on the wooden floor, falling into a deep, uncomfortable sleep.

40

Offering

My head hurts.

That was the first thought that came to Ash's mind when he woke up.

I really need a wee.

That was the second.

He was aware that he was lying on hard ground. He gritted his teeth and clenched his hands, his mouth dry and throat painful. Memories began to trickle back into his head. Had he actually collapsed at the feast? Was he still there?

No. Mother Sun burned the back of his head. Snow kissed his skin. He was lying on his front, his cheeks and furs damp from morning frost. That, or he *had* wet himself.

I really need that wee.

He shivered, and became aware of a noise getting louder and louder. It was the sound of people cheering. *Lots of them.* The world slowly blurred into view, bright and painful.

With a groan Ash picked himself up. He swayed unsteadily, but caught his balance. Holding his hand to his head, he tried to make sense of his surroundings. Hundreds of Isolai were gathered on the interweaving platforms and bridges that formed their Stronghold, cheering, whooping, and calling out. All eyes were on the labyrinthine passages of the hunting maze below.

"What's going on . . . ?" Ash mumbled, his tongue feeling thick and at least two times too big for his mouth.

"He awakens!" came the voice of Shaard.

Ash turned to see the man standing behind him with a small grin. Under his arm he held the spherical archeomek casing he'd shown Ash while changing the sunstone enjin. Ash rubbed his face, trying to clear the fog in his head.

"Followers of the great Leviathans!" boomed a voice, and Ash cringed at its loudness. His groggy mind recognized it as Song Searcher Temu. The leader was standing on a raised platform, holding his staff up high and addressing the crowd. "People of the Isolai, we stand together, unified in our worship of our Leviathan masters!

We aim only to please them, and now our masters demand their tithe!"

A tithe? What is this guy going on about? Something felt very wrong.

"Every year we make an offering to the Leviathans in exchange for their forgiveness. It is what they demand! And look what gifts they bless us with in return! Song Weavers have been guided to us. They will show us how to communicate with our masters. We shall use their Song to learn of the Leviathans' Great Plan, and of what we must do to return the world to order! And with this mighty offering our masters shall be appeased for years to come!"

T-teach them?

Ash's eyes were focusing better now. He looked among the applauding throng of the Isolai, but couldn't see the *Frostheart* crew anywhere.

I've got a bad feeling about this . . .

Ash looked down into the labyrinth of wrecked sleighs, and finally saw what the crowd was jeering at.

There, all alone, was Captain Nuk. Her large fists were clenched, and she looked defiantly up at her audience. Ash's brain couldn't comprehend what it was seeing. He stumbled over to the opposite side of the platform, and down below saw Lunah making incredibly rude gestures at the roaring spectators above. He fell to another railing, and saw Kailen in a corner of the maze, still struggling to stand up. The entire *Frostheart* crew were scattered here and there about the labyrinth, alone and separated from each other

"What—what's going on?" Ash cried.

"I'm so sorry, Ash," Shaard replied, coming to stand next to him. "I did all I could."

A cold wave of dread washed over him as Isolai hunters began to turn large wooden wheels, which in turn rotated various spokes and gears connected to huge doors that lay within the hunting maze. With a creak and a groan the doors began to open. Ash could see something in the darkness behind them. Something large and slithery. Something with razor-sharp fangs and claws the size of daggers. The things roared and hissed, scratching at the ground, eager to be let into the maze with the Pathfinders.

"Under the gaze of the Song Weaver, let the sacrifice begin!" Temu announced.

The crowd erupted with even louder cheers and Ash's head suddenly felt as clear as day.

Sacrifice. The drinks we were given last night—they were drugged!

Three Lurkers stalked out of the doorway in front of Lunah, tasting the air with their long tongues, multiple eyes glistening, blinking in the sunlight. Another two emerged from a doorway close to Captain Nuk. More appeared before Kailen, in front of Twinge. Here, there, everywhere. The maze had been filled with them.

Without a second thought Lunah was off. She ran as fast as she could away from the monsters. Slower, but no less determined, Nuk slipped round a corner and made her way through the narrow snow-covered trenches, the Lurkers taking a moment to gather their bearings, then rushing after her.

"*We have to stop them!*" Ash cried out to Shaard.

"Do not worry, Song Weaver!" An Isolai man laughed. "This is what the Leviathans demand. It is what they are owed. Join us in our worship!"

Ash could only gawk in disbelief.

"I have tried, Ash, but they would not listen," Shaard said. "They spared you because you are a Song Weaver, and me because I made a deal to teach them all we know about the art of Singing."

Ash gripped the wooden railing, watching in horror as his friends ran for their lives below. The Lurkers sped through the passageways, writhing over and under each other, ramming against the walls in their eagerness to

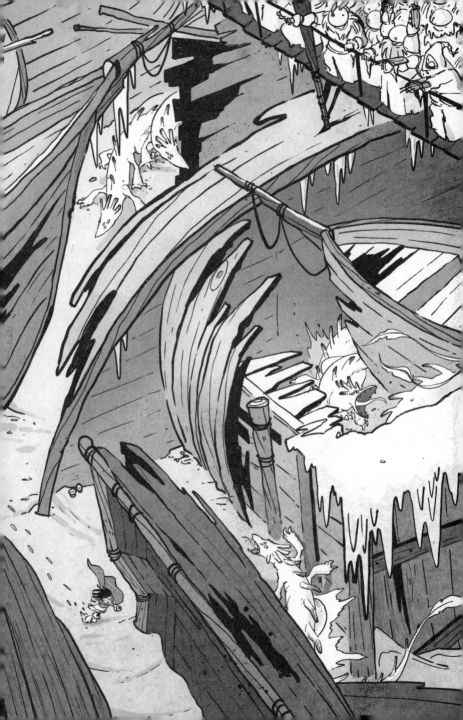

catch their prey. Ash felt like he was going to be sick. "I have to help them!"

He prepared to throw himself over the railing into the maze, but Shaard pulled him back.

"Don't be foolish!" Shaard hissed. "I know what you're thinking. But if you go down there, if you try to Sing, then the Isolai will fill you with arrows, if the Lurkers don't kill you first. This is their custom, and they will not have outsiders ruin it for them, Song Weaver or not. Do not throw away your life, Ash. This is your chance to start again!"

"What—what are you saying?" Ash whimpered.

"I hate what's happening to the *Frostheart* crew as much as you, believe me. It's awful and unfair, but so is life. You have fought so hard to survive in this uncaring world. Trust me—I know all about that. Come with me now, Ash," Shaard pleaded. "Think what we could learn from each other! With your father's Song, you can lead us to the hidden Song Weaver Stronghold. We could find your parents in a matter of days!"

"I—I can't—" Ash began.

"The *Frostheart* only took you aboard since you benefited them. You think they would've taken you if you had no powers?"

Ash paused at this. "Yes, I—they—"

"Wherever you go, people will hate you," Shaard said. "I have traveled this world, and all I see is hatred toward your kind. You'll never truly be part of their crew. Never. You belong with your parents, Ash. With your people, people who will care for you because of who you are!"

Ash couldn't think straight. He felt as though he were being torn in two. He heard a Lurker screech and the crowd whoop with excitement. Down in the maze he saw Twinge stumble in the snow, a Lurker only a wall's width away.

"Ash!" Shaard called his attention back. "We could set off right now. The Isolai have ulk sleighs—we could steal one and set off before they're any the wiser!"

Ash felt as though he were free-falling off a cliff face. His mind could barely keep up, and his heart threatened to rise up into his throat.

Shaard extended his hand. "Please, Ash. You don't belong with them. You belong with *us*."

I'm so close . . .

His parents, the Song Weaver Stronghold, it was all right before him, and all he had to do was follow Shaard. That was all he had to do.

All I have to do . . .

He heard a terrible scream. It was Lunah. She was in trouble. All of them, they were all in terrible danger.

Ash took one last look at Shaard's hand. "I'm sorry," he said, before vaulting over the railing.

"Ash, *no!*" Shaard shouted out, but it was too late.

Ash had dropped into the labyrinth.

41

Twists and Turns

Down in the maze Ash noticed something he had not seen up on the platform. Almost camouflaged, half-buried in the snow, were bones. Lots of bones.

His blood went cold. He tried to swallow, but his throat was too dry.

They were not just any type of bones. They were human bones.

He didn't waste a moment. Like an arrow he sped into the chaos of the maze as fast as his wobbly legs would allow. He clipped the edge of some wreckage with his shoulder and nearly went spinning to the ground, but managed to regain his balance and surge forward.

I have to find the others!

He could hear screeching and keening all around

him, Lurkers eager for blood. He was aware of large quick shapes darting in the maze with him, behind him, in front of him. Was it the *Frostheart* crew, or the Lurkers?

The crowd roared with excitement. He heard someone shouting: "It's the Song Weaver! The Song Weaver's down there! We have to get him out!" But he refused to take help from the mad Isolai, the ones who were doing this to his friends.

Ash turned left, but heard a monstrous thrum, the terrifying purring of a predator on the hunt.

He swerved right, but saw a slithering, coiling shape lurch past.

Not that way.

He headed forward, only to be confronted with a gaping, salivating jaw.

Definitely not that way.

He did all he could not to panic. He tried to control his breathing. Tried to remember what Tobu had taught him—to always be in control, to focus. Ash climbed through the rotting ribs of a sleigh and darted forward, only to collide with something that was moving at great speed. Ash whipped himself back to his feet, ready to run away.

"*Ash?*" Lunah cried, picking herself up, her thick locks flecked with snow. "Watch where you're going, yeah?" she said, giving Ash such a hug she nearly took him off his feet again.

"We need to find the others!" he gasped. "Do you know where they are?"

"I don't even know where I am! I saw Teya rush past with Kob, but I couldn't get to 'em in time." Lunah swallowed. "They were alive. Least, they were then." Her face was strained with fear but full of resolve. "Let Leviathans take the Isolai!" she panted as they rounded another corner. "Looks like I've finally got someone to add to my enemy list!"

They entered a larger enclosure and with a sickening lurch skidded to a halt before the long whipping tail of a Lurker. It had cornered Captain Nuk and Kailen, who were backed up against the sheer wall. The Lurker prowled toward them, thick drool dripping from its snarling maw.

Lunah gave him a nod. "Now's about the time I'd start Singing if I were you!"

Without a second's hesitation Ash began to do exactly that. His aura met the Lurker's blood-red one, which immediately lashed out at him.

With a terrible roar the Lurker charged toward him.

I'm too close, there's not enough time to control it!

Fangs clamped shut inches away from Ash's head as

he dived out of the way. He rushed across the clearing, using his momentum to run up the sheer surface of a wall. The Lurker crashed into it just below, cracking and splintering the wood, missing Ash's foot by a hair's breadth. Ash pushed off the surface with all his might and landed on the Lurker's moist back with a loud squelch, before rolling off and leaping away from its snapping jaws. He spotted a boy-sized crevice between some ruined prows and dived into it, the Lurker moments behind. He squeezed through the gap and backed away as the Leviathan snapped and reached for him, the sleigh prows creaking and trembling but thankfully holding. Ash backed away as far as he could go. The Lurker's tongue whipped around the space, covering Ash in foul-smelling slobber.

"*Go! Go! Go!*" Ash shouted back to the Pathfinders, who were using the now fractured wood of the wall as handholds to climb up and out of the maze.

"*Not without you!*" Nuk yelled.

"Go! I can Song Weave, remember?!"

Nuk and the others hesitated, but time was short and they saw the sense of it.

"Whack 'im with yer voice, fire-boy!" Lunah called back.

Around them the Isolai howled their displeasure,

hunters racing to cut the Pathfinders off.

Ash was glad to see them get out, but knew he was in quite the pickle. He tried to Song Weave, but his voice was too shaky, his body too panicked. He was trapped.

The Lurker strained and pushed against the wood, trying its hardest to reach its prey. It was inching forward bit by bit, the wood bending and tearing with the Lurker's strength. He could hear other Lurkers arriving. He was surrounded.

What am I gonna do? There's nowhere to go!

As the fearful grip of panic tightened he heard a strange sound. It was deep and sharp and ululating. It filled the air and reverberated through his bones. It stood out against the roaring of the crowd, the cheering that was becoming unsure and confused at this new sound.

It was raw and primal. Guttural and harsh. *Powerful.*

It was a Song.

It was the Song of a Song Weaver!

42

There Is Another

The Lurkers hissed and recoiled. The one that had been moments away from biting Ash slowly pulled its head away. It let out a somber sound and lowered its head and tail, slinking away.

Gathering all the courage he could muster, Ash tentatively crawled out of his hiding place and into the open. There skulked four Lurkers, all under the Song Weaver's spell.

And the Song Weaver . . . was none other than Shaard himself.

Standing tall above the sacrificial maze, Shaard Sang out his harsh, powerful Song. His aura was blacker than black, slithering like an oily eel, wrapping itself round the Lurkers' Song-auras, choking away any free will.

Ash would not waste this chance to escape. He ran

past the Lurkers, whose heads were dipped low in submission. Their auras were small flickering lights, their Song a pathetic whine. It hurt Ash's heart to hear their Song reduced to this, even if they had just been about to eat him. He raced up the broken wall the Pathfinders had used to escape, Nuk hoisting him to safety as he neared the top. The Isolai audience gasped with outrage, their warriors encircling the escapees.

Shaard ceased Singing his sharp Song, the Lurkers hissing in relief as they were freed from his grasp. He had followed Ash from above, and now stood tall above the sacrificial maze.

"I will not let you throw your life away, Ash," Shaard sneered. "You are *far* too valuable for that."

Ash could do nothing but open and close his mouth in disbelief. The Pathfinders stood on guard beside him, forming a defensive circle as the Isolai surrounded them, furious at being denied their sacrifice.

"*What is the meaning of this?*" demanded Song Searcher Temu, storming toward Shaard, his face red with fury. "*We had a deal!*"

"Calm yourself, Temu," Shaard said, annoyance twitching the corners of his smile.

"*You said the child would teach us how to Song Weave!*" Temu continued, poking an accusing finger into Shaard's chest. *"You promised! We kept our side of the bargain. You must keep yours!"*

"Enough," Shaard said dangerously.

"Why would you stand in the way of our deal? We demand that you finish this!"

"I agree," Shaard said.

Then, quicker than Ash's eyes could follow, Shaard kicked Song Searcher Temu in the chest, sending him flying off the wall into the maze. Ash looked away in horror as the Lurkers fell upon him. He didn't even have time to scream.

"Thought the fool would never shut up," Shaard commented, watching the grisly spectacle unfold. "No one can be *taught* how to Song Weave. It is in our blood, born only to us. It is what makes us *greater* than the others."

Ash couldn't believe what he was seeing. *"Y-you're a Song Weaver,"* he managed to say. "All this time . . ."

"It's true," Shaard replied as the Isolai recovered from their surprise and ran at him with vengeful anger. "But can you blame me for having to hide it?" He barked out a harsh sound again and again. It took Ash a moment to realize it was his Song.

The Lurkers began to behave strangely. Their movements became twitchy and erratic, as though they were being pulled against their will by invisible reins. One rammed itself against the wall, and then another climbed onto its back, and then another, and another.

They're using each other as a ladder! Ash watched in horror. He'd never seen Leviathans act in this way. It was as wondrous as it was terrifying.

The Isolai warriors stumbled to a halt, suddenly aware of the danger they were in. Then the topmost Lurker pulled itself over the wall. Another followed, and the one below that grabbed its brethren's tail and pulled itself up as well.

The Lurkers were loose in the Isolai Stronghold.

The villagers exploded with panic, but the Pathfinders held their nerve. They formed a defensive wall, ready to fight with fists and teeth.

"You knew that the Isolai would do this to us!" Captain Nuk spat.

"Of course. The Isolai were a tool, a means to an end. It became disappointingly obvious that I would never convince you to leave the *Frostheart*, Ash. Not even the lure of your parents was enough to convince you. And so I had to take matters into my own hands and remove the *Frostheart* crew from *you*." Shaard's voice rose above the screams of the villagers and the howling of the Lurkers.

Kailen bared her teeth. "You'll pay for this, you *monster!*"

"The Song your father left to you is the only map to Solstice, Ash, and only *you* know its secrets. You will guide me there," Shaard said.

"I will *never* help you!" Ash shouted. *"Never!"*

Shaard sighed. He seemed genuinely disappointed. "If only you'd simply see the light, Ash. I see so much of myself in you, I thought you'd see reason."

"He's *nothing* like you!" Lunah protested.

Shaard smirked. "Isn't he? I too was outcast from my Stronghold for being a Song Weaver. I too have been hated and scorned simply for being . . . *different.* I was thrown into the wilds to die—like *all* our people! But like you, Ash, I too refused to fade, refused to die quietly. I fought with every ounce of strength I had. And learning to survive in the wilds made me more powerful than my Stronghold could have ever imagined. I revisited them years later, and I showed them what a Song Weaver was truly capable of."

"FEAR. BEWARE. OUTCAST." The crow-witch's voice filled Ash's mind once more.

It was Shaard. She was warning me about Shaard! Oh, Tobu, what have I done?

"There are others who have joined me, Ash. Soon I

shall gather *all* the Song Weavers together, and then you will see the sense in my vision." Shaard held his spherical archeomek casing aloft.

Ash saw that it glistened with frost, a chill white vapor pouring from it like a cloud. He remembered what Shaard had said about the device being able to withstand extreme temperatures—clearly that went for extreme cold as well as heat. But what could be that cold . . . ?

The frost-heart! Ash realized. *He's stolen the frost-heart!*

Seeing that Ash had worked out what he'd done, Shaard laughed. "None of you idiots had any idea of the power the frost-heart holds. You hung it up as a decoration! But your father knew, Ash. He heard its call. And now I will use it to lead Song Weavers into a glorious new future, where we rule our own destiny, where we will be looked upon with awe and reverence. The Strongholds of the world will have true reason to fear us! We'll be changing history, Ash. We'll be rewriting it in the Song Weavers' name!"

"How are you still talkin'?" Lunah spat.

"I won't let you do this, Shaard. I will stop you," Ash said.

The lullaby told me to protect the frost-heart! I have to get it back!

Shaard laughed again. "Ash, my boy, you don't have a choice! You truly are your mother's son. That fool refused to see reason, just like you. She tried to convince your father not to follow me in our righteous crusade. But your mother was no Song Weaver—she could never be one of us! At least your father wasn't so shortsighted."

Ash reeled at this. "No! He would never follow you!"

"And what would you know? You can't even remember him! Perhaps I'll tell you more about him on our travels. You're coming with me, Ash, one way or another," Shaard snarled, and he began to bark out his guttural Song.

A Lurker twitched round to Shaard's side, hissing with discomfort, writhing under his control.

"No, he's ruddy not," Captain Nuk said.

The Pathfinders pushed Ash behind them for protection, raising their fists, ready to do what little they could against the encroaching Lurker to defend Ash.

Shaard's hungry grin spread across his face as he raised his hand, ready to order the Lurker to attack.

Suddenly Ash noticed something move high above on the rooftops. The thing rushed down at great speed, and with a *crack* hit Shaard with tremendous force. With a yelp, he fell backward, roaring and writhing on the ground in pain. The now released Lurker hissed and ran to join the chaos that had overtaken the village.

The figure who had struck Shaard was huge, muscular, and covered in white fur.

"Run," it growled.

"*Tobu?!*" Ash managed to say in utter disbelief.

Tobu turned round and frowned. "*Now!*" he roared, before spinning to block an attack from the Isolai hunters who charged toward him, his spear whirling like a storm.

43

Friendship's Token

Ash had known Tobu was a great warrior, but he had never seen him fight, not properly. What he saw before him now was nothing short of awe-inspiring. The Isolai hunters didn't stand a chance.

Tobu's movements were almost too fast to follow, his spear spinning their attacks aside with ease, cracking into their bellies and skulls, scattering them as though they were nothing but a nuisance. A hissing sound came from behind them as Shaard got to his feet and drew two wicked daggers from either side of his belt. "Damn yeti," he growled, before leaping into the fray.

"Tobu, look out!" Ash cried.

Shaard fought with blistering speed, slashing his daggers with vicious precision. But none came more skilled than Tobu, who blocked every blow Shaard sent his way. He dodged and parried, sweeping his spear with brutal strength, each swing nearly taking Shaard off his feet. But Ash could see that despite his skill something was bothering Tobu. His left side dragged as though under some invisible weight. Tobu kicked Shaard to the ground, but grunted in pain. Shaard leaped back up with incredible dexterity, ducking a low swing of Tobu's spear—and rammed all his weight into the yeti's wounded shoulder. Tobu roared, staggering back, and only just avoided a slash from Shaard's blade.

It was the poisoned arrow wound! It was sucking the energy from Tobu.

The Pathfinders saw what was happening, and Ash charged at Shaard, who simply swatted him away with the back of his hand.

"*Yaaaaaaa!*" Lunah cried, leaping atop Shaard's shoulders and pummeling him with her fists. Nuk slammed right into his midriff, sending him careening into a wall with a gasp. Kailen cracked him across the head with her fist.

As the others kept Shaard busy Ash helped Tobu up. "Tobu, are you OK?"

"The poison." Tobu winced.

Ash inspected Tobu's bandage and gagged. The

wound stank, black rot spreading across the white fur like a spiderweb.

"The salve hasn't worked! The poison's still hurting you!" Ash said in horror.

"Oh, how forgetful of me." Shaard laughed, throwing Lunah down and dodging another of Kailen's punches. "I must have given him the wrong antidote. You can resist it, yeti, but it *will* kill you."

"*OH, WILL YOU JUST SHUT UP!*" Nuk roared, knocking Shaard to the ground.

Ash tried to ignore the fury roiling inside him. He had to concentrate. He had to save Tobu.

"I'll get you out of here," he said, trying to support him. Kailen raced to his aid. "Tobu, I'm so sorry. I'm so, so sorry!" Ash repeated, but he could feel Tobu slipping out of consciousness. "I was such an idiot. I—I—"

"*Aaaaash!*" Shaard roared, free of Nuk now, bloodied and rushing toward him with manic eyes. But before he could reach him a flock of crows dived from the sky and rushed about him, sweeping, pecking, and tearing at him with their sharp talons. He struggled and squirmed, shielding his face from the sudden onslaught.

Ash hadn't noticed it at first amid the absolute ruckus, but suddenly it was all he could hear.

Another Song.

This one was broken, starting and stalling like the cry of a crow. It was guiding the birds—asking them for their help instead of dominating them.

"*JOIN, FIGHT*," the rise and fall of the melody Sang.

"*JOIN. FIGHT. FIGHT. FIGHT.*"

Ash peered from under Tobu's arm. There, arms raised, hood drawn, ragged black rags flowing in the breeze, was the crow-witch.

Crows circled her, joining their Song to hers.

"*You!*" Shaard shouted at the crow-witch as she continued to guide the crows with her Song.

Where had she come from? Ash puzzled. Had she been on the *Frostheart* this whole time, or was she really magic?

"Can't move for Song Weavers now!" Lunah said, arriving at Ash's side and shouldering Tobu's arm in Ash's place. "Oof, bit heavy, ent he?"

"Please, take him to the *Frostheart*, Lunah. Keep him safe!" Ash said.

"Ash, we're not leaving you!"

"And you won't have to! Get the *Frostheart* ready, and I'll meet you there. I need to help the crow-witch. She's on our side. She's trying to help, I'm sure of it. I think it's why the lullaby led me to her—I can't just leave her!"

Lunah rolled her eyes, but she heaved Tobu's heavy arms up regardless, helping Kailen take him toward the sleigh docks.

"Show him what a real Song Weaver can do, Ash!" Kailen shouted back, hauling Tobu into the tangle of Isolai desperately trying to get away from the monsters.

Three Isolai warriors spotted the Pathfinders and leveled their spears, anger in their eyes. But however angry they were, it paled in comparison to Captain Nuk.

"I have had some unpleasant farewells in my time,"

she rumbled, teeth clenched, tusks gleaming, "but this is far and away the most inconsiderate goodbye party I have ever witnessed! Isn't that right, Master Podd?!"

"Indeed, captain!" Master Podd agreed, appearing on a rooftop and leaping down onto the headwear of one of the warriors, pushing it down in front of his eyes.

The warrior swung his spear wildly, whacking the warrior next to him in the belly, the man crumpling over as Master Podd leaped to the head of the remaining warrior and pummeled him with his little fists.

"No one tries to sacrifice *my* crew and gets away with it!" Nuk bellowed, crashing the warriors aside with her huge weight. She gripped a ladder that led to an upper platform and with a grunt ripped it off its brackets. "Come, Master Podd!" she yelled. "We have a crew in need of a ladder!"

"Don't we always, captain," Master Podd said, following her back toward the edge to the hunting maze.

And with that Ash turned back to the battle of the Song Weavers and prepared to fight.

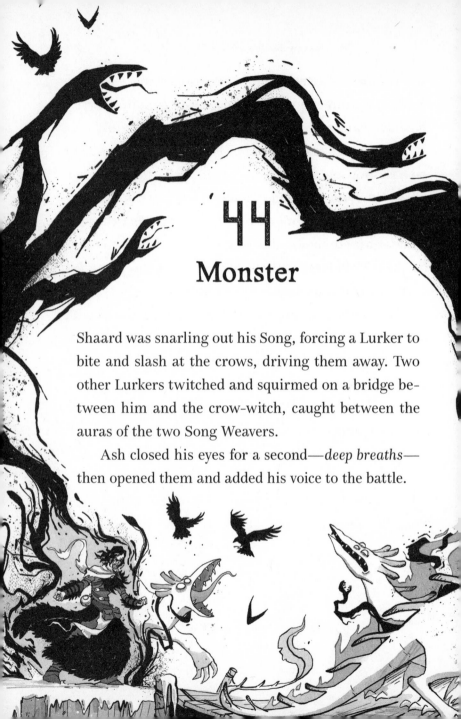

44
Monster

Shaard was snarling out his Song, forcing a Lurker to bite and slash at the crows, driving them away. Two other Lurkers twitched and squirmed on a bridge between him and the crow-witch, caught between the auras of the two Song Weavers.

Ash closed his eyes for a second—*deep breaths*—then opened them and added his voice to the battle.

The shrinking auras of the Lurkers were being pulled in opposite directions—Shaard's awful aura of darkness strangled and tore at them, while the crow-witch's Song, disjointed and shattered, tried to free the Lurkers from his grasp.

"*Join. Weave. Together,*" came the crow-witch's voice in Ash's mind. She was using a similar Song to the one Ash had used before. But as tempting as it was to join forces Ash thought it was a useless technique. It didn't achieve anything. He was trembling with anger, furious at Shaard's betrayal. It was time to fight fire with fire.

"*I trusted you! I thought you understood, but you were just using me!*" Ash's emotions poured out in a torrent through his Song. "*I won't fall for that again!*"

In the whirlwind of his dark aura Ash put all he had into attacking and dominating Shaard. His aura pushed through Shaard's with surprising ease, surging forward like the *Frostheart*, and, intoxicated with his new power, he went right for the heart of Shaard's Song.

"How dare you try to use me! How dare you try to hurt my friends! I'll make you pay for this!" Ash's Song bellowed.

"DON'T. Outcast. POWERFUL. Talons. TIGHTEN!" Ash could dimly hear the crow-witch pleading. But what did she know? Ash had controlled Gargants with this Song!

"You are powerful, Ash, but remember who taught you this Song," sang Shaard, strangely calm, *amused* even. *"You are NO MATCH for me."*

Like creeping sticky tree sap, Shaard's aura began to form an impenetrable wall, trapping Ash's in a stranglehold. Ash struggled to break free, his voice becoming strained and hoarse, his melody sounding more like the growls of a cornered animal than a Song. He was stuck, just like the Lurkers.

Of course it had been too easy to push through Shaard's aura—he'd *let* Ash do it. He'd rushed headlong into a trap! Tobu was right. Ash was too impulsive, and it would be his undoing.

Shaard was just too powerful. Every time Ash thought he'd found a space in his Song, an opening, *anything* to wriggle his aura through and flee, Shaard would weave

darkness in its place, mending the gap and blocking his escape.

"*You have so much promise, lad! Don't waste it. You could be a great Song Weaver, if only you'd listen! Well, here's a lesson in doing what you're told!*" Shaard's grip was tightening. Ash cried out in pain and fear. The crow-witch tried to break through, but her fractured aura was no match for Shaard's.

Ash's breaths came out in ragged gasps as though Shaard's hands were clasped round his neck. His vision dimmed, filling with dots and flashes of light. Fury and desperation blinded him. He wasn't sure if he was Singing or screaming—his voice sounded the same. He had never felt so isolated, so very, very alone.

But then I've always been alone, Ash lamented. *Why should the end be any different?*

His fists opened and his hands fell to his sides.

Ash could barely draw breath. He thought of what he was about to lose. The *Frostheart* crew. Captain Nuk. Lunah. And Tobu.

Tobu, I'm so sorry. I've been such an idiot! I've lost everything all over again. Just like the Fira. Just like my parents. I'm alone again. I'm always going to be all alone.

He let go. He stopped Singing. Then another voice Sang in his ear, gentle yet urgent.

"NOT. ALONE."

Ash recognized, somewhere in the back of his head, that it was the voice of the crow-witch.

"NOT. ALONE. NOT. ALONE. NOT. ALONE. FOCUS. LISTEN. WEAVE. FREEDOM."

Suddenly Ash heard another new voice.

"SING!" came the familiar Song of the frost-heart, through its archeomek prison. Ash felt as though invisible hands were lifting his chin up, trying to help him to stand tall.

"Don't give up!"

"*JOIN*," the crow-witch Sang. "*LISTEN. WEAVE. TO-GETHER.*"

"*Just give up, Ash. Accept that we are the same, you and I,*" Shaard's voice resounded.

"*No. We are not the same. I am not a monster.*"

Concentrate. Focus. Listen.

"*I am a Song Weaver. And I'm NOT alone!*"

Then came another voice. "*HELP.*"

It sounded like the Song of the crow-witch, but Ash knew instinctively that it wasn't. For one thing it wasn't human.

"*CRUSHING. DARKNESS. PLEASE. HELP,*" the Song whimpered.

It was the Lurkers, still being forced to keep the swarming crows off Shaard. Despite how small it was, how defeated, he would know that Song anywhere. It was the Song that made him feel safe and warm, and as though he was in a place where he belonged. Ash almost burst into tears at hearing it.

So Ash wove a new Song.

The dark, disgusting void of his aura was gone, and out burst a flurry of starlight, a snowstorm of warming brightness. This wasn't Shaard's Song. This was his own. A rush of energy surged through Ash's body, lifting him to his feet. A thrill of joy buzzed from his center to his toes and fingertips, the joy of Song Weaving burning within him like a warming fire. His Song exploded, more powerful than ever. He felt Shaard recoil and the crow-witch push forward, joining Ash's resistance. Ash entwined his aura with hers, fortifying and doubling their strength. Their Song would not be so easily smothered by Shaard. Together they wove their aura through a tiny gap in Shaard's all-encompassing darkness.

Within was a weak ice-blue light. It squirmed, desperate to escape from the prison of Shaard's aura. *It's the Song of the Lurkers.*

Ash and the witch wove their Song about the light, trying to help release it.

"It won't work!" Shaard howled, the greasy coils of his aura lashing out at the two Song Weavers while applying even more force onto the Lurkers. *"You can't win!"*

"You want to be free?" Ash Sang to the Lurkers, ignoring Shaard.

He focused. He listened. The Leviathan Song was so weak it could barely be heard, but Ash sensed the whisper of agreement.

"YES! HELP," it Sang.

"We can help you, but you have to push with all your strength!" Ash replied.

The Lurker Song lit up with determination.

"*Together we can do this—we can break you out of there! Fight with us! Fight with us!*"

"*FIGHT. FIGHT. FIGHT,*" the crow-witch chanted.

Ash, the crow-witch, and the Leviathans pushed and pulled—they resisted with all they had against Shaard. The barricade seemed to waver. It began to crumble.

"*That's it! Just a little more!*"

With a final push the entwined, powerful Song ripped out of Shaard's grasp. They were all free.

A rush of gratitude came from the Lurkers. "*ALLIES. FRIENDS.*"

It washed over Ash like warming sunlight. It felt amazing. It felt *right*.

Shaard staggered back with a groan. "*What?*" he said in disbelief, preparing to attack again.

Ash readied himself for the barrage when he caught a glimpse of the frosted archeomek tied with rope to Shaard's belt. It gave him an idea. "*Please,*" he Sang to the Lurkers, "*the heart! We need to get the heart!*"

The Lurkers Sang a Song of Understanding, eager to aid those who had helped them. As one they bounded across the bridge toward Shaard. He swerved out of the way just in time, but not before a Lurker clamped the sphere in its jaws, ripping it from his belt.

"No!" Shaard shouted, true terror in his eyes. He

roared another Song at the Lurker, the Leviathan reeling back as though it had been physically struck. The sphere spilled from its mouth, a torn piece of Shaard's cloak trailing behind it like a ragged tail. As the Songauras of Shaard and the Lurker struggled for supremacy, Ash skidded forward and scooped it up. Despite the archeomek shell, it was freezing to touch, a cold so strong it felt like fire. Ash held it tight nonetheless.

The Lurker howled as Shaard forced it to leap down into the maze, before he tore toward Ash, who held the casing over the edge of the bridge in warning.

"*Don't!*" Shaard yelled, and immediately ground to a halt. "You do not know what you hold! That is our future, Ash. The future of all Song Weavers!"

Ash considered this. Shaard, for the first time ever,

looked like he wasn't in
control of the situation, his
vivid blue eyes pleading, panic threatening
to break free. His smile was gone.

Ash almost felt sorry for him. *Almost.*

"It's no future I want to be a part of," Ash said, before
dropping the archeomek case over the side and into the
maze.

"No!" Shaard screamed. Then, with no concern for
his own safety, he leaped after it and disappeared below.

With a cry of relief the remaining Lurkers scurried
away, desperate to escape this terrible Stronghold.

Ash knew the feeling. He looked across at the ghost-
like form of the crow-witch, crows swooping and swerving round her. "We need to go. *Now!*"

45

Doubt

The Isolai Stronghold was in utter turmoil.

The Lurkers stalked and chased the fleeing villagers, the warriors throwing down their weapons and running with the rest of the villagers to scramble onto waiting sleighs. Ash and the crow-witch struggled against the fleeing crowd, the Isolai too full of terror to even notice it was the Song Weaver who ran in their midst.

They finally made it to the dock and skidded to a halt, panting and wheezing, looking on in despair.

The *Frostheart* was nowhere to be seen.

"They've *left* us?" Ash cried out in disbelief. A cold chill ran through his body, Shaard's voice laughing at him in the back of his mind. *The* Frostheart *only took you aboard since you benefited them. You'll never truly be part of their crew. Never.*

Had Ash finally proven to be more trouble than he was worth?

A group of Isolai warriors stood upon the ramshackle pier, the only ones with enough wits about them to notice the newcomers.

"*There!*" one of them shouted, and the warriors charged forward. "It's them! The ones who did this!"

"*Wall,*" the crow-witch hissed. With apparent effortlessness she bounded up to a higher level, then again up to the battlements that formed one of the Stronghold's outer perimeters.

"*Wait up!*" Ash called out, running up some stairs with the warriors in hot pursuit. His lungs burning, his legs aching, Ash made it to the wall, the crow-witch's dark shape waiting for him. Together they ran along its length, the warriors close behind, shouting for vengeance. "What now?"

"*There,*" the crow-witch Sang.

Familiar blue sails rose above the battlements. Timbers creaked, a sunstone roared. The *Frostheart*.

"They waited!" Ash cried with joy.

He was sure he'd never seen anything more beautiful in his life. It followed the length of the wall, trying to stay at a speed Ash and the crow-witch could keep up with.

The Isolai warriors called out in alarm, afraid they might lose their quarry.

"I say, you're going to have to jump, you two!" Captain Nuk shouted.

"Are you ready to do this? If we—" Ash began, but in a blur of black the crow-witch had already leaped aboard the *Frostheart*'s deck. "O-OK then—" Ash panted. He prepared to do the same when the *Frostheart* pulled away, avoiding the sleigh wrecks jutting out from the snow. They couldn't get any closer.

They're too far—I'm not gonna make it!

The Isolai warriors were almost upon him. He could hear their huffs and puffs, their furious grunting as they rushed to catch him.

"*Ash!*" Lunah cried, holding on to the rigging with her arm outstretched. "*You have to jump!*"

"*It's too far!*" he cried. His legs were screaming out, his breaths ragged and raw.

"*We're not leaving without you!*" came Kailen's voice. She gripped Lunah's hand with one hand and the rigging with the other, allowing Lunah to dangle over the edge, closer to Ash.

"*It's now or never, fire-boy!*" Lunah cried.

With a roar of effort, finding the very last drop of energy he could muster, Ash leaped from the wall. He flew through the air, the grasping hands of the Isolai warriors missing his furs by a hair's breadth.

He reached out his free hand.

He stretched with all his might.

Time seemed to stop.

The distance was still great.

But the Pathfinders were doing everything they could to reach him.

His friends.

His family.

He snatched hold of Lunah's hand and hit the side of the sleigh with a loud *thump*. Lunah grunted with the strain, but did not let go, and Kailen kept hold of the rigging strong and true.

"Stars above, Ash, how much do you weigh?" Lunah wheezed through gritted teeth. The *Frostheart* pulled away from the horrors of the Isolai Stronghold, surging forward into the distant Snow Sea.

Ash savored the feeling of the *Frostheart*'s cold wooden deck beneath him. He might have even given it a little peck. He'd been convinced he wasn't going to make it, that he'd never see the sleigh or its crew ever again. Lunah and Kailen huddled around him, making sure he was OK.

"*Heart? Where? Gone?*" the crow-witch hissed, fear in her Song.

Ash let go of the torn piece of Shaard's cloak he'd been gripping on to with all his might, which had gone rigid with a coating of ice. The frost-heart rolled out, cold and vibrant—and safe.

"You got it back!" Lunah cried out.

Ash grinned. "Managed to slip it from the casing while Shaard fought with the Lurker."

The crow-witch's shoulders dropped in relief.

Lunah laughed. "You gave him the ol' sleight of hand! Who knew you were so devious?"

Ash's smile suddenly left his face. "Where's Tobu?" he asked, fearing the worst.

"The healing tent!" Lunah said, pointing.

Ash wasted no time in getting there. He found Nuk and Arla beside Tobu's bed.

Tobu's wound looked foul, and the smell turned Ash's stomach. An evil-looking darkness was spreading from where the arrow tip had been, filling Tobu's veins with angry-looking rot. It seemed to let out a heat, for the healing tent was humid and close. "It doesn't look good," Arla the healer announced. "The poison has been spreading. It won't be long before it sickens his blood entirely."

"Is there no way to stop it? An antidote or something?" Ash asked, his face strained with fear. "We have to help him!"

"I've done all I can do," Arla said, shaking her head. "We need to get him to a Stronghold; he needs proper medicine!"

Ash felt dizzy. *This can't be happening. Not to Tobu. He's invincible!*

"*Wolversbane.*" The crow-witch's voice resonated in Ash's head. From the fearful looks on the rest of the crew's faces, they only heard strange wordless Song coming from her lips.

"*HYFERIS herb. FOXBREATH thistles. COMBINE.*" She was telling him the antidote! Ash checked the pouches and vials Arla had in the healing tent, making quite the mess in his haste.

He snatched up two pouches and held them high. "We have the ingredients for the antidote!" Ash said, hope rekindling.

"You'll—you'll have to do it," Tobu managed to say through gritted teeth. "You must learn."

"Me? I—But why not Arla?" Ash began, incredulously. "This is no time for your survival lessons, Tobu, this is life or death!"

"Precisely. You can do it."

Of all the times to be worried about training! Ash's mind was a storm. Seeing Tobu like this, he couldn't think straight. He tried to remember his survival lessons. All the things Tobu had told him about healing herbs and salves.

Tobu placed a weak hand on Ash's shoulder. "I know you can do this."

Ash gulped down sour spit, grabbed a small bowl, and gathered the herbs. He put them in his mouth, chewed them, and spat them back out. He smeared the wet paste over the wound.

"Nnnnngggg." Tobu gritted his teeth in agony.

"Am I doing it wrong?" Ash asked, his voice close to breaking in panic.

"N-no! Just—*hurts*—"

Tears clouded Ash's vision. He'd always looked to

Tobu for the answers when it came to survival. Now Tobu was dying and it was up to Ash to save him.

"So we've gathered, furball!" Nuk said. "Now stop your yammering and save your strength. Ash has this in hand."

Ash chewed the rest of the herbs. He signaled for the cup of water that was sitting by Tobu's side. Lunah handed it to him, and he spat the glop into the cup, then swilled it around and then put it to Tobu's mouth, helping him drink the concoction to a chorus of "*eeurgh*" and "*uuuuurgh.*"

Ash laughed at this, his eyes hot with tears. Tobu managed a smile. He stirred and groaned in pain as he turned on the bed. He mumbled something to Ash, so quietly it was barely audible.

"T-Tobu?" Ash asked.

"You . . . you did well," Tobu croaked. "Your Song. Your healing. You did well."

Ash blinked in surprise. He couldn't believe what he was hearing. Maybe the herbs he'd given Tobu were making him speak like this?

Or maybe I didn't survive the battle with Shaard? Maybe I died, and this is the afterlife after all . . . ?

"To have defeated Shaard . . . you . . . you must have exercised careful technique . . . and . . . control."

"I'm so sorry, Tobu. You were right about him— about everything!" Ash gripped his fur.

Tobu's breathing was shallow, his eyes barely open. "Not everything," Tobu whispered. "I was wrong . . . to doubt you."

Suddenly Tobu gave a great sigh . . . and stopped moving.

Ash's eyes widened. "Is . . . is he . . . ?" Ash began, his eyes hot and wet, his body shaking.

Arla listened to Tobu's chest, and sniffed at the wound. "He's asleep."

Ash let out a cry of relief.

Nuk beamed. "You did it, Ash!"

Lunah punched his shoulder playfully. "Looks like you might actually earn one of them mighty names! Ash the Hero, Who Is Also Really Gross and Spits Goo into Cups. Has a nice ring to it, don't you think?"

Ash could do nothing but laugh. He grabbed Tobu's hand and gave it a squeeze. He got up, taking one last look at his sleeping guardian, before joining the others in leaving the tent to give Tobu some space to rest.

46

Home

Ash and Lunah approached the crow-witch out on the main deck, her tattered rags billowing in the wind, her face hidden in the shadow of her hood. "Thank you," Ash said to her. "For all your help." The witch remained silent, a crow cawing at Ash from her shoulder. "You've helped me so much, but I don't even know your name."

"Yeah!" Lunah agreed. "Who is it hidin' back there?"

The crow-witch slapped Lunah's hand aside as she reached for her hood and hissed.

"Yikes!" Lunah exclaimed. "No touching, I get it! You coulda just said!"

"Who *are* you?" Ash asked again.

"*Broken. Shattered,*" her voice Sang, and Ash could hear the pain in it.

"Quite the name," Lunah remarked, once Ash had

translated. "You really understand what she's saying?"

"She speaks through Song. Something's happened to her. I don't—I don't think she can speak, not like we do . . ."

"You're just one big, fat mystery, ent ya?" Lunah said to the witch.

"*What's your name?*" Ash Sang to her.

The witch thought about this, the crow on her shoulder rustling its feathers. "*Rook*," she Sang.

Ash smiled. "Thank you, *Rook*. For all your help back there."

"Yeah, 'n' welcome aboard the *Frostheart*! Fastest growin' Pathfinder crew on the Snow Sea, so it seems." Lunah put her hands to her hips with pride.

"*Knew. Father,*" Rook Sang tentatively, pointing toward Ash.

Once the meaning of this sank in, Ash felt as though he'd been dunked into cold water.

"What's she sayin'?" Lunah asked.

"I—I think she's saying she knew my father," Ash stuttered, though he had begun to suspect it. His father had guided him to her after all. Ash felt the flame of hope rekindle within him. Rook still offered him a connection to his missing parents. It hadn't disappeared with Shaard. The thought that his father had been friends with Shaard was a dark one, one Ash daren't contemplate. But if Ferno had also been friends with someone like Rook, well, there was hope yet that he was a good man.

"*Follow. Lullaby. Find. Father,*" Rook said.

"I've been trying, but I don't understand the verse you gave me!" said Ash.

The witch—Rook—shook her head vigorously. "*Didn't. Understand. Didn't. LISTEN.*"

The crow on her shoulder began to call the strange ululating Song the crows had Sung at Skybridge. This time Ash wasn't scared. He listened and focused, reaching for the hidden meaning.

"*Where spirits dance behind walls so great,
the wayfinder's Song will reveal your fate.*"

Ash recited this, picking out the words that were whispered beneath the bird's harsh cries. "Oh! That thing about the outcast . . . that wasn't the next verse . . . that *was* a warning about Shaard!"

"What? What do you mean?" Lunah demanded.

"*Lullaby. Incomplete,*" Rook hissed. "*More. Awaits.*"

"What is goin' on?"

"She's saying that I don't have the whole lullaby, that there's more to it . . ." Ash explained, unable to hide his exasperation. This wasn't so much a lullaby as a whole epic saga!

"Well, at least we have the next clue now!" Lunah beamed, excited. *"Treasure hunt!"*

"But . . . it doesn't make any sense. The spirits dance in the sky, how are we supposed to get up there? It's impossible!"

"Aurora," Rook hissed.

"What?" Ash asked.

"Place where spirits dance . . . ?" Lunah repeated, stroking her nonexistent beard in thought. "It's Aurora . . ."

"That's what Rook is saying. I don't understand! What's a Stronghold got to do with spirits dancing in the sky?" Ash said, frustrated at being the only one who didn't get it.

"Doik," Lunah said, knocking Ash on the head. "Stories say that the name the World Before used for the place where spirits dance . . . was *Aurora*. Same as where we're goin'!"

Ash's mouth gaped at this information, before turning into a joyful smile. "You've done it!" he cried out in joy, grabbing Lunah by the arms and spinning her round. Rook took a step back, not wanting to get caught up in such undignified happiness. "We've not hit a dead end! We're still on the right track!" He couldn't stop grinning.